ELI EASTON

A Second Harvest

Dedication

To my own silver fox farmer.

A Second Harvest by Eli Easton

David Fisher has lived by the rules all his life. Born to a Mennonite family, he obeyed his father and took over the family farm, married, and had two children. Now with his kids both in college and his wife deceased, he runs his farm alone and without joy, counting off the days of a life half-lived.

Christie Landon, graphic designer, Manhattanite, and fierce gay party boy, needs a change. Now thirty, he figures it's time to grow up and think about his future. When his best friend overdoses, Christie resolves to take a break from the city. He heads to a small house in Lancaster County, Pennsylvania to rest, recoup, and reflect.

But life in the country is boring despite glimpses of the hunky silver fox next door. When Christie's creativity latches on to cooking, he decides to approach his widower neighbor with a plan to share meals and grocery expenses. David agrees, and soon the odd couple finds they really enjoy spending time together.

Christie challenges the boundaries of David's closed world and brings out feelings he buried long ago. If he can break free of the past, he might find a second chance at happiness.

Acknowledgements

Thanks to my ever-faithful beta readers Kate, Veronica, and RJ! You always help me to be a better writer and I owe you all so much. Also thanks to the folks at Dreamspinner Press for giving this book a first publication and helping me edit the initial draft into shape. The new (second) cover was done by the talented Anna Tif Sikorska.

I love the idea that it's never too late to change your life, to take up a new degree or profession, a new love, or even a whole new family. Because the opposite is tragic, isn't it? Being doomed to forever walk the same path can be a kind of living hell. It's not easy to leave a well-worn road, but ultimately it is worth it. This is the story of one man's second chance.

ACT I: PLANTING

Chapter 1

David sat against the rough wooden boards of the cow stall and watched Gertrude die. She opened her big brown eyes once toward the end and gazed at him for a long moment. In the glow of the lantern light, her lashes cast deep shadows so David couldn't see what emotion might be in those eyes. Was she grateful he was sitting up with her? Did she know it was time to go? Was she relieved to finally be leaving this farm where she'd spent her entire long life?

But she was just a cow. Probably she thought none of those things. When she closed her eyes again, it was for the last time. An hour later she stopped breathing, and she was gone.

It felt like an era passed with her, silently and stealthily. David was there when Gertrude was born. She was the first cow that was *his*, designated as such while still in the womb, a birthday present from his parents. He raised her and showed her at the Harrisburg farm fair when he was in eleventh grade. She was a beautiful brown jersey with classic lines, and she won a third-place ribbon that day. David was proud enough to burst. For years afterward Gertrude was a reliable, strong milking cow.

A farmer didn't get sentimental about animals. That was plain stupid. But David was not able to kill Gertrude when her milk production fell off. She'd half performed for another decade until he eventually retired her to pasture. If anyone asked, he told them it was good to have a mature cow around to show the rebellious younger ones what was what, teach them the routine. And Gertrude was a leader by personality. She knew how to put other cows and heifers in their places. But the truth was, David just couldn't bear to load her in the truck and take her to the slaughterhouse.

She was a part of his boyhood, and it was right she was dead now. God knew the boy in him was a far distant memory.

He turned off the lights in the barn and walked back to the house. It was foolishness to have stayed up with her. The day's work had to be done whether or not he had a good night's rest. He was too old for this.

The light in the kitchen was on as he approached the house. He checked his watch. It was just past 5:00 a.m. Amy must be up.

For the past two years, Amy had come home from college for the summer to work as a nursing intern at the Lancaster hospital and to help him run a CSA program on the farm. It was Amy who did all the customer work. She made up the flyers, packed the boxes of produce, and met with the customers every week when they came to pick up their shares. She was good at that sort of thing. He wished he could pay her more, but like every other operation on the farm, the profit from the CSA was a very faint line of green. David honestly didn't know how most farmers made it. His grandfather had paid off the farm, but still, between property taxes, upkeep and maintenance, animal feed, and everything else, he made just enough to get by. As his dad used to say, the gravy was thin.

He opened the sliding glass door and saw Amy in her bathrobe pulling some fresh eggs from the fridge.

"Hey, Dad." She yawned. "What are you doing out at the barn so early?"

"Gertrude passed."

"Aw! That's a shame." Amy didn't sound too broken up about it. Then again Amy learned young not to get attached to the animals.

He grabbed a glass from the cupboard, went to the fridge, and poured himself some orange juice. But when he went to lift it to his mouth, he was surprised to discover a hard, thick lump in his throat. He put the glass back on the counter and breathed. Ridiculous. He hadn't gotten particularly choked up, even when Susan died. But then she was sick for a few years. Her death was a blessing in the end.

"Things live. Things die. That's the way of it." His voice was gruff, but the lump eased. He drank his juice.

When he put the glass down, Amy was watching him with a frown. "You sound so cynical. I worry about you, Dad. You should take Mrs. Robeson up on her offer for dinner. I think she really likes you."

"I'm not interested in Mrs. Robeson."

Amy rolled her eyes. "You should give her a chance. Mom's been gone two years now. She wouldn't want you to be alone forever. And Mrs. Robeson taught both Joe and me in Sunday school. She's a very nice lady."

David gave Amy a warning look. "I don't care to discuss my love life, thank you. Are you gonna cook those eggs, or are you waiting for them to hatch?"

Amy snorted a laugh, but she opened a cupboard and

brought out a skillet. "Slave driver! I just worry about you. I hate that you're all alone here when I go back to school. Joe hardly ever comes home."

"I don't mind."

"I know! That's the problem. You're turning into a crusty old hermit. Next time I see you, you'll have a beard down to your belly button. I know you live on TV dinners, hotdogs, and chips. It's not healthy. You *should* get remarried. I know Pastor Mitchell thinks so."

"Pastor Mitchell wants to get some of his old maids and widows married off so he doesn't have to handhold them so much. I'm not interested."

David was half teasing, but Amy still gasped. "Dad! That's a terrible thing so say!"

David waggled his eyebrows, unrepentant, and exited the kitchen.

He went upstairs and took a shower. The sleepless night hit him along with the hot water, and he knew it would be a *long* day. Why had he felt compelled to sit up with Gertrude? She probably hadn't even known he was there. But at the thought of her, another wave of sadness hit him. An image ran through his mind—one of falling leaves and the boy he'd been playing in them, laughing. He had no idea where that came from or why.

Out of the shower, he used a hand to wipe off the fogged mirror. He looked at himself critically to see if he could get away with not shaving this morning. His reflection surprised him briefly, as it always did. He felt so old. He always expected to see white hair and a sagging face when he looked in the mirror. But there were only a few strands of gray at the temples of his dark-brown hair and in his close-cropped beard. His face was not young, but it wasn't sagging yet either. He'd lost a good thirty pounds since Susan died, so he actually looked younger.

Fine. He might not *look* old, but he sure felt it. And he suddenly understood why he sat up with Gertrude. He wanted to watch her as she escaped the farm at last, as she simply left her body and went away, gone where no one could prevent her going and no one could follow.

One day David would leave too, maybe just that way. He'd shut his eyes and vanish, leaving a shell behind. But dear Lord, he was only forty-one this past May. Even if he died when his dad did, at age fifty-eight, he had years to wait yet.

Just to... *wait.*

He couldn't bear the melancholy look of his reflection. *Foolishness!* With a huff of self-disgust, David dried himself off and brushed his teeth, avoiding glancing in the mirror again. He was in a hurry now. Chores awaited and no one was going to do them for him.

*   *   *

Christie got to his feet in the small bathroom stall. He had to put his hand on the wall to help himself up, though whether it was due to the booze he'd consumed or his thirty-year-old bones was anybody's guess. The *thump thump* of the bass from the music out front made the black stall quiver under his hand.

"That was great! Can I return the favor?" The young Latino hottie looked at Christie hopefully.

"No thanks. I'm good."

Christie hadn't gotten off, but he was cool with that. He got hard, and he had some fun with his hand down his pants, but he'd lost the urge to climax. And *that* was definitely down to the dirty martinis. The martinis and his own ennui. He only agreed to hook up with the guy because he was obviously a tourist, and he screwed up his courage to come over and talk to Christie. He hadn't wanted to reject the kid. And yeah, the guy was hot too, with light caramel-colored skin and big soulful eyes. He was so young and green he was practically fluorescent.

"Fantastic. Oh—wait. I have something." The guy dug a baggie containing three blue pills from his jeans pocket. "X, man. Guy gave me a sample. Says it's awesome stuff." He opened up the baggie, took out one pill, and held the baggie open for Christie.

"No thanks. I've had too much to drink already."

The guy shrugged and swallowed his pill dry. "Save 'em for later, then. And think of me." He winked, closed the baggie, and stuffed it in the front pocket of Christie's tight jeans.

"Thanks." Christie smiled. He didn't plan to take the pills, but it was nice of the guy to offer.

"Have a good night!"

The young hottie left the bathroom. Christie followed at a slower pace, washing his hands at the sink and rinsing out his mouth. In the mirror his pupils were large, the black surrounded by only a sliver of blue. He looked washed-out too, old. He suddenly felt on the tired side of drunk. He wanted to go home.

Out in the club, he made his way through the crush of bodies. It was Saturday night and The Boiler Room was packed to health-hazard levels. Christie didn't have the patience for it. He'd been feeling off lately, more critical of his usual scene. He surveyed the crowd looking for his roommate, Kyle.

The dance floor and bar area held the usual mix of tourists looking for the "gay New York club experience" and the regulars, who were dotted here and there in clusters. Christie knew all the regulars. He was one himself. And of course there were the assorted jack-offs with their eyes focused on their phones. *What are you looking at? Grindr? You're at a club, douchebag.*

The flash of annoyance reminded him of why he was tired of this scene. It was so shallow, so transient. The tourists came and went and the regulars stayed, growing bitchier and more cynical by the year—not to mention older. Christie included.

And Jesus Christ, was it just him, or were the twinks getting younger every day? Babies, all of them. That was Christie once. Now he felt like aged beef. The thrill of it had definitely begun to wane, but it was hard to break the habit of eight long years. All his friends in the city were into this scene, especially Kyle. His best friend was nowhere close to wanting to rein in the party just yet.

Christie spotted Kyle on the dance floor with Billy. Billy was a local too. He was a big, sweet-hearted muscle guy who had a massive crush on Kyle. They slept together now and then, but Kyle was the last guy on earth to settle down. He'd hooked up with at least one other guy tonight Christie knew of for sure, a cute redhead. He also looked plowed.

Christie made his way over to them. "Hey!" he hollered. "I'm ready to head out."

Kyle pouted and took both of Christie's hands, forcing him to dance. They danced together for a few minutes, but Christie really was over it. It was after 1:00 a.m., and he just wanted to leave. "You gonna stay?" he asked Kyle.

Kyle shook his head. "No. I'm good. Let's go." He kissed Billy hotly, and they waved good-bye to the regulars as Kyle pulled Christie out the exit.

They walked the six blocks to their place. Christie loved living in the East Village, but he had to admit the proximity of The Boiler Room was a huge factor in his decision to sublease his pricey but tiny apartment. And it certainly was a factor in Kyle's moving in. Their place was only a one bedroom, but Christie paid more rent, so he got the privacy. Kyle slept on a pull-down wall bed in the living room. It was a constant battle to keep the place from looking trashed. But despite its many disadvantages, the apartment had three undeniable perks: location, location, location.

They all but carried each other up the six flights of stairs. As was their postclub routine, they kicked off their shoes, scooted out of their tight jeans, and settled on the couch for a final round in their underwear. Kyle lit a joint, and Christie grabbed a half-full bottle of red wine from the kitchen and uncorked it. He slouched back on the couch and held the bottle aloft on his palm, testing his sobriety. It wobbled. A lot.

"You're gonna spill that, idiot!" Kyle complained. "And that's, like, wed wine!"

"Wed wine?" Christie giggled. Kyle handed him the joint, and Christie took it with one hand, put it to his lips, and inhaled. Just one toke. He was still drunk on the martinis.

"Wed!" Kyle tried again. "W-Rrred! Red! Wine!"

They both cracked up. The red wine in question tipped dangerously. Christie passed Kyle the joint and brought the bottle to his lips. "Guess we'd better hurry up and drink it, then, before I spill it."

Kyle took a hit, held it, and let it out in a fragrant cloud. He took another immediately, toking so hard the paper on the joint flamed red. Man, that guy could smoke a joint down to a nub in minutes. He held the joint out to Christie.

"Nah, I'm good."

Kyle shrugged and took another deep drag.

"Thank God I don't need to get up early tomorrow. Sundays rule," Christie sighed. He was already dreading the hangover.

"Except the day after Sunday is Monday," Kyle bitched, sounding funny because he was trying to hold in the smoke.

"Don't remind me."

Christie used to love his job as a graphic designer. But lately he'd been uninspired, and his relationship with his boss had soured too. He knew it was his fault. He wasn't working up to his usual level. He needed to hit up an art gallery or something. Find some fresh motivation. Maybe he would do that tomorrow—a lazy Sunday art stroll.

His eyes fell on the stack of legal documents lying on the coffee table. Or.... Lancaster County, Pennsylvania. Could that provide some fresh motivation? He snorted. It'd provide fresh manure, more likely.

Kyle noticed what he was looking at. He started singing, loud and purposefully off-key. "Old McDonald had a farm, eeii-eeii-ooo!"

"Shut up!"

Kyle snorted like a pig and snuffled against Christie's shoulder. Christie laughed.

"I keep telling you, it's not a farm, it's just a house," Christie protested.

"'S not the city, ergo it's a farm. Flies, pig shit, and really, really, *really* tall corn or green beans or whatever."

"You're so wasted. It's a little house in farm country. Quit drooling on me, and put that out before you burn your fingers." Christie shoved Kyle over. Kyle blearily put the nub of his joint in the ashtray.

"Wish some rich relative would leave something to me," Kyle muttered.

Christie's Aunt Ruth hadn't been rich, but she was sharp and frugal. She left her house to Kyle, free and clear. The lawyer thought he could sell it for a hundred grand. But Kyle wanted to at least go see it before he sold it off. He had fond memories of visiting that house as a boy.

"Was that the last joint?" Kyle complained.

"Yes. Anyway, we've both had enough. Time for bed."

"*Fuck*." Kyle sounded despondent. He ground his eyes with the palms of his hands. "What about pills? You got anything?"

Christie looked at his watch. "Jesus, Kyle, it's almost 2:00 a.m."

"Oh, come on! Weed just doesn't do it for me anymore. I won't be able to sleep. Do you have anything or not?"

Christie looked at his friend, or tried to. Everything was a bit blurry. Damn, he really had drunk too much tonight. He had five dirty martinis at the club, plus a shot Mick bought for him. It was all over the course of at least three hours, so it didn't seem like a lot. But one thing about being a regular at The Boiler Room—the bartenders went heavy on the booze in your drinks, and he hadn't had much dinner. The single toke on the joint pushed him over the edge into the unpleasant side of stoned. His head swam.

Kyle, however, was sitting up looking at him expectantly. Was he genuinely not high enough? Whatever. Christie wasn't his babysitter. And it wasn't like they were going out anywhere.

He took the baggie the hookup gave him from his pants

pocket and tossed it to Kyle. "A guy gave those to me. Said they were X. I didn't actually know him, though. So maybe we shouldn't—"

Kyle was already opening the baggie. He popped both of the blue pills into his mouth and swallowed.

"Hey!"

"I'm sorry, did you want one?" Kyle put a hand over his mouth. He looked truly abashed.

"You're such a bogart!"

Kyle giggled, then giggled harder, until he was half lying on Christie, laughing. "I'm sorry! So, so sorry! That was rude! And they were your pills too! Oh my God!"

"Dork."

"I'm not a dork!" Kyle sat up and put his shoulders back, flashing his best clubbing smile. No, Kyle wasn't a dork. He was fucking glorious. He had platinum-blond hair, big blue eyes, and a fragile build, just like Christie himself. They were practically twins. Guys loved Kyle, and he was a sweetheart too. He was a total slut, but he'd give you the shirt off his back. Then again, Christie had no room to slut shame.

Kyle wobbled a little as he posed. His eyes went funny. Worry niggled at Christie. Kyle should not have taken both those tabs. "You need to drink some water, Ky. I'll get it."

He went into the kitchen to get them both some water. It was definitely time to call it a night. Would Kyle be able to sleep after taking two tabs of X? Or would he be up for hours, trying to get Christie to talk? God, please don't let him freak out like he did a few months ago after taking some pills at the club. He scared Christie that night.

He stood at the sink, letting the water run cold for some

time. He blinked, coming out of his daze. He filled two tall glasses of water and went into the living room.

"I want you to drink this whole glass. You'll—"

Kyle was slumped over on the couch. His eyes were rolled back, showing a sliver of white under parted eyelids, and foam came out of his mouth. His body convulsed in soft jolts.

Christie screamed. "Kyle!"

Instantly the evening changed. The two glasses Christie carried hit the floor and shattered, sending water everywhere. "Kyle, oh my God!"

Glass cut Christie's stockinged feet as he stumbled to the couch, but he just winced and kept going. He shook Kyle's shoulders and pulled down his jaw, fighting against the clenching of Kyle's teeth. "Kyle, are you all right? Kyle!"

Christie looked around, desperate for something to keep Kyle's mouth open. How could he even breathe through all that foam and gunk? Christie ran back into the kitchen, cutting his feet again, and grabbed a towel. He twisted it into a rope as he ran back, and he forced it between Kyle's teeth. "Oh God. Oh my God!"

He fumbled for his phone on the coffee table and dialed 911. "Help me! Please! My friend, he's OD'ing. He's having convulsions!"

"Calm down, sir. Give me your address."

Christie gave her the address. "We're on the sixth floor, apartment 613. Please hurry!"

"The ambulance is on the way. Now sir, I need you to stay calm and help him. Can you do that?"

The operator—God bless her every firm and caring word—gave Christie directions for clearing Kyle's airways. He wasn't convulsing anymore, but now he was unconscious. The operator walked Christie through moving Kyle onto his side so he wouldn't choke.

Christie did everything she said, but he felt like he was fucking it up. He was a mess and still too drunk to think clearly. He grabbed Kyle's phone with one hand and sent a quick text to Billy. He needed help *now*.

It felt like mere seconds before Billy pounded on their door and Christie let him in. Billy said nothing, merely fell to his knees beside Kyle on the couch and took over CPR like he knew what he was doing. His face was white with fear and tears swam in his eyes.

"Sir?" Christie had forgotten he was still holding the phone to his ear.

"My friend is giving him CPR," Christie whispered to the operator.

He felt like he might throw up. The room went gray. The phone slipped from his fingers and terror seized him.

What if I'd been too high to call the ambulance?

What if I'd taken those pills instead, or if we'd each taken one? Would I be like Kyle now too? Who would have called the ambulance then?

Is Kyle dying? How the hell do I live with myself if Kyle dies?

For the first time in eight years, Christie prayed. He prayed absolutely and sincerely and with everything he had. *Please God, please let Kyle live. I swear, I will give up partying forever, never touch another drug or drink. Just let Kyle live!*

From the distance came the sound of sirens, and then Christie's world went black.

Chapter 2

"Christie? Are you awake?"

Christie opened his eyes. He was in a hospital bed. A doctor stood over him, shining a light into Christie's eyes. "There you are. I need you to tell me what your friend Kyle took tonight. It's very important. Do you understand? And I need to know what you took too."

He was in the hospital? He must have passed out and ended up going in the ambulance too. Jesus. He tried to sit up. The doctor let him, watching him critically. He had an IV and felt reasonably coherent, even though his head was killing him.

"Is Kyle okay?"

"No," the doctor said with no trace of softness. "He's not okay. We've pumped his stomach, but we need to know what's in his bloodstream."

Christie told him what drinks Kyle likely had at the club, the red wine, the joint, and the two pills that were supposedly ecstasy.

The doctor's face was hard. "Do you know how dangerous it is, Christie, to take street drugs from strangers?"

Christie knew. But everyone did it at the clubs, shared

drugs. And normally it was fine. But not this time. "It was stupid," he agreed.

I never should have shown Kyle those pills. I should have dropped them in the waste can as soon as that guy left the restroom.

The judgmental look on the doctor's face made Christie feel like shit. How had his life come to this? He'd had a strict upbringing, an enviable education, a good professional job, decent looks, and an apartment in Manhattan.... He had it all. So how did he find himself in a scene from a bad reality show like *Intervention*?

This isn't me. He wasn't an addict or an alcoholic, he just liked to party on the weekends. Everyone he knew did the same. And yet here he was.

"Well, I don't know what those pills were, but they weren't ecstasy. You don't know any more about them?" the doctor pushed.

Christie shook his head. "The guy who gave them to me took one, so he must not have known they were bad." He described the pills to the best of his memory—which was basically small and blue. He couldn't remember if they'd had any markings.

The doctor frowned and wrote it down. He had Christie describe the Latino too. He said nothing when Christie couldn't remember his name. "I'll let the police know. This guy who gave you the pills—he may be in trouble somewhere if he took one too."

"I'm sorry," Christie repeated pointlessly.

"And you didn't take any pills like that?"

"No. I told you what I had tonight—booze and one toke of weed. That's it."

"You were passed out when the ambulance got there and your feet were all cut up. Your blood alcohol level was

.24. That's seriously intoxicated. Are you aware, Christie, that levels as low as .35 can kill you?"

"We were home for the night," Christie said lamely, but his gut burned. He *had* been too drunk. He was almost too drunk to help Kyle. He moved his feet under the sheet and felt bandages. Now that he remembered cutting his feet on the glass, they started to ache. "Will Kyle live?" The words caught in his throat.

The doctor's expression finally softened. "He'll live. He's lucky. This time. As for you, we're giving you fluids, and we'll retest your blood every hour. Once you get below .08 blood alcohol, you'll be free to go. But if you can think of anything else that will help Kyle, I hope you'll let us know."

Christie nodded, relieved. He watched the doctor go, looked at the IV needle in his arm, and decided right then: it was time for a change.

"The new husbands may now kiss."

Christie watched Kyle and Billy kiss each other with sweet gusto. The sight provoked a weird mix of hope, jealousy, and worry. Was this truly what Kyle wanted? Would he be okay?

Since the night Kyle almost died three months ago, he was a changed man. Both Christie and Kyle saw that night as a serious wake-up call, but Kyle's transformation was extreme. He was a party boy ever since Christie met him, but he went cold turkey—no booze, no weed, no drugs, no clubs. He started seeing Billy exclusively. It was even Kyle who popped the question, insisting he was ready to settle down.

All of those were good changes, but Christie was

worried about the manic speed with which it all happened. He hoped Kyle stuck with his new resolve and was truly happy.

It was hard to believe one of their duo—Kyle and Christie, fierce boy toys extraordinaire—was married. Of course Christie longed for that too. He wanted a stable relationship, a chance to build a permanent home with someone, to have someone to love and count on through thick and thin. But wanting it was one thing; *finding* it was another. He had a hard time seeing himself settling down with any of the guys he knew or had dated. His relationships always started with heady infatuation and ended with disappointment.

Probably he expected too much, but he didn't want to come second after someone's career or desire to play the field, or sometimes even after his partner's own vanity. There was one memorable Prince Charming who wasn't willing to disrupt his gym routine to come to a birthday dinner Kyle arranged for Christie. That was the end of that "boyfriend."

But Billy truly was a sweet guy. At least Kyle chose well.

The ceremony over, Billy and Kyle hugged their guests. There were about twenty people in the room at the city clerk's office on Worth St. Most of them were friends, but Kyle's mom was there, looking elegant in a peach suit, her mascara running all over her face from her tears. Billy's parents were there too, quiet and looking a little shell-shocked.

Kyle threw his arms around Christie. "I'm married. Can you believe it?" he whispered in Christie's ear.

"You're so lucky. Billy's an amazing person." *Please don't break his heart.*

"I know! He's too good for me, but I'm selfish that way."

Kyle pulled back and gave Christie a starry-eyed smile. "Now we just need to find you a husband too."

Christie laughed. "Probably not going to happen in Lancaster County."

Kyle looked sad at that, pouting his lower lip. "Can't believe you're leaving me." He hugged Christie again.

"You left me first."

"Yes, but it was for a good cause."

Kyle announced four weeks ago he was moving out of their shared apartment. Christie could have found another roommate, but he decided against it. The apartment was too small a place to live with anyone who wasn't practically a brother. Besides, it was too close to the clubs and to all their party friends. Too tempting.

Christie needed a change too—a complete and total change. That's why he decided to let the apartment go, take a six-month hiatus from Manhattan, and go live in the house he inherited from his aunt. That would give him plenty of time to look over all her stuff, get the house ready for market, and sell it. It felt like the right thing to do. She left him the property along with all her worldly possessions. He should look after it himself, not hire some stranger to pick through her things. And he was ready for a break from city life. He'd had a strong sense of nostalgia for the country lately. Ironic. Growing up, he couldn't escape it fast enough. He never thought he'd miss it in a million years.

"You'll come back, right?" Kyle asked, studying Christie's face. "Once you've sold your aunt's place. You'll be back?"

"I'll be climbing the walls in a month. Of course I'll be back! I can't exactly build a big old gay life in rural Pennsylvania."

Kyle frowned at that. "Be careful, okay? There are probably a lot of rednecks there. And, you know, Republicans!"

Christie laughed. "I don't think they hang gays, Kyle." *At least I hope not.*

Billy joined them, putting his big arms around both of them and squeezing. He looked so happy it hurt Christie's heart. "You two both look gorgeous today. Babe, come say hi to my parents."

Kyle kissed Billy's cheek. "I'll be right there, love."

Billy moved away and Kyle gave Christie one last embrace. There was a trace of fear in it. "Who would have ever thought? Me married and you leaving the city. We're going to be okay, right?"

Christie murmured reassurances, but inside, he was scared too.

Chapter 3

A stranger had moved into Ruth Landon's house. David saw the guy from a distance. He was young, blond, and very "city-looking," from his expensive boots and tight jeans to his long haircut. He was probably Ruth's heir. David heard through the neighborhood grapevine that she left her house to a nephew.

He put off his duty, uneasy about talking to the young man. But at last he couldn't put it off any longer. So after Earl finished the second milking on a Wednesday and went home and all of David's own work was done for the day, he made up his mind to go over there. He showered, put a TV dinner in the oven to cook while he was out, donned his best suede-and-sheepskin jacket, and walked down the gravel farm lane that led between his place and the Landon property.

The lights were on in the small brick house, so he figured the stranger was home. *This is just business. No need to be nervous.* He knocked on the front door. There was no answer. He tried again.

"Hello?" The stranger came walking around the side of the house. God, he was even more swanky than he looked from afar. This close up, his good looks took David aback.

He had light-blond hair, which was cut short at the nape but had long sides and bangs that hung over his forehead. He had big blue eyes. His face was delicate, with a long, thin nose, small chin, and a finely drawn mouth. He was of average height but quite thin, and he wore his blue jeans skintight. Small silver rings and balls marched up the curve of both ears. He had on a light-blue long-sleeved T-shirt that matched his eyes, a black down vest, and fur-topped hiking boots. Somehow the entire outfit looked more fashionable than anything David had ever worn in his life.

David's gaze skittered away, and he found himself focusing on the guy's vest to avoid his eyes.

"I thought I heard someone knocking on the door. Hi! Who are you?"

The man's voice was friendly, but it was a little high in pitch, as if he were younger than the midtwenties he appeared to be.

"Hi. I'm David Fisher. I own the farm next door." He stepped forward and held out his hand. The stranger moved closer and shook it.

"Oh, hi! Yeah, I've seen you out working in the field. I'm Christie Landon. My Aunt Ruth used to live here."

David stuffed his hands in the pockets of his jeans, feeling awkward. "Ruth was a good woman. I'm sorry for your loss."

Christie frowned. "Thanks. Yeah. I hadn't seen her for a few years, unfortunately. But she was a very cool lady. Hey, do you mind if we walk around back? I'm burning some leaves, and I'm sort of afraid I'll set the eastern part of Pennsylvania on fire if I leave them unattended."

Christie laughed at himself, and David relaxed a little.

City or not, Christie didn't seem judgmental or stuck-up. "Sure."

Christie led the way around the side of the house. The grass, David noted, desperately needed cutting. It was early October, so it had stopped growing for the year, but it probably hadn't been mowed in months. It was too long and shouldn't be left like that over the winter. Maybe he should offer the use of his tractor mower.

Or maybe he should just stay out of Christie Landon's business.

Ruth had kept an old rusty barrel in the corner of her backyard for burning. David saw her use it many a time. Now puffs of smoke curled out of it, limp and black.

"Um, I wasn't sure what to do with all the leaves, so I googled it. I read that you can burn them, and Aunt Ruth had this barrel, so I figured that's what she did. But I'm not sure I'm doing it right."

He *googled* what to do with fallen leaves? The thought boggled David's mind, but Christie sounded unsure, and David's instinct was to be neighborly and help. If there was one thing he knew about, it was the endless task that was fall leaf disposal.

He walked up to the barrel and peered in as best he could with the smoke, but he already knew what was wrong. "The leaves are too wet. That's why they're not burning well."

He allowed himself a glance at Christie's face to see his reaction. Christie bit his lip and looked sheepish. "Oh. That's completely logical, isn't it? I just raked them up and stuck them in there."

"It rained pretty hard last night. Best to let them lie until they mostly dry out before raking them up."

Christie nodded. His blue eyes sparkled with wry

amusement. "Good to know. Guess I suck at this home ownership thing."

David blinked at the language. "Suck" wasn't a word most people he knew would use. He stared at the barrel of leaves, unsure what to say next. *You'll get used to it? Ask me about leaves anytime?*

"So did you just come over to introduce yourself? Or is there something I can do for you, David?"

David felt his neck heat. Right. "Yeah, I, um, wanted to discuss your field."

"My field?"

David pointed to the west, toward his farm. "Your property extends that way. Two acres of it are part of that cornfield there. Your aunt let me farm it with my acres, and I paid her rent for it once a year in December. So I was wondering if you want to do the same, or if you have other plans for the land."

"Oh my God!" Christie looked at the field in surprise. "I own *corn?*"

David hid a smile over the amazement in his voice. "Well. Not exactly. You own the land. Your aunt rented it to me for this past year, so technically the corn is mine."

"How much of that field is mine? Two acres, you said?"

He sounded like he had no idea how to eyeball two acres, so David took a step closer to Christie so he could point. "You see that tree there on the lane? The one with the crooked branch? That's about where your aunt's property ends. Follow that straight across toward that red barn over there. What's in front of it is your two acres."

"Sick!"

David looked at Christie doubtfully, but he appeared to mean it as a good thing. "Uh, there are markers in the ground, but you can't see 'em from here."

Christie took a step back as if to see better, and that put him rather close to David. David wanted to move out of the way, but he didn't want to appear skittish. His heart started pounding.

"Do you always grow corn there? When do you, um, plow it down? Under? Harvest! That's the word. When do you harvest it? Is it good to eat? That would be amazing to eat corn that grew on my own land."

Christie looked over his shoulder at David. His blue eyes had long blond lashes, and they were pretty, too pretty, girl pretty—*and too darn close*. But they were also inquisitive and lively eyes. Christie's face, on the other hand, was entirely masculine from this distance. A faint trace of fuzz grew on his chin and above his lip, and his nose and brows were strong. Something about the mix made David feel hot and cold at the same time.

He forced his feet back two steps. "Um. No. Not always corn. Every few years I plant soybeans or a cover crop."

Christie kept looking at him, curiously now. David half turned away. A light sweat broke out on his back. Why did Christie make him so uncomfortable? He was a grown man, for God's sake. He'd always been shy with new people, but he should be able to talk over business without getting so nervous. "So... do you still want to rent the field to me? Or maybe you plan to sell this place."

"How much?"

"What?"

"How much did you pay my aunt to rent the field?"

"Seven hundred a year."

"That's all?"

David scratched his neck. "It's actually high compared to the average price per acre around here. But since it was just two acres, I wanted to make it worth your aunt's while." And he also wanted to give the old woman a little bit of income. He didn't say that.

"Hmm. Well, to be honest, David, I do plan to sell the place. I'm just not sure when. I figured I'd be here for at least six months, but—"

David looked toward the house in an effort to escape Christie's gaze. It took him a moment to register what he was seeing—smoke coming out of the back screen door. "Hey! Something's burning!"

"Oh shit!" Christie yelled. He ran for the house.

He banged inside the back door. David stood there stupidly. He didn't know if he should follow, but it would be rude—not to mention cowardly—to leave Christie to deal with a house fire alone. He ran for the back door.

The kitchen was just inside, and he found Christie taking a cookie sheet of smoking charred lumps out of the oven, coughing.

David held open the back door. "Take it outside!"

Christie nodded and pushed past him with the smoking tray. He put it on the little table Ruth always kept out back. The smoke ascended into the open air.

"I can't believe I did that!" Christie rolled his eyes at himself. "I set a timer, but I didn't even hear it out here."

"Don't you have a smoke alarm?"

"I... have no idea?" Christie said sheepishly.

David sighed. "Come on. Let's look for one."

They went back inside the house. When David visited Ruth in the past, he was only ever in her living room near the front door. It was their December ritual. He came by with his annual rent check and a wrapped ham. She gave him a tin of Christmas cookies and wished his family Merry Christmas. They had a perfectly amiable business relationship, but not a close one.

The little house was sorely in need of updating, David noticed. The wallpaper, paint, and curtains hadn't been changed in at least two decades. He helped Christie open windows in the kitchen to clear the smoke. Several stuck badly. Then he walked into the attached living room looking for smoke detectors. He didn't see one.

Christie followed him, not saying a word. When David reached the short hallway that probably led to the bedrooms and bathroom, he stopped and glanced at Christie questioningly.

"Please." Christie waved a hand at the hallway. "I'd like to know if I need to have one installed. Apparently I'm not to be trusted with anything involving combustion."

David smiled despite himself at Christie's choice of words. He liked the smart way the kid talked. He went on. At the end of the small hallway, there was an old smoke detector on the ceiling. It was once white, but it had aged to a gnarly yellow. The light wasn't on. Given its location, David would bet good money it was the only one in the house.

He needed to take the cover off and check the battery. The ceilings weren't very high, and he found he could just grasp the unit if he stretched up as far as he could, but his bulky coat restricted his movements. He took it off and laid it on the floor. He reached up with both hands and tried to twist off the cover. It hadn't been removed in a long time, and it was stuck. Probably that's why Ruth gave up putting in new batteries. She wouldn't have had much arm strength at her advanced age. The cover wasn't sitting in the grove right. He jiggled it with his fingers.

There was a sound like a whimper of protest from Christie. David looked at him, wondering what the problem was, but Christie was studiously looking at the wall, his cheeks a little flushed.

"Sorry, I'm trying not to break it."

"No, it's fine."

The cover finally gave way, turning. David removed it slowly. The inside showed an old battery and a few spiderwebs. "Have you got a nine-volt?"

"There's a junk drawer in the kitchen. I'll check."

Christie went down the hall. There was the sound of rummaging. David wiped his brow with the sleeve of his plaid shirt. Why did Christie discombobulate him so? Yeah, he was better looking and more worldly than anyone David knew. He had multiple earrings in both ears, and his smile was white and perfect. Still, he was very friendly. He even tugged at David's sympathy a bit, being so clearly out of his depth. There was something appealing about him with that slender face and warm blue eyes.

Heck, he was just a kid, probably not much older than Joe, David reminded himself firmly.

When Christie returned he wore a determined look and carried a pack of nine-volt batteries. "Found some."

David took one from the pack and replaced the dead battery in the smoke alarm. The little indicator light went green. He put the cover back on carefully, making sure to get it in the right grooves this time so Christie wouldn't have any difficulty if he needed to change the battery again.

"Well, that should do it."

"Thank you so much. I should have thought to check that."

David shrugged. "There's a lot to do when you move into a new place."

"Yeah. I've been slowly boxing up all my aunt's stuff." His voice was a little sad.

David knew exactly what that was like—boxing up the pieces of someone else's life. He'd packed away all of Susan's things in their bedroom, but he still hadn't touched her sewing room. Had no idea where to even start in there.

His sense of discomfort returned. They were standing together in the small hallway, which meant they were too close—again. "Well. If you want to think about the field and let me know. My contract with your aunt doesn't run out until the end of the year, so you have time. I also wanted to let you know I'll be taking the corn down next week. My tractor is loud, but it won't take longer than a day."

Christie nodded. "Okay. No problem. Um...." He gestured over his shoulder toward the kitchen. "I put on some coffee."

David stuffed his hands in his coat. "I should probably get going."

"One cup?" Christie's face screwed up hopefully. "I can't leave you with the impression I'm completely helpless!"

The anxiety in David's stomach tightened some more. He wanted to escape, but Christie's expression made him reluctant to force the issue. Maybe the kid was lonely. He probably didn't know anyone in the area.

"All right. One cup. Thank you."

Christie smiled gratefully and led the way to the kitchen. The coffeemaker was on the counter, hissing and percolating away. It was probably Ruth's because it looked ancient. Christie took two china cups and saucers from a cupboard, humming happily. "Do you like cookies? The ones I burned were the last of the batch. I have some good ones from earlier."

It seemed rude to refuse, though the lingering smell of burned pastry and his own nerves left David without much of an appetite. "I'll try one."

Christie poured the cups and put them on the table with saucers and spoons. He put out a small carton of half-and-half and a bowl of what looked like sugar. Then he loaded up a plate with cookies that had been cooling on a rack. David took a seat at the small pine table, and Christie brought the plate over and sat down too.

He looked up at David and smiled shyly. "I found Aunt Ruth's box of recipe cards and decided to try a few of them. There's not a whole lot to do around here." He pushed the plate a tiny bit closer to David. "I thought these sounded interesting. They have coconut, cherries, dates, and walnuts in them."

They looked delicious, lightly golden and chock-full of the ingredients Christie had mentioned.

"Your aunt was a good cook. She baked cakes for weddings and such."

"She did? I didn't know that."

"Yup. She had a good reputation. Do you bake a lot too?" David was having a hard time getting a handle on Christie. None of the men in David's family—his father, himself, nor his son—ever did more than boil water and grill meat on the barbeque. But then he already knew Christie wasn't like anyone he'd ever met.

Christie shrugged. "I can cook. I took home ec in high school, and I really liked it. But when I lived in New York, I just did the basics. Pasta. Salads. Things like that. It's kind of fun, though, to get into it with this bigger kitchen. And,

I don't know... it just feels like the homey, country thing to do."

He said *the homey country thing* as if it were a novelty. David took a bite of a cookie. It was actually quite good. He hadn't had decent home-baked cookies lately. Susan hadn't felt well enough to do much in the kitchen her last few years. After the funeral the church ladies inundated him with food for a few weeks. But lately the only one who tried to feed him was Evelyn Robeson, and her food was practically inedible.

David finished the cookie and drank a sip of coffee before saying anything. He still felt awkward. "The cookies are very good."

Christie's smile was wide and genuine and so immaculate it looked like an advertisement. "Thanks. Would you, um, like to take some with you? For your kids? Your wife?"

Christie licked his lips nervously. David's eyes flickered down to follow the motion then back up to Christie's eyes. "I live alone," he said stiffly. "My wife passed a few years ago, and my son and daughter are both in college."

"Oh." Christie's smile faltered. "I'm sorry to hear about your wife."

"Thank you." David stood up. "Well. I appreciate the coffee and cookie. I really should be going, though. I have a lot of work to do."

"Okay. Hang on a sec." Christie got up, grabbed a plate from the cupboard, and started piling cookies on top of it. "Please do me a favor and take some of these. I'll blow up like a balloon if I eat them all."

"Nah. I shouldn't."

"Honestly. Please take them." Christie's big blue eyes implored.

David's resolve crumbled. "Well… if you're sure."

"I am *so* sure!" Christie brought the plate over to David with an odd little sashay in his hips. "And I'm sorry about the whole burning oven thing! I got distracted in the backyard and totally forgot I'd put in a sheet of—"

David suddenly gasped. His jaw dropped open.

"What's wrong?" Christie asked.

"I have a TV dinner in the oven! I have to go!"

David grabbed the plate and ran out of the house. He ran all the way back to his place on the farm lane, trying not to spill the cookies. When he got close to his old fieldstone house, he could hear the shrill of the smoke alarm.

He yanked open the kitchen door to the acrid scent of smoke. His two dogs fled the house and the horrible noise, nearly knocking him over. He tossed the cookies on the counter, grabbed an oven mitt, and pulled the silver tray of blackened food from the oven. He took it outside, coughing, and threw it in the trash can by the garage.

His coughs became chuckles and those became laughs. Holy Toledo! How could he have forgotten the TV dinner? He and Christie Landon had better avoid each other from here on out. Or as Christie foretold, they might end up burning down half the state of Pennsylvania.

Chapter 4

Christie's pen flew over his Wacom tablet in a blur. His sketch took life on the large monitor, and it was good. The rolling farmscape and the swirling clouds above it had a woodcut feel.

He'd been put on a brand identity campaign for a young organic dairy company. His boss joked it was appropriate given where Christie was now living, and today, looking out the window, he'd been inspired to just sketch.

It had been a while since Christie used serious sketching as part of his design work, but this brand wanted something old-fashioned yet hip. The Wacom filter he was using made his strokes look like a fine charcoal pencil. It was fucking *awesome*.

He saved, considered, erased, redrew. He liked thick lines for this, almost a Grant Wood style, but modern. He wanted to *feel* the life in the soil on the foreground, making it look solid from a distance but actually comprised of a dozen swirling lines and a few cool-looking beetles too.

He looked up photo reference for a cow on the net, then started sketching it on a new layer.

The hours flew by as he worked. When he finally

became conscious again of his surroundings, it was thanks to the loud sound of a motor. Christie blinked and looked out the window. He could see the top of a tractor approaching through the towering stalks of corn out back. Right. David Fisher said he'd be harvesting the corn soon.

Christie paused his pen over the Wacom tablet. He watched as a green tractor came through the corn like a land-eating monster, made it fully into view, and turned. Through the glass window in the cab, Christie could see David manning the wheel and watching the side mirror as he drove. He was dressed in a tan canvas jacket that was unbuttoned. Underneath he wore a green plaid shirt buttoned to the collar.

Nothing about this outfit should have been remotely sexy. But damn, it was. The *man* was hot, that was all.

Christie put his elbow on his desk and his chin on his palm and watched the tractor. He should not be perving on his farmer neighbor, but then entertainment was a bit scarce here in Amish country. When David came by two days ago to talk about the field, Christie probably hadn't subtle about his immediate attraction. Luckily David was too clueless to get it. He was hetero with a capital H and probably unaware of what a silver fox he was or that Christie was even gay. Talk about different worlds!

David Fisher was the first man to give Christie honest-to-god butterflies in ages. He had an attractive, honest face with full lips framed by a short brown-and-gray beard. His smile, which made only a few brief appearances, was shy and real. He was butch and earthy, so different from the metrosexuals and club types Christie knew in New York. He found that unpretentious manliness super sexy.

David was in good shape too. His hips were narrow and his thighs toned in his baggier jeans. And when he took his coat off—mama mia. He had the body of a hard-working man, lots of upper body strength, way broad shoulders, and a trim waist. There was something to be said for working on the land, Christie decided.

He sighed. Then he frowned with worry. David's belt was cinched to within an inch of its life too. He'd obviously lost weight recently. When did he say his wife died? Two years ago? Sad. Really sad. David lived alone and he was eating TV dinners. It was surprising some lucky woman hadn't snatched him up already.

The tractor had by now driven back toward the other end of the field. Christie went back to his sketch. After trying to work on the cow and not feeling it, he created a new layer and added the small figure of a farmer walking through the field in the distance. He had very broad shoulders.

Christie's boss adored the sketches. They had a conference call about an approach for the dairy company's logo and website. Christie was going to move forward with a white, black, and red design with a modernized woodcut feel and his original farm sketches. He had a week to put together clean mock-ups for the client, and he was excited about the direction.

It felt good. No, it felt fantastic. It was several years since he'd been this engaged with his work. This was just what he'd hoped for—that getting out of the city and moving to the quiet countryside would be inspirational. That and help him back off the partying. So far it was working.

He didn't miss the booze, thank God. His episode of "scared straight" had definitely worked. He didn't miss the clubs or even the city so much, but he did miss Kyle. He missed company. It was *awfully* quiet here, and the house was so empty. He'd been reading in the evenings or watching Netflix and drinking lots of coffee. He joined a local gym so he could work out. But it wasn't enough.

On Saturday morning he decided to tackle some of the house. Aunt Ruth's house—now *his* house—was a modest single-story ranch with three small bedrooms and one bathroom. One of the bedrooms was his aunt's hobby room, full of plastic flowers and baskets and drawers of cloth and thread and all sorts of things Christie would have no use for in his entire life. It would make a nicer office than the little table he was using in her bedroom, but first he had to clean it out.

He enjoyed seeing the evidence of his aunt's creativity. She was religious, just like his parents, but she had a sweet and generous nature. He remembered the way she "loved up" Christie when he was little—her words for it. She would tickle and hug and kiss him until he could hardly breathe for laughing. The two weeks he spent at her house every summer were some of the best memories of his childhood. She continued to write to him regularly over the years—actual letters with actual stamps—even after he came out, and his relationship with his parents was strained.

She was an artist too, apparently. He hadn't realized. Her quilts and needlework were gorgeous. And he found a photo album of the fancy cakes she baked, which she probably showed to prospective clients. There were trains and ladybugs, tall wedding cakes, and tiers of cupcakes. Her attention to detail was epic, and she'd had an irreverent sense of color. It was nice to feel that connection to her, that some part of her lived on in him through his art. It also made him feel sad he hadn't tried harder to come see her in the last five years.

After hours of packing up bags of craft stuff for donation—and putting aside the best finished pieces for himself—Christie finally got to the closet. On the top shelf were neat stacks of magazines. One stack was a craft magazine. The pile next to it was *Bon Appétit*.

"Huh." Christie carefully pulled the entire stack of magazines off the shelf and took it over to the rocking chair by the window. The magazines weren't old. The top one was dated only a year ago. It looked like Aunt Ruth subscribed for several years and kept every issue. They'd been used too. They were in good condition but definitely read, and there were dustings of flour or dried drops of liquid here and there. She must have tried at least some of the recipes.

The issue on top was a Thanksgiving issue. Christie opened it to a page with the corner folded back. "Oh wow," he muttered. The photo was of an amazing-looking bright-orange soup with a dollop of white cream and green cilantro leaves in the center. It was in an elegant white serving bowl on a perfect table. "Curried carrot ginger soup" read the caption.

The picture and even the name of the soup invoked images of the perfect Thanksgiving table with a large, good-looking family in cozy sweaters, a log fire, a big shaggy dog who did not shed, and a hunk of a man smiling at him from the table as Christie entered with the soup tureen.

Christie was dressed in a white shirt and white pants in this fantasy, and he looked fierce, of course.

"Hmm," Christie hummed to himself as he read the ingredient list. It was a fairly healthy dish. He got absorbed looking at other recipes in the magazine. Then he went to rummage around in his aunt's kitchen.

He found her cabinet full of spices. They were high-quality ones and not out of date. She had a zester, a whole stack of graters, cheesecloth, a double boiler, and other gadgets he had no idea what they were for. So Aunt Ruth had not only liked to bake, but she liked to cook as well. It made him sad to think she had no one to cook for. She'd never been married, as far as Christie knew, nor had she had any children.

Maybe she'd had an older gentleman friend Christie knew nothing about? He'd have to ask his mom. Or maybe David Fisher would know.

It was Saturday and the idea of doing more cleaning held little appeal. What else did he have to do with himself? Nothing. The temptation to go into Lancaster or Harrisburg was there, to seek out a gay bar, or even get on Grindr. Gay men had to exist out here. But... that wasn't why he moved here. He came here to get away from all that for a little while.

His mind made up, he went to the grocery store in town with a long list. It was a big-chain grocery store, and he was pleased to find nearly everything he needed. The October day was bright with crisp leaves and a blue sky. When he got back home with his sacks of goodies, it was still early afternoon. He opened the windows in the kitchen—struggling against the one over the sink that stuck—turned up the music on his iPhone, and started dancing around, organizing his supplies and digging out pots and pans.

He made the curried carrot ginger soup, a lovely dish with fresh peas, green onion, and radishes, some savory cheese-and-herb swirled biscuits, and a basic herb-roasted chicken. He truly did love to cook, though the past few years, it never seemed worth the effort. There were so many great takeout places in the East Village. Plus Kyle was such a picky eater. He basically ate pizza and stripped-down salads, and that was it.

It occurred to Christie while he was prepping this meal that it was going to be a beautiful repast, and it was a shame he didn't have anyone to share it with. He could freeze some of it, but it wouldn't be the same. He thought of David next door, living alone, and of his TV dinner. Would that be weird? That would be weird, right?

Pushing it from his mind, Christie spent the rest of the afternoon jamming to tunes in the kitchen and working his way through the recipes, having fun and dancing in his stocking feet.

When everything was ready, Christie decided the meal deserved some pomp and circumstance. His aunt had a drawer of tablecloths, but they were not quite his style. He used a white linen towel for a place mat and put each dish on the table in the best china dishes he could find. He used a red cut glass for his water and lit a candle in an old silver candlestick he found in the cupboard.

He looked at the table and chewed his lip. Everything looked beautiful. It smelled amazing too. He sucked some chicken juice from his thumb—*yum*. It almost seemed like a waste to eat it. He wished someone were here to share the meal with him. Anyone, really. The idea he'd avoided thinking about while cooking poked its head out again.

Well. He'd never been exactly shy. If he was going to do this, he had to do it quickly. The food was getting cold.

With a nervous shake of his head, Christie decided. He cut the roast chicken in half and put it on a large plate with a little bit of everything else, covered it with aluminum foil, and ran out the back door.

He hadn't been to the Fisher's farm before, and it turned out to be a longer trip down the gravel lane than he anticipated, maybe a quarter mile. He kept up a jog, worried about the food getting ruined. Between that and his nerves, he had a fine sheen of sweat when he got there.

David's farm was beautiful. The white barn Christie had seen from a distance was huge and picturesque. It made Christie's fingers itch to draw it. The farmhouse was fieldstone with black shutters. Electric candles in the windows gave it a cozy Colonial air and made Christie realize how dark it was getting outside. Why hadn't he grabbed his coat? It was fucking freezing. He was an idiot—a shivering idiot at the moment.

Determined to drop off his gift without further delay, he marched to the back door and firmly knocked.

Enthusiastic barking commenced. More than one dog—two or three. Christie felt a little nervous. He liked dogs, but these farm dogs might be territorial. And he *was* holding a plate of chicken. He might as well have bathed in bacon grease.

A deep voice silenced the dogs and the door opened. David's face looked stern and worn for a moment, but when he recognized Christie, a smile softened it. "Oh, hi."

"Hi. Sorry to bother you, but I spent the day cooking, and I made all this food. No way can I eat it all, so I thought I'd bring you a plate. You know, to make up for causing you to burn your dinner the other day, fixing my smoke detector and all." God, he was overdoing it! *Shut up, Christie.*

"Oh." David looked surprised. He glanced at the foil-covered plate in Christie's hand. "You didn't have to do that."

"I was bored." Christie's shrug turned into a shiver. He held out the plate. His mouth was dry. He was starting to wish he hadn't done this.

There was a reserve about David, a way he kept himself at arm's length. Christie sensed that when David stopped by his house, but he put it down to the fact they were strangers. The vibe was stronger here, on David's turf. Christie felt like an intruder standing at the back door. David was looking at the plate with an unreadable expression. *Please just take it.*

Then the wind shifted and a delicious aroma billowed up. David's face grew curious. "Roast chicken?"

"Yeah. It was from a Thanksgiving magazine. I made some sides too."

Suddenly David moved. "Heck, you must be freezing. Come inside."

"Thanks. I can't stay. I just wanted to drop this off." But Christie was stepping inside as he spoke, welcoming any relief from the cold air.

"River. Tonga. Sit." David shut the door. The dogs sat obediently. One was a golden retriever and the other a large furry black mix of some kind.

"Tonga?" Christie asked.

"It's an island," David said with an adorably bashful duck of his head. He took the plate from Christie and raised the foil, looked at it, and smelled. "This looks really good. You made this?"

"Sure. I just followed the recipes." But David's words made Christie feel infinitely better about bringing it by. "Well. I'll leave you to eat it before it gets cold. I have mine back at the house."

"Thanks. It beats the heck out of frozen food." David sounded sincere. He put the plate on the counter. "Hang on." He opened up an accordion door in the hall, revealing an overstuffed closet with a collection of coats, hats, and shoes. He selected a black woolen pea coat with large buttons and pulled it out. "You're going to freeze to death."

"It was stupid not to wear my coat. I didn't realize it was so far over here."

David got an amused smile, but he wasn't looking directly into Christie's eyes, so he still seemed uncomfortable. Instead of handing Christie the coat, though, he held it open and moved behind Christie.

Christie blinked. He couldn't remember the last time anyone had helped him into a coat. He held back his arms and let David slip the coat onto him. It fit in the shoulders okay, but it was big around the waist and hips. David turned Christie in a matter-of-fact way and started doing up the buttons.

Christie's eyes widened, and he swallowed hard. *What the hell?* Did David think he was a child? But there was something titillating about being taken care of, or maybe it was David's proximity, his handsome face focused on his task, his rough hands so close to Christie's body.

Yes, it was definitely the proximity. Wow, David was a good-looking man. Who knew rugged could be so hot? And to think of all the money Christie had spent on grooming!

There were only five buttons, and when David finished the last of them, just below Christie's chin, he looked up and saw Christie's face. He suddenly blushed, his nose and cheeks going red. He dropped his hands and took a step back. "Sorry. That was... sorry."

"I didn't mind." Oh God, Christie's voice had dropped in register and sounded rumbly to his own ears. That was a smexy voice! What the hell was he doing? "Um... thanks for the jacket, David. I'll bring it back later."

"No hurry." David was avoiding his gaze again.

Christie yanked the door open, escaped the house with a silly little wave, and walked fast back to his aunt's place.

Once inside he found his own food was only tepidly warm, but still flavorful and delicious. The herb glaze on the chicken was to die for, and it went beautifully with the floury-cheesy biscuits and the curried soup. He hoped David liked it too.

He kept the coat on while he ate, snuggling into the fabric and holding the collar close under his chin. It smelled of earth and hay, a slight trace of motor oil, and the smell of a working man—piney, sweaty, and altogether appealing.

He remained in the coat all through dinner. But only because he was cold.

*　*　*

"Yoo-hoo! David?"

David was in the free stall, trying to pry a stone out of the hoof of one of his milking cows, when he heard the call. It was a woman's voice. *Dang it.*

He smoothed out his scowl as Evelyn Robeson opened the latch door and walked into the feed aisle next to the stall. She looked much like she always did. Her red-blond hair was pulled back into a long braid that wound around like a bun on the back of her head. Her black wool coat was long but not as long as her skirt, which was a dark-green color and down to midcalf. She had on thick hose and churchgoing dress shoes, which were not going to do her any favors in the barn. Like the other women in his congregation, she wore no makeup. She was plainer than Susan had been, quite thin, and about David's age.

"Hi, Evelyn," he nodded. "Sorry, I'm a bit tied up here at the moment."

The cow tried to get away from the post it was tied to, even though its leg was cinched up tight in a rope. It hopped and shuddered, pulled taut.

"Whoa, whoa," David murmured, petting its flank. He did not need a stranger in the barn right now. He didn't need this cow to get riled up and break its fool neck.

"I was just over at Roots market, so I thought I'd stop by already. It's warm for October. Isn't it warm?"

"Yup, it is."

"You still getting tomatoes?"

"Yup."

"I'm still getting tomatoes too! Small ones, mind. But I made a big batch of tomato sauce, and I brought you some jars. I left them by the back door. All you have to do is heat up some pasta—"

Evelyn described exactly how to make the dish, as if David couldn't have figured out that much. He worked with a flat-head screwdriver to pry the stone from between the cow's split hoof.

"My, we really missed you at church on Sunday. I hope you weren't ill?"

"No." David didn't offer any justification. He felt like relaxing with the paper after chores this past Sunday, so he did. Without Susan there to get them both out the door, he missed church more often than not these days.

"Well... we feel the loss when you're not there, David. I hope you know that. It's important for us all to commune together, especially those who live alone. I even got Jessie to go this past Sunday, thank the good Lord. He's got a job now over in New Hope—"

Jessie was Evelyn's grown son. He was Joe's age, around nineteen, and he was a mean-spirited boy, from what David knew of him. Rumor was he took after his father. Evelyn's late husband, Luther, wasn't the churchy type. In fact, he was an alcoholic. He died just before Susan did, crashed a car while driving drunk. Susan said it was probably a blessing for Evelyn, though a shame for the poor man's soul.

"I wish you'd've heard Pastor Mitchell's sermon. He talked about seeing God's plan for your life, and following God's will, and doing things that are good for others and for building up the community."

"That so?"

The stone came out of the hoof with a pop. The cow tried to jerk away again, probably in pain. David steadied her, clicking his tongue. If he'd been alone, he would have said something to the cow like "I had to get it out of there, girl. You'll feel better now." But with Evelyn standing there, he refrained. He needed to put some unguent up in the hoof, make sure it didn't get infected.

"David?"

"Yes, ma'am?" David looked at Evelyn.

She blinked at him, then gave him a shy smile. "I'm sorry if I'm interrupting your work. I can wait 'til you're done?"

God no. If Evelyn hung around, she'd expect them to chat over coffee or something. "No, ma'am, I can hear you fine. Hang on a minute." He went to the shelf in the corner and got the unguent, went back to the cow, and started treating the wound.

"Anyway, about seeing God's will," Evelyn continued. "You know I... well, I've been praying a lot. About things. Jessie, of course. He's my baby. He's had a wild streak, but I'm hopeful that God's been softening his heart. But also for poor Luther and Susan. And... and for us."

David had done all he could with the hoof. He started to untie the rope that held up the cow's leg. Her words sank in. He looked at her over the top of the stall, and she looked back at him steadily, her mouth pressed in a determined line. "For us?"

The cow moved away from him the moment it was free and shook its leg, stomped it. *That's got to feel better.*

"About you and me, David. I've been praying."

David turned his back to Evelyn and indulged himself by closing his eyes and sighing. *Lord, I'm so not up for this today.*

He composed his face and let himself out of the stall.

"I believe it's God's will that we... well, that we at least get to know one another better!" Evelyn said patiently. "Susan is gone, and my Luther is gone, practically at the same time! I know you must be at sea trying to run this farm and take care of yourself too. It's too much for any man. God gave man a helpmeet in woman so that they might hold each other up and provide support."

David pulled off his gloves and moved them from one hand to the other, shuffled his feet too. Now that he didn't have a task to do, he wasn't sure what to do with his eyes. He looked at Evelyn, looked away again. He couldn't bear the determined openness in her eyes . "Well. I don't know about that. I don't know that I'm ready to think about that quite yet."

"Well." Evelyn's voice was a little pinched. "The Bible

says it's not right to mourn forever. Please just mull it over. Pray about it. Will you do that, at least?"

"I will do that. Yes," David promised.

Maybe he could pray Evelyn found someone else. He felt sorry for her. She'd had a rough life. But he wasn't attracted to her, not even the least little bit. After Susan he wasn't about to let himself get pulled into another yoke. Why couldn't he choose to remain single? Being a widower, he sometimes felt like a bull at auction. There were far too many single women in their Mennonite community.

Evelyn's face softened, and she gave him a smile. "It's just that I know you believe the same as me. You're a good, God-fearing man. I promised the Lord that if I ever, well, married again, it would be to someone with strong faith."

"That's wise thinking."

"I'm sure you feel just the same!"

David nodded. "I, uh, thank you for stopping by, Evelyn, but I have some more doctoring to do this afternoon. Can I walk you to your car?"

Evelyn hesitated, the expression on her face saying she wasn't sure how to take this. She apparently decided to take it as a compliment. "Of course, David. You may walk me to my car."

"This way." David walked around Evelyn carefully and opened the barn door.

There was absolutely nothing wrong with Evelyn Robeson, he reminded himself as they walked up the driveway. She was a decent Christian woman. It was purely David's own fault he wanted nothing to do with her.

Chapter 5

They were in for a dry few days, according to the weatherman, so David mowed the far pasture on Monday. It had been a mild autumn, and the grass had grown tall enough for a late cutting. On Wednesday he ran the baler over the felled grass, leaving bound square bales dotting the field. A shift in the forecast called for rain on Friday, so on Thursday late afternoon, he had to pick up all the bales on the flatbed truck and get them safely stored in the barn before rain ruined them. A farmer lived and died by weather text alerts these days, and David loved his smartphone as much as anybody.

Storing hay was one of the many preparations he made every year for winter. Once he saw how much hay he'd gotten off his own land, he'd know how much he had to order from the Millers down the road. He needed enough to get his herd through 'til April. His cows had access to the pasture all year round, and they'd dig through the snow to find grass, so he didn't need as much hay as confinement operations. But there were weeks sometimes when the weather was too bad to let them out. Besides, they loved the soft hay like it was candy.

He backed his flatbed truck, overloaded with bales,

through the huge, wide-open doors on the top story of his bank barn. He set the brake and began unloading the bales and stacking them in front of the bales from previous cuttings.

River and Tonga were in the barn with him. River lay watching him work, and Tonga hunted the corners for mice. When River gave off a sharp bark and stood up, David turned to see Christie Landon in the open doorway.

"Hey there, neighbor." Christie's voice had a lilting quality that echoed in the big barn.

"Hey." David nodded at him and pulled another two bales off the back of the truck by the twine that bound them, but his stomach did an uneasy slide. He still felt humiliated about the way he'd buttoned Christie's coat for him the last time he came around. He had no idea what he'd been thinking, just that it came automatically to him, an urge to take care of Christie, make sure he was warm. He couldn't even remember doing that for Joe, at least not since he was a little tyke.

He shoved the bales in place in the stack he was making.

Christie fussed over River, who ate it up. He was all about receiving kindness from strangers. Then Christie wandered closer as David moved two more bales from the truck, one in each hand. "Wow, impressive. I bet those aren't as light as they look."

His easy tone made David relax. "Why don't you try one and see?"

Christie was carrying a white box that looked like a cake or pie box, and he had the old coat David lent him over one arm. He put the box and the borrowed coat on a beam and then lifted one of the bales from the flatbed. He made a face. "Yeah. What is that, like, forty pounds?"

"Forty to fifty, I guess."

"I should come over here to work out instead of going to the gym in town," he joked.

David grabbed two more bales and swung them into place. "Anytime you want to break your back working for me, you're more than welcome."

Christie raised a challenging eyebrow. "Maybe I will. I brought you more cookies. I've been channeling Betty Crocker lately, so I could use all the weight lifting I can get."

"That's nice of you, but not necessary." He stopped and wiped the sleeve of his work shirt over his sweaty forehead. "That reminds me. That plate you brought over.... That was something else. I think that chicken's the best I ever ate."

Christie's smile was instant and bright. "Really?"

"Surely. Those biscuits were good too."

"I'm glad you thought so, because I wanted to ask you something, actually. But let's get this done first."

To David's surprise Christie took off his own coat—a puffy black ski jacket that looked expensive—and put that on the beam as well. Underneath he wore a gray sweater and jeans, both of which were tighter and fancier than was practical on the farm. He had such a trim physique, like he'd never eaten a cookie in his life. David didn't want to be caught staring, so he didn't allow his gaze to linger.

He said nothing as Christie started to move bales. He moved one at a time, but he wrangled them just fine. He had more upper-body strength than David would have expected, and strong hands. Probably he did go to a gym. The idea of having to pay someplace for the privilege of exercising was bewildering to David. He always worked his body harder than was probably wise on any given day. His aches and pains were witness to that.

Christie stuck with the task. David found himself moving a little faster, pushing a little more, with someone there to impress. They swung bales like the truck was on fire. In ten minutes the flatbed was empty and all the hay was stacked.

"We definitely deserve a cookie for that," Christie commented as he brushed hay off his sweater. There was a fine sheen of sweat on his face that made him glow. He went over to the beam and picked up the box. He opened the lid and brought it over to David.

The box contained at least two-dozen cookies—chocolate chips, some kind of oatmeal with crisp brown edges, and fancy chocolate ones. David took an oatmeal. "You didn't have to bring me all these."

"It's strategic." Christie took a bite of an oatmeal cookie too and licked his lips to catch the crumbs.

David didn't know what he meant by that and didn't ask. He looked away at the bales of hay and took a bite of his own cookie. It was perfect—there was a caramel taste mixed with the oatmeal and a hint of saltiness that set off the sweet. But Christie still made him nervous, dang it. It wasn't a bad nervous, necessarily. He was a little intimidated, perhaps. Christie's city clothes and all that modern frippery and haircut and earrings and such made David feel like a homebody and a country bumpkin, like an old squash left out in the field.

Christie took a deep breath and spoke in a firm rush. "Okay, so here's the deal. I'm working a lot of hours right now, from the house, you know? But there's not a whole lot else for me to do around here. I tend to be a compulsive type. When I get into something, I really get into it."

David's gaze was drawn back to Christie's face. His eyes were shining with enthusiasm.

"And... well... lately it's been cooking. Aunt Ruth had stacks of gourmet cooking magazines, and it's fun to try the recipes. But then there I am with all this extra food, and my freezer is already full after less than a week. Plus it feels like a waste to make all that just for me. It's not like a drawing or a painting. It needs to be consumed right away."

All the stuff about cooking being fun wasn't something David could relate to. But he thought he knew where this was going, and he wasn't sure he liked it. He wasn't going to be anyone's charity case, and he didn't like feeling obliged. It reminded him of the way Evelyn Robeson kept bringing food over. There was an implied favor there, almost an implied possessiveness, like she was staking a claim. He could manage on his own, thank you.

That must have showed on his face because Christie held up his hands. "Hang on. Let me finish. This would help me out too. It's not cheap to buy the ingredients, though Aunt Ruth already had a lot of the spices and things, so that helps. What I thought was this.... I could keep track of what I pay for ingredients, you could pay half, and get half of what I make. Most recipes serve four, so you'd get two servings, and you can freeze one or have it for lunch the next day. That way I get to cook my little heart out, it's cheaper for me, my freezer is saved from chronic bloat, and you get home-cooked meals delivered. What do you say? Want to try it for a few days and see how it goes?"

He said all of this in a rush, as if anticipating David's arguments and trying to outpace them. David took off one of his work gloves and rubbed his chin. Why was Christie even offering this? Was it as straightforward as he said?

Wanting help paying for ingredients? Food *was* pretty expensive.

David reverted to the practical. "How much would these meals likely run?"

"Good question. I figured up what the chicken dinner cost me to make and half of that would have been sixteen dollars. But if you have a dollar limit in mind, I can take that into account too."

David would have paid sixteen dollars for the meal Christie brought over, if he'd been in a restaurant. And the food wouldn't have been half as good either. If he got two meals out of it, it was certainly in his budget. But he still felt uncomfortable, like he'd be taking advantage of Christie.

Then he heard Amy's voice in his head. *For Pete's sake, Dad, all the chemicals in those frozen meals will be the death of you. Promise me you'll do better.* She'd be all over him to accept Christie's offer, if she were here. And since he would be paying, there'd be no strings attached. Right?

"What kind of things do you like to make?" he asked.

Christie gave him a brilliant smile. "Oh my God, there are so many amazing recipes! I'm trying to avoid the super fatty or heavy stuff. Or lighten it a bit. You know, cut down the sugar and things like that. There's a *Bon Appétit* issue on Moroccan food that looks delicious, and Indian food too." His face became wary. "Or if you're more of a meat-and-potatoes kind of guy, there're some good steakhouse recipes. Oh! And there's an issue on Southern barbeque and New Orleans cuisine."

"Hmmm." David needed a moment to think. He took the push broom that was against the wall and started sweeping the stray bits of hay toward the large pile. Heck, just hearing those words piqued his appetite. He'd never had Moroccan food. And everything else Christie mentioned made him so hungry he could eat the hay. It was well past lunchtime, and he hadn't had a thing to eat since early that morning.

Christie waited patiently while David tried to collect his thoughts. "I wouldn't want to put you to any trouble," he said, still sweeping.

Christie waved a hand. "Like I said, I'm already making the food. But maybe we could start out three nights a week, so if I don't feel in the mood to cook, I won't worry about it."

"If you ever don't feel like it, just text me to let me know. I can fend for myself."

"Perfect!" Christie appeared to take that as consent. "Want to exchange phone numbers?"

David leaned on the broom and took his phone out. Soon his number was in Christie's phone and Christie's in his. *Christie Landon.* For some reason the sight of it gave him a little thrill. He couldn't remember the last time he'd added a new contact to his phone, especially one that wasn't for church or business.

Christie grabbed his ski jacket from the beam and put it on. "What about tomorrow night? Does anything I mentioned sound good?"

All of it. It all sounded good. For some reason words lined up to press their way out of David's usually taciturn throat. "Well... I've never been very far from here. Susan always made meat and potatoes, country cooking. I guess... I wouldn't mind trying new things. See what people eat in other parts of the world."

The confession made him feel awkward, but Christie tilted his head and looked at David with interest. "Spirit of an adventurer, hey? I like it. Moroccan it is, then. I'll text you tomorrow when it's about ready!" Christie skipped out the door, leaving behind the box of cookies and David's old coat.

David put down the broom and went over to look in the box. He chose a chocolate-chip cookie this time, and it practically melted in his mouth. He felt... excited. Nervous. He felt like he'd either just done something very foolish or incredibly fortunate. Time would tell which, but he was sure looking forward to eating more food as good as that chicken dinner.

He whistled to the dogs, shut the huge barn doors, and decided to leave the flatbed truck in the barn for the night. It wasn't hurting anything. Once in the house, he put on some water for tea, stuck a cup of soup in the microwave for a late lunch, then went into the living room.

One of the bookcases in there had four shelves of *National Geographic* magazines carefully arranged by date. They were some of his most prized possessions. He'd read them so often it only took him a moment to find the two issues he was looking for. One had an article called "Monkeys of Morocco" with amazing photographs, and the other was on the ancient spice trade with pictures from a Moroccan food market. He took the magazines with him back to the kitchen, where he could read them and look at the pictures while he ate his soup.

He felt a giddy surge of anticipation stir in his heart. Tomorrow night he'd be eating food just like the people in these articles ate. He'd be dining in Morocco.

Chapter 6

Christie set his alarm so he'd get up early. He settled down to work by 7:00 a.m. with a cup of coffee and a piece of toast. He knew if he got his usual slow start, he'd be distracted all day, and he couldn't let his new enthusiasm for cooking derail the progress he was making at work.

By three he finished his mock-ups and uploaded them to the cloud where his manager could look at them and comment. With happy relief he signed off for the day and allowed himself to think about tonight's meal. By three thirty he was at the grocery store to pick up the fresh ingredients.

He was stupidly excited about making Moroccan tonight for himself and David. He had a warning voice in his head. *Be careful. Don't get too friendly with this guy. David Fisher is not gay.* This wasn't like meeting some nice New Yorker to date. Hell, David probably didn't even want to be his friend. They had nothing in common.

Except, possibly, an interest in exotic food.

Even though those warnings were all true, Christie was a left-brain, instinctual kind of guy. This was a trait that had gotten him in trouble more than once, but generally his instinct was sound. He genuinely liked David—liked his honest, attractive face and the shy get-'er-done vibe about him. He was obviously a hard worker and a nice man. He lived alone and seemed... sad. It was simply a nice gesture to share meals Christie was cooking anyway. And God knew he could use a few ticks on the positive side of the karma balance sheet.

Beyond all that there were little flashes of something else—things that had gotten under Christie's skin. There was the way David seemed uncomfortable and awkward around him, couldn't look at him for long, the way he'd buttoned up that coat. The logical part of his brain said David was being fatherly, and not in a "hot daddy" kind of way. But Christie's gut.... His gut was not so sure. David taking care of him like that, the touch of his hands.... Yeah, that started any number of alarms happily ringing deep down in Christie's gay little heart.

Anyway, instinct, aka *wishful thinking* notwithstanding, Christie knew nothing would happen with David. He was just sharing expenses and helping out a neighbor at the same time. He was also lonely as fuck. So who did it hurt?

He picked out three recipes from the Moroccan issue. There was a spiced cauliflower and almond soup, a chicken dish with lemon and olives, and a pastilla made with filo dough and stuffed with a mixture of almonds, cinnamon, and turkey sausage to replace the duck in the recipe. The pastilla would look impressive, but it wasn't all that hard to make with prepackaged filo. For another easy and cheap side dish, he picked up a head of broccoli to roast. With some olive oil, sea salt, and cracked pepper, the broccoli would go well with the meal's more exotic flavors.

He was home by four fifteen and started pulling out pots and spices. He texted David to let him know dinner would be coming around six. Then he put on some tunes and got to work. Everything came together pretty well, though the filo on the pastilla got too dark in a few spots. It smelled fantastic, though, and a dusting of powdered sugar covered up the black bits.

He was done just before six, so he shot David a quick text that he was bringing the food over. Feeling suddenly nervous, Christie changed into a fresh sweater, a dark-blue one that brought out his eyes, and brushed his teeth and hair. It only took a few minutes, but when he came out, ready to pack up the food, David was knocking at the door.

Christie let him in. "Hi. I was going to bring it over to you."

David shrugged. "You did all the work. I figured the least I could do was pick it up." He sniffed the air. "Wow. That smells incredible. How much do I owe you?"

"I spent thirty-six dollars, so eighteen dollars would be great."

David took out his wallet and pulled a twenty.

"I think I have some ones."

"Heck no. I should be paying more for my share anyway since you cook it."

Christie stuffed the twenty in a pocket. "Thanks. Um. The recipes made six servings, so you'll get a couple of meals from this. You can just reheat the leftovers in the microwave."

"Great."

David was still standing in the doorway in his coat, his cheeks rosy with the cold. As usual he wouldn't meet Christie's gaze for long.

"Would you like to eat it here or take it to go?" Christie suddenly very much wanted David to stay, to sit in his aunt's small dining room with him and share the meal.

He wanted to see David's reactions, what he liked and didn't like. And yeah, he would love the company. But that wasn't exactly the deal they'd negotiated.

"I'll take it to go. That would be great, thanks," David said quickly.

Christie forced a smile. "Sure. Just give me a second to pack it up."

He went into the kitchen and opened the big drawer that held his aunt's Tupperware. He decided to put half the pastilla in a pie tin covered with foil, but the rest went into various sized containers. He put all of it in a fabric bag and took it out to the living room. "Here you go. I hope you like it."

"I'm sure I will. Thank you, Christie." The words were sincere, and David even met Christie's gaze when he said them.

Christie handed him the bag. "You're welcome. Thanks for helping me pay for it."

David started to go and hesitated. "I wanted to tell you—anytime you don't feel like cooking, just text me and let me know. I can always do for myself with what I've got at home. I don't want you to feel obligated. I know what it's like to have to do a job you don't feel like doing."

Christie supposed farmers had lots of chores they had to do, rain or shine, sick or well. He'd never had a job that demanding. "Okay. But like I said, it's fun for me. I enjoyed cooking today."

"All right, then." David gave Christie a grateful smile and left.

Christie sat down to his own meal. He wasn't a big eater, so he liked to take his time and taste every bite. The chicken breasts could have been juicier, but the olive and lemon sauce on them was tangy and scrumptious. The soup was perfectly spiced and filling. The pastilla was to die for—flakey and savory and sweet all at once. He couldn't make that often or he'd get fat. It wasn't long before he was full and had to pack up the rest for the fridge.

It was a lovely meal, but eating it wasn't as much fun as cooking it, or as much fun as eating it *with David* would have been. But there was no reason David should feel obliged to eat with him.

As he was cleaning up the kitchen, his text chime went off. He looked at the phone.

Enjoyed every bite of that. Thank you for taking me to Morocco.

It was a simple enough "thank-you," but not what Christie would have expected from his neighboring farmer. He wouldn't have expected David to be so openly interested in world cuisines, much less so appreciative about it. There was a glimpse of longing in David's words that touched something inside Christie, the same spot where David putting on his coat planted a seed.

Then again, maybe Christie was just "touched" altogether and reading too much into it.

He hesitated for ten minutes before replying. *How does Indian sound for Sunday lunch? Maybe 1 pm?*

David responded at once. *Sounds perfect. Thank you.*

Feeling suddenly much better and full of an energy he needed to burn off, Christie changed into his running clothes and went for a long run around the neighborhood in the dark and chilly October evening.

David should have gone to church on Sunday morning, but he decided to skip it once again. He felt guilty when he didn't go. The importance of church had been drilled into him since before he could walk. And the congregation was so supportive after Susan died. Also Pastor Mitchell called to "check in" if David missed more than a few weeks, and David dreaded that "visitation of shame." But he just wasn't up for it today. There were some church teachings he'd been uncomfortable with for years but silently ignored. He wasn't sure where his faith stood, but right now it seemed to be buried under a dissatisfied and restless part of himself that grew bigger and heavier each and every day.

At least this Sunday, he had a good excuse not to go. He wanted to neaten up the house.

It was a beautiful warm fall day. The sky was blue, the sun was bright, and there were lots of orange, russet, and gold leaves around the farm, vibrant against the still-green grass. He cleaned up the kitchen, wiping down the counters and the inside of the microwave in case Christie wanted to heat up anything. He swept up dog hair and opened the windows for fresh air. He found some Pledge and used it to polish the big plank table in the dining room.

He hadn't missed the disappointment on Christie's face when he opted to take his meal to go last time. And it was Sunday today. David didn't have to do any work except for the chores that could never be skipped—feeding and watering the animals, and the twice-a-day milking. He might as well invite Christie to eat over here. He might appreciate escaping his aunt's small house for a few hours, and the view from the big windows in the dining room was real pretty. Golden-leafed trees marched down to the farm's pond, which sparkled in the bright sunlight. It was foolish for both of them to eat alone on a Sunday, and the same darn meal yet. It didn't mean they had to eat together *all* the time. It was just a nice thing to do for once.

He texted Christie midmorning. *It's a nice day. If you want I can pick you and the food up in the truck, and we can eat over here.* He sent it, then had second thoughts. He quickly added, *Unless you have other plans.* Maybe Christie was going to the gym today. Or maybe he'd met some locals his own age. He probably wouldn't want to hang out with an old man.

But Christie's reply came quickly. *That would be great. See you at 1. Food looks good so far.*

David read the text with a smile and then went about his mission. He set the table with some old plain navy placemats—he preferred them to the frilly ones Susan favored. He made sure the silverware, plates, and glasses were nice and clean. Then he pulled some *Nat Geo* magazines. There were lots of articles on India, but he grabbed the ones that were mostly food related—one on traditional Indian weddings and their feasts, and another on temple food offerings. There were photographs of exotic-looking plates of food. What would Christie bring over? A curry? Some kind of eggplant dish? Tandoori?

David had been to an Indian food restaurant in Lancaster several times. But Susan didn't cared for it, so he didn't go often. He liked it at the time. But Christie cooking it himself made it a more authentic experience somehow. Or maybe David was just less busy and better able to appreciate it today.

He decided apple cider might go okay with the food, so he grabbed a jug from the basement and put it in the freezer to chill. After he'd done everything he could think of and taken a long shower too, it still was only just past noon, so he settled down to reread the magazines.

* * *

Christie made chicken tikka masala, paneer naan, aloo gobi, and basmati rice. He bought mango sorbet for dessert and got sprigs of mint to spruce it up.

It made him stupidly happy David invited him to eat at the farm. God, he was cracking up living out here all by himself, and it had only been three weeks.

The spices suffused Aunt Ruth's little house with aroma and left him in an extra-good mood. Everything tasted amazing when he sampled it. He put on a cream turtleneck cashmere sweater and a blue down vest the color of his eyes. Then he packed up his precious cargo and sent David a text.

A few minutes later, there was a knock on the door, and Christie opened it.

"Smells fantastic." David's expression was one of pure anticipation when he stepped inside. He put his hand unconsciously on his stomach.

"Wait 'til you taste it."

David's gaze fell to the bag in Christie's hand, and he reached out to take it. "All ready to go, then?"

"All set." Christie handed over the bag. He wasn't going to complain if David wanted to schlep it, though he wasn't used to people being quite so courteous.

They both commented on the fine weather as David drove them over to his place down the farm lane. At the house River and Tonga were excited to see him—or more likely to smell the bag of food David had.

"Hey, guys!" Christie gave each dog attention. They were nice dogs, super friendly. The black mix, Tonga, was a little hyper, but the yellow lab, River, was placid as could be.

"I've already set the table. This way." They moved into the dining room, and David set the bag on the table.

Christie looked around. "Wow! I love this room."

The original stone farmhouse had been added onto at some point. One whole wall of the dining room was made of fieldstone and was clearly once an exterior wall. Tall windows made up the opposing wall. There was an expansive view of gold-leafed trees, a sloping lawn, and what looked like a small lake at the bottom.

"It's the best room in the house," David admitted with a trace of pride, unloading containers from the bag.

"I guess! Did you build this addition?"

"Me? Nah."

Christie opened the tikka masala and put a spoon into the container. It was a shame not to have real bowls for the meal, but he didn't know David well enough to start getting greedy with his hospitality, and the Tupperware would work just fine. The table looked nice with simple placemats, heavy cream-colored plates, and shiny silverware.

David groaned as he opened the pie saver where Christie had put the naan. "Oh man. This looks incredible."

Christie felt a wave of pleasure. "Thanks. Chicken tikka masala, aloo gobi, naan, and rice."

David poured them both cold apple cider from a nearby Amish farm. Then they loaded up their plates and settled into their seats for some serious food appreciation..

Christie picked up his fork but David hesitated. "Do you say grace?"

Oh. Right. Christie put his fork down. "Please go ahead."

David closed his eyes. His blessing was brief, thanking

God for good neighbors and the wonderful food, which was actually very sweet. It was still strange. It had been years since Christie was at a table where prayers were said.

They both dug in. David was enthusiastic. His eyes practically rolled back in his head as he tasted each dish, and Christie tried very hard not to think about his little moans of appreciation in another context.

"You should open a restaurant. You have a gift. I can't imagine even attempting complicated dishes like this."

"It's really not that difficult," Christie replied modestly, though he soaked up the praise like a sponge. "I just followed the recipes."

"That's like a builder saying it's not that hard to build a house if you have a blueprint."

"Maybe it's not hard," Christie smiled wryly.

David wiped his mouth with a napkin. "Speaking of houses, you asked earlier about this addition. My father put it on when he discovered my mother was expecting me."

"Oh really? That sounds like a sweet family story."

"I guess. They didn't think they could have children. My mom got pregnant with me when she was forty. And yes," he said, smiling at Christie shyly, "the family story goes that my dad was so excited about it he expanded the house. Not that it was necessary, mind. I was one boy, not a new herd of cattle. Farmers tend to think big."

"Maybe it was his way of preparing for you emotionally. He must have doted on you."

"I wouldn't say that." David's face grew carefully shuttered. "He was a tough man, my dad. Very strict."

"Mine too." Christie decided neither one of them needed to talk about their childhood traumas, though it sounded like they had more in common than he'd thought. "So... you have children?"

His eyes went to a framed photo on the wall. It was a professional family portrait, taken near the barn. The family of four wore lots of denim and red, like a matched set. Besides David there was a woman with dark hair pulled back severely and a pretty, chubby face. She wore a long denim dress over a red turtleneck There were two kids—a girl and a boy in their early and midteens. It was a good-looking family but very conservative Midwest.

It was also a strong reminder, in case Christie needed it, that David Fisher was not on his team or, indeed, even in his universe.

"Yes, Amy and Joe. Amy's the oldest. She's twenty-one. And Joe's three years younger."

"They're both away at college?"

David nodded. "Amy's up in State College studying nursing at PSU, and Joe's just over in Lancaster at Franklin and Marshall. But he lives in the dorms and he's pretty busy, so I rarely see him. He wants to become a minister."

Christie's eyes flickered back to the photo. Both Amy and her mother wore long dresses and had their long hair back in buns. They clearly weren't Amish, but they weren't exactly modern either. "A minister in what denomination?"

"Mennonite. Our church is fairly progressive—for Mennonite."

Christie couldn't hold back his snark. "Is that like saying a dog is gentle for an attack dog?"

David studied Christie's face for a moment, a frown between his brows. *Yeah, way not to show bitterness with that analogy, Christie!* But then David shrugged, and the corners of his mouth turned up a little. "I suppose it's all relative."

"Sorry. I shouldn't have said that. Actually I was raised Southern Baptist. I bet it's not all that different."

"You were?" David looked surprised.

Christie nodded and took a bite of rice—the tikka masala sauce was so yummy over rice; he could eat just that for days. He gave himself a moment to think about how honest he wanted to be. "I haven't been to church since I moved away from home when I was eighteen. You could say I have some issues with religion."

David looked thoughtful rather than shocked or disapproving. "How old are you now, if that's okay to ask?"

"Thirty. My youth is behind me, alas."

"You're thirty? I thought you were closer to Joe's age. I would have guessed twenty-four or five at the most."

"Thank you?"

"Even so you're still just a pup."

"I guess it's all relative." Christie smiled wryly. "How old are you, David?"

"Forty-one." He ducked his head down when he said it like he was... what? Embarrassed? Lying? Christie didn't think he was lying; he had no reason to. Maybe he didn't feel his age.

"That's pretty young to have two grown children."

"It's not that young. I was twenty when my oldest, Amy, was born."

"Most twenty-year-olds are still trying to decide on a major."

David looked out the window. "By the time I was nineteen, I was married and running this farm full-time." It was a statement that might have been said with a prideful tone, but it wasn't. There was a weariness to it that made Christie's stomach clench.

"Why? What about your dad?"

"He died when I was a senior in high school." David tore off a piece of naan and dredged up some sauce with it. "He was only fifty-eight. Had a massive heart attack while driving the tractor. Died almost instantly, they said. I had to drop out of school to run the farm full-time."

"That's terrible! Fifty-eight is so young."

"It is. He worked too hard, and he was... not a happy man."

"That must have been so hard, having that much responsibility so young and dealing with your dad's death too."

David shrugged, but his neck got bright red, as if he were feeling much more than he showed. "It wasn't such a bad deal for me. The teachers at my school helped me finish my high school degree from home, plus I got the farm. Most young adults have to work and save a long time to buy a house. When I got the farm, it was already paid off, plus I had job security to boot."

"It is a beautiful place," Christie agreed, looking out the window. David was right. Christie knew a lot of people his age who were still searching for their path in life. Maybe being born with a path all laid out wasn't such a bad thing. But his host didn't have the vibe of a contented man.

"Are you happy, David?" The minute Christie said it, he wished he hadn't. He had a tendency to be too pushy, and that was a very personal question for virtual strangers.

David blinked at him in surprise. "I'm... I guess I don't think about it like that." He looked down at his plate. "What about your family?"

"My dad was a dentist, and my mom a teacher. I grew up in a small town too, in Illinois."

"Do you have brothers and sisters?"

"Nope. Only child."

"Christie is an unusual name. Is your family Swedish or something?"

Christie laughed. "Pretty all-American, really, though my dad has Swedish roots. It's Christopher on my birth certificate, but my mom started calling me Christie when I was little, and it stuck. I tried a couple of times to get people to call me Chris, but it never lasted."

It brought back a wave of memory—himself in high school trying briefly, and pointlessly, to be more butch. But trying to change his name just made him more of a target, as if he were admitting shame about who he was. In the end he was just grateful if the other students didn't call him faggot or fairy.

"I like it. *Christie*. It's... foreign-sounding. Italian maybe, like something in Latin."

Christie looked at David curiously. "Are you serious?"

David shrugged, his cheeks going a little pink. "Do you see your parents much?"

Christie was very careful to keep his voice light. "No. We're not close."

David looked like he wanted to ask why not, but he didn't. Thank goodness he wasn't as blunt as Christie himself.

"What about your mom?" Christie asked.

"She lived with us for a while when the kids were little, then her older sister's husband passed, so the pair of them moved to Florida together. She loves it down there." David looked at Christie thoughtfully. "Did you go to college?"

"Art school. I'm a graphic designer."

"Oh? Well, I can see you're very creative in the kitchen." David's gaze lingered on the earrings in Christie's ear. "I don't know that I've ever met a real artist before."

Christie laughed. "You make it sound like I'm an

aardvark or something. A person can be artistic in all sorts of ways."

"I s'pose. And you look nothing like an aardvark." David smiled wryly, and Christie thought, *He has a sense of humor after all.* "What do you do as a graphic designer?"

Christie talked about his job for the advertising agency. David wanted to see some of Christie's work, so he pulled out his phone and showed his sketch of the field with the cow and farmer. "This is for a campaign for a dairy company."

David took the phone and looked at it for a long moment while Christie ate his food. "I like the way you did the soil, with all the lines and rocks and beetles. Well, it's all good. You're very talented."

For some reason the compliment meant a lot to Christie. Maybe it was because David didn't seem like the type who said things he didn't mean. "Thanks. You might recognize the barn as yours. I had to guess some of the details. I can't see it very well from my house."

David handed back the phone. "You're welcome to come over anytime if you need to sketch something close up."

"That wouldn't be intrusive?"

"Nah. What are neighbors for?"

"That would be great. So what all do you raise here on the farm?"

David shifted in his chair, sighed. "This farm's a hundred acres, and I lease another hundred down the road. I raise conventional crops—corn, wheat, soy, alfalfa. I have a small dairy herd too. I sell the milk to an organic co-op. Then I run a chemical-free CSA with my daughter Amy during the summer. We grow the vegetables and herbs for that in a small field by the barn."

"By conventional crops you mean nonorganic?"

"Yup."

"Why not organic?"

David shook his head with a grimace. "Money. A farmer's always got to be looking into what's selling and adapt to that. Raising organic crops is very labor intensive, and it takes years to get certified too. It's a big investment for no extra return until you've got the official paperwork. On the other hand, organic dairy is not that hard to convert to and earns twice that of nonorganic. We switched over six years ago."

"Sounds complicated."

David looked embarrassed. "Well. I could never do what you do. I meant what I said. You're welcome to sketch whatever you like here. And you don't have to always bring food either, though this is a wonderful meal." He hesitated. Then his gaze met Christie's head-on. "Thank you for offering to cook something special like this. I want you to know I appreciate it."

There was so much warmth in his eyes it was like being handed gratitude in a brightly wrapped gift box. All the excuses and platitudes that came into Christie's mind felt trivial by comparison. *It's fun for me. I like having help paying for groceries. I like having company. I like your company.* Damn it, he so did. He shouldn't, but he did. Hell. He was crushing on David Fisher.

He mumbled a "you're welcome." And for a while, they focused on their food.

The Indian food was excellent—better than David remembered from his few restaurant visits. Sharing the meal with Christie was nicer than he expected too. Very nice.

There was a hot feeling in David's chest that grew over the course of the meal and took him by surprise. He genuinely liked Christie Landon. He didn't normally take to people so easily. Even at church he tended to keep to himself. He found himself wondering about it as he savored the meal.

He was flattered, if he were honest with himself. Christie was a smart, interesting, and attractive young man—not as young as David thought, but still considerably younger than him. He imagined Christie would have no trouble finding people his own age who desired his company, especially young women. Yet here he was, spending time with David. He asked a lot of questions, looked directly into David's eyes a discomforting amount of the time, smiled and laughed at the things David said like he was actually paying attention.

It struck David that it had been a long time since anyone truly *saw* him. To Amy and Joe, he was just "Dad." They asked him how the farm was doing, or about his health, but that was about it. And when Susan was alive, they'd gotten far too comfortable with each other. She was always wrapped up in her sewing or church work or books. She'd ask what he wanted for dinner or talk about the kids or people they knew. But he couldn't remember the last time she'd really looked at him.

Are you happy, David?

When was the last time anyone cared if he was happy, as long as he continued to maintain the farm and put money in the bank for school, clothes, and food?

That isn't fair, he chided himself. Amy worried about

him, he knew. And Joe was a good kid. His family loved him, but he still felt invisible most of the time.

Then again Christie was just a stranger making small talk. It didn't mean anything. Still, the company was stimulating. He liked the fact Christie spoke his mind, like he'd done about religion and his parents. He didn't pull punches or give what he thought was the *right* answer, or simply quote scripture. David was both taken aback and admiring of that fact.

After they ate David put the leftovers in the fridge and started dishwater in the sink. He washed the dishes and Christie dried.

"How old is this farmhouse?" Christie asked as he took a wet plate from David.

"The main house was built in seventeen fifty-three. That's pretty much the front two rooms."

"No shit! Can I take a look after we're done here?"

"Sure." David wasn't used to the profanity, but Christie didn't seem to mean anything bad by it, so he decided it didn't matter. It made Christie seem even more worldly and mysterious in David's eyes.

After Christie's bag was repacked with clean and empty containers, David led the way to the front of the house. The front two original rooms had high ceilings, old-fashioned crown moldings, deep windowsills because of the thick stone walls, and a huge fireplace. Susan had turned them into a formal parlor and a study, but they were rarely used even when Amy and Joe lived at home. These days David spent all his time in the kitchen, where a small table and TV served his needs. It was easier to heat too. Which meant the front rooms were tidy but could use a good dusting.

Christie wandered around looking at everything. He

ran his fingers over the fireplace's old lintel and ended up in front of the bookshelf with its shelves of magazines. "Someone likes *National Geographic*."

"Those are mine."

Christie turned to look at him, one eyebrow raised in surprise. "What do you like about them?"

David hesitated. It wasn't something he talked about much, but he felt an urge to show Christie he thought about things other than the farm and the next crop. "I like to learn about other places. It's my way of traveling, I guess."

"Yeah?" Christie's smile was soft. "What's your favorite issue?" He trailed his long, thin fingers over the spines.

David immediately knew the answer to the question, but he felt a twinge of doubt. Probably Christie would think he was ridiculous. He hesitated then reached out, pulled a magazine, and handed it to Christie.

Christie looked at the cover. "Polynesia?"

"Yeah. Maybe because we're so landlocked here, but I like islands. Polynesia has the best ones, like Bora Bora."

The magazine was still in Christie's hands. David carefully turned to an oft-viewed page. The double-page title spread had a gorgeous picture of a white sand beach, a turquoise ocean, and little beach huts built right over the water. How many times had David looked at this picture and tried to imagine himself there?

He looked up at Christie from under his lashes, ready to back off the subject with excuses and dismissal.

But Christie grinned. "Oh yeah. That's gorgeous! I love beaches. I haven't been to Polynesia, but I've been to Cancún. The beaches there are fantastic."

"I have an issue on Cancún." David scanned the titles and unerringly pulled the issue. He found the page quickly and handed it to Christie. "More than a third of all Mexican tourism dollars come from Cancún. That's a lot when you consider the size of the country. They call it the 'Mayan Riviera' in that article."

Christie got a curiously amused frown between those blue eyes. "You know these magazines backward and forward, don't you?"

David shrugged, uncomfortable. "I'm not much of a TV watcher. I prefer to read, and facts stick in my head. That is, they do if I find them interesting."

Christie flipped through the Cancún article. "Have you been able to travel much yourself?"

David laughed. "No. It's hard to leave a farm. When Joe was in high school, I could trust him with the place for a few days at a time. I went to a farming conference up in State College and another one in Washington DC. I enjoyed that. I have a guy who works part-time for me now, but I still need to be here myself."

He remembered the excitement of that trip to DC. Time had made the details fade, but he clearly remembered standing in front of the massive Lincoln Memorial and thinking how much bigger and *realer* it was in person. It was as real as the bark on a tree or the shingles on the farmhouse roof when he repaired it one sweltering summer, as though, if he touched it, some residue would come off on his skin and be there forever. And all the time Lincoln's Memorial existed out there—massive and real and solid—heedless of whether or not a man named David Fisher ever went to see it, or that he even existed at all.

Head in the clouds. Daydreaming never got a lick of work done. Yup. Just like his dad always said. Maybe daydreams didn't get work done, but they sure helped pass the time. His thoughts were his own in a way nothing else was.

They kept him company while his body was busy doing repetitive tasks.

Christie was watching him with a penetrating gaze, as if he could see all of David's thoughts and secrets. It felt intimate and yet comfortable, which was a bit unnerving in itself. Christie was a stranger only this morning, but he didn't feel like one now. In fact, David couldn't remember the last time he'd connected to someone like this.

He cleared his throat. "So. You ready for that sorbet? I can put on some coffee. And if you're up for it, I'd love to hear about your Cancún trip."

"Deal." Christie turned away and the strange moment ended. David carefully put back the magazines.

"God, I'm going to have to run six miles tonight to burn off that tikka masala," Christie groaned, patting his stomach.

"You're welcome to swing the hay bales around in my barn if you want to."

Christie laughed. "Nice try."

Chapter 7

Everything changed after that Sunday. Nothing earth shattering happened during that comfortable fall afternoon when Christie took Indian food over to David's house. And yet something shifted between them in a fundamental way. Christie had enjoyed David's company, and the feeling seemed to be mutual.

Christie wanted *more*—more exotic cooking, more shared meals, more time in David's company. It was an itchy feeling that gave him little peace until he indulged it.

On Tuesday Christie went over to the farm in the morning with his sketchbook. He walked around the barn until he found a vantage point he liked—one with the big white silo peeking over the front of the barn and two big windows facing him. It was so quaint it made his teeth ache. He took a chair from David's porch and carried it to the spot, sat down, and opened his sketchpad. It was a little cold to be drawing outside, but not so cold he couldn't stand it. He drew a line sketch first and then started to fill it in with the woodcut swirls he'd established as the style in his other drawings.

After an hour or so, David came by and brought him a travel mug full of coffee. They chatted for a few minutes about the weather and the features of the barn. David said it was several hundred years old and was called a "bank barn" because it was built on a slope. The back of the barn could be driven up to for delivering hay and feed to the second story, while the lower level opened onto the pasture and was where the animals were kept.

"Well, I should let you get back to work. And me too," David said after a bit.

Christie smiled. "Have a good afternoon."

David looked like he was about to walk away, but he hesitated, gazing at Christie. He clenched his fist, then left abruptly. It was weird, as if he were resisting an impulse to ruffle Christie's hair or something.

Christie mused over it as he worked on his sketch, a low warmth in his belly. Had David really wanted to ruffle his hair, maybe the way he'd buttoned up the coat? Or perhaps touch his shoulder? Brush the hair out of his eyes? Kiss him?

Don't get excited. It's probably a paternal instinct, if anything at all. Yes, because it would be just his luck if the hot farmer next door saw him as a son substitute.

And yet... that didn't explain the little frissons of tension Christie sensed there sometimes. Though admittedly those frissons could be entirely one-sided.

He loved that things with David were so... *not* blatantly sexual, actually. Christie had been getting jaded; there was no doubt about that. Picking up men was so easy in the city: flirt for ten minutes, have sex, and it was over. But being back in the country, being around Aunt Ruth's things, and David—definitely David—it felt like he'd shifted to a simpler, more innocent time. It was softening his cynicism like stiff leather soaked in brine.

It reminded him of where he'd come from, of who

Christie Landon was before he became fierce Christie Landon, Manhattanite. He'd left small-town Illinois with a lot of anger. He earned it, bitter drop by bitter drop. He never fit in either at school or at home. And he hated the church his parents dragged him to, mostly because he knew they'd hate him if they knew who he really was. He understood from a young age he was gay, and even though he didn't come out 'til right after high school, he'd stored up slights like broken shards of glass. Didn't they say living well was the best revenge? Christie *had* lived well in New York. A little too well. But maybe... possibly... when he left his small-town home, he threw out the baby with the bathwater.

Maybe there was something to this simple life after all, especially if it included a guy like David Fisher.

That night Christie made blue cheese stuffed burgers with grilled mushrooms and herbed sweet potato oven fries. When it was almost ready, he debated with himself and then sent a carefully worded text:

Dinner is ready. You're welcome to eat with me over here or just pick it up.

He didn't want to make assumptions or give David the impression he had nothing better to do. But the answer came back quickly.

Might as well eat there. Be over in a few.

Christie smiled and hurried to set the table.

"Oh my God. That was too good. I'm going to get fat." Christie pushed back his chair and patted his stomach. It looked flat to David, if maybe slightly full. It was hard to tell under the blue sweater Christie was wearing, especially since he didn't allow his eyes to linger.

"You always say that, but I haven't seen you gain an ounce yet," David remarked, scraping some peanut sauce from his plate with his spoon. Tonight Christie had made pad thai, a salad with spicy sliced beef called "crying tiger," and tom yum soup. He even played some instrumental music from Thailand on his phone, which was new. It helped make the food taste even more authentic. "Anyway, you have a long way to go before you have to worry about getting fat."

"A long way to go is right. I'm going to have to run a couple of extra miles tomorrow. Thank God it's Saturday."

"How far do you normally go?"

"Four miles during the week, but I like to go longer at least one day on the weekend. I might do six tomorrow. I don't suppose you need to worry about getting out of shape." Christie smiled at him indulgently.

"No. But I see the appeal. I used to run track and field in school. I liked it a lot."

"Oh yeah? Did you compete?"

"For a few years. The private high school I went to had a track team."

It was one of the things David liked best about school. He traveled around the area for track meets. His team didn't go as far away as the bigger public schools. Never to New York or Boston or even Philadelphia. But it was still a treat just to visit someplace new, to get away for a while. He had to fight his father to stay in school as long as he did.

You'll go to Mennonite school or none at all. You don't need to be exposed to a lot of worldly wickedness or subjects you'll never need. I don't know why you want to go in the first place. You can home school and help more on the farm, earn more money to put away. You don't need all that learning to be a farmer.

But he stayed in school, at least until his father died, and he had no choice. Thank heaven his mother was on his side in that debate.

"Would you like to run with me sometime?" Christie asked. "Might be fun."

David was startled by the question. He barked out a laugh. "Oh no. I'll run the day you do farmwork."

Christie cocked an eyebrow. "Is that a dare? I will if you will."

David passed it off as a joke and changed the subject. They finished their meal without any further dangerous references to running.

But on Sunday, a rare night Christie didn't bring a meal over, David ate leftovers in the quiet house and then found himself staring out into the night. There was a full moon, and it was fairly bright out. Before he could change his mind, he went upstairs, put on some long underwear, a pair of sweats, and some older tennis shoes. He slipped out of the house.

He jogged slowly down the driveway to the road to warm up, and then set the timer on his phone. It was a mile to the old stone bridge. Surely he could go that far. He'd be damned if he'd run with some young pup and look like a worn-out and tired old man.

He made it to the bridge in twelve minutes. He worked hard on the farm, but little of it was cardio. His lungs felt like they were on fire, and his heart pounded like an engine that needed oil or it would soon start smoking. But he made it. He hung over the side of the bridge, breathing hard and staring at the rushing water. The white foam glowed in the moonlight. That wasn't bad, he told himself, not completely humiliating for someone who hadn't run in twenty years. If he could practice for a few weeks and get down to a ten-minute mile for three miles, he might dare run with Christie Landon.

Why did he even want to, though? That was what he should be asking himself. In the past week, he'd shared four meals with Christie. That should be enough time spent in his company.

It still wasn't quite enough.

Not enough for what?

The water coursing in the stream below was real—water over rocks. But nothing else felt all that real anymore.

He enjoyed Christie's company; that was all. Looked forward to it. It was ages since he had something like... a friend? Someone to talk to. Why shouldn't he run if he wanted to? If Christie wanted somebody to run with?

It wasn't something to worry about, for goodness sake. It wasn't a big deal. He turned and started back for the farm, running harder than before.

The next day David was in the barn checking on a pregnant heifer he'd confined when Christie appeared at the half door to the stall.

"Hi." David felt his heart lift like it always did around Christie. He couldn't help but smile.

"Hi." Christie smiled back. "Who's this?"

"This is a very pregnant mama-to-be."

"Does she have a name?"

David hesitated. The truth was he named all the cows in his head because it was simply easier to keep track of them with a name rather than "the reddish one" or whatever. But some farmers would find that ridiculous.

"Buella," he admitted. He palpitated her stomach.

"Holy cow! No pun intended." Christie's eyes got wide

as he got a good look at her massively swollen udders. "She looks like a balloon about ready to pop. Those udders are ginormous."

"Yeah. This is her first calf, and her body's reacting hard to the hormones. She should still have a few weeks go to, but with her this swelled up, it's safer to separate her 'til then."

"What do you do if she doesn't go into labor on her own?"

David smiled at the naive question. "Oh, she will. She'll go when she and the calf are ready."

Christie looked fascinated. He bit his lower lip, eyes on Buella.

"Come on in if you want."

"Really?" Christie looked delighted. He quickly figured out the door latch, let himself in, and shut it tight behind him. He came over through the fresh straw David had put in the stall. This was a small pen he used when one or two animals had to be separated from the herd, so Christie didn't have to walk far. He was wearing tall rubber boots, David noticed, which was good. Chances were if you walked into a cow's stall, you'd walk out with a little bit of nature on your shoes, no matter how recently it had been cleaned.

Christie looked at Buella, and she looked at him. She was a bit irritated, probably because she felt lousy. She shook her head, but when Christie reached out a hand, she sniffed it and let him pet her nose. She relaxed under the touch.

"Best to scratch her up here." David demonstrated behind her ears. "If you touch her face, you encourage her to head butt you the way cows greet each other. Believe me when I say a cow head butting you is not something to be desired. They don't know you're not as strong as they are."

"No, that doesn't sound like an outcome to be desired." Christie petted her behind the ears.

"So what can I do for you?" David felt carefully around Buella's sides, trying to determine the size of the calf.

"Actually I was wondering what can I do for *you*. Something that involves lifting and sweating, hopefully." He waggled his brows.

David snorted. "You know I was joking about you doing farmwork. You've got enough on your plate, what with your artist job and all the cooking you do."

Christie shrugged. "I've been at the gym in town for a month, so I had to decide whether or not to renew my membership. I wasn't crazy about the place, to be honest. I don't exactly fit in there. So I figured I might as well save the money. Is there something I can do that would require muscles for an hour or so? If I run without any weight-lifting, my upper body gets too lean."

He spoke a little fast, like that time he proposed sharing meals and meal costs. He sounded worried David would say no. David couldn't see a single reason why he would, though.

"I'd be happy to put you to work. I can't guarantee you'll get the same results as the gym."

Christie eyed David up and down. "Your body looks good to me. I'll take my chances."

David blushed down to his toes. Literally he felt the soles of his feet flush hot inside his boots. He turned his back on Buella and Christie and wiped his face with the crook of his arm, trying to hide his reaction. Surely Christie was only looking at him objectively. But it was a long time since anyone looked at his body like that, and it stirred up more than just embarrassment. "There's a, um, delivery of feed bags that could be binned. They're fifty-pound bags."

"Perfect. Just show me where."

David led Christie out of Buella's stall to the back of the barn where the feed guy had dropped off a hundred large bags of a grain mix. "These get moved downstairs, opened up, and dumped into that large green bin next to the cow stall."

"You got it." Christie squatted down, picked up a bag, stood, and put it on one shoulder. "You realize this means you'll have to run with me, though."

David rubbed the back of his neck. He'd never admit in a million years he'd been practicing for just that. "Maybe I will. Soon."

"This weekend?" Christie pushed in that persistent way of his.

David sighed. He could easily put Christie off, but the truth was, he had a hard time saying no to any opportunity to spend time with Christie. Besides, his run to the bridge was already down to ten and a half minutes.

"Yeah, all right. I'm gonna ruin your pace. You know that."

"I'll survive. It's just one run." Christie looked quite pleased with himself as he carried the bag off into the barn.

David wondered if one of anything would ever be enough for Christie Landon.

The first time David came over to run with Christie, it was early November. They did an easy-paced five miles at eight in the morning, which was early for Christie, but apparently David had already done a bunch of chores by then.

Christie took David along his usual route. It went around some neighborhoods and along the backside of the town's quaint main street. Christie wore compression tights and an Old Navy thermal half-zip, but David's sweats were the old-fashioned kind—like something Sylvester Stallone wore in *Rocky*. He looked good in them, though. Manly. He had sexy narrow hips with a small belly. The sweatpants hung just right off those hip bones and over his round ass. Not that Christie was staring. Much.

They didn't talk a whole lot. Christie got the feeling David was focusing on his gait and breathing, so he didn't want to distract him. He was a good runner, not fast, but steady and solid. The few times he started to breathe too hard, Christie slowed down.

They got back to Christie's place in just over an hour.

David was wearing at least two layers under his sweatshirt, but his front and back both had a deep V of sweat, and he panted, head hanging over his knees, in Christie's front yard.

"This is... I should...."

Christie bent one leg up behind his back to stretch it. "What's wrong? You okay?"

David nodded, nostrils flaring as he tried to catch his breath. "Cut your grass. Needs it."

Christie laughed. "Stop judging my pathetically long grass. You'll make me self-conscious."

David gave him a disbelieving look, as if to say, *You made me dress like this and run with you, and you feel self-conscious?*

Christie rolled his eyes. "You did good, old man. Ran like a pro. Come in while I make a pot of coffee." Christie led the way inside and headed right for the sink. He poured them both a glass of cold water and handed one to David before he went to the coffee machine. Water after a run was necessary, but coffee was what he craved. "I haven't been able to get Aunt Ruth's mower to run. It's ancient, and apparently they no longer make the arrowheads or stone gears or whatever that it needs."

David drank his water down in one long, mesmerizing draught. He wiped his lips on his sleeve. "I'll come over with my rider mower and do it. It'll take no more than a half hour."

"You don't have to do that. You already fixed the windows in my kitchen and my showerhead."

"Gotta pay you back somehow for all the meals."

"You *do* pay me."

"Money. You've also earned the milk of human kindness."

David's eyes twinkled with humor. Christie smiled and turned away, trying to banish the lingering image of David's throat as he drank the water. He fussed with the coffee pot. David was joking around more lately, and that was a good sign. He was so serious and solemn when they met, maybe even depressed.

My father was not a happy man. Maybe depression ran in the Fisher family. Only David didn't seem depressed now.

Christie started the coffee dripping. "You just feel sorry for me because I don't know how to do anything."

"You know how to do lots of things, just not stuff that requires a screwdriver."

"Mmm." Christie turned and leaned back against the kitchen counter.

The coffee percolated with pops and hisses. David stood there in the kitchen in that gray sweatshirt, all sweaty and rosy -cheeked from the cold. His brown eyes were warm and his lips quirked in a smile. His close-clipped beard gave him a scruffy vibe, and his hair had gotten a little longer at the nape and curled against his ruddy neck, damp with sweat.

And suddenly Christie wanted him so badly it *ached*. He wanted to take a step forward and touch David, wanted to press up against that hot, sweaty body, feel the hungry slick of his lips. The pain of frustrated longing was sharp. His body reacted to the rush of lust in other ways as well. He turned back to the cupboard and started opening up doors randomly, as if looking for cups. Dear Lord, he so did not need an erection in these spandex tights.

Behind him he heard a chair pull out from the table. David had backed off. Thank God. Christie pulled out two mugs, his hands numb from the sudden evacuation of blood to parts south.

"Hey, mind if I grab the coffee to go? I need to get back for the dairy pickup."

"Sure." Christie pulled out a travel mug. By the time he'd filled it and put in a dollop of milk the way David preferred, he had his body under control. He turned and offered it, his face carefully blank.

"See you at six?" David asked. He was avoiding Christie's eyes, though. Had he guessed?

"Sure. I was going to do shrimp and grits, New Orleans style."

"Can't wait." David gave him a brief glance and a smile and was out the door.

Once he was gone, Christie banged his head against the fridge. God, he was way too young to be this horny and frustrated with no relief in sight. But he wasn't sure he had a solution—at least nothing but a long shower and his good right hand.

"I'm glad things are going so well for you and Billy," Christie told Kyle over the phone. *And I'm not jealous at all.*

"Me too. Hey, we want to go to Cancún in February. You in?"

Christie opened his fridge and scanned the contents. He needed something light for lunch—a salad would do. "I don't know. I don't want to be a third wheel, Ky."

"You wouldn't be! Come on, we're an old married couple now. It's not like we think of nothing but sex."

"That's not what you just told me."

"I said the sex was *amazing*, not that we do nothing else. Come on, I miss you, and Billy would love to see you too. Maybe we can find a fourth."

Christie grimaced. "No, that would be weird. It would be like you were setting us up, and there we are stuck on vacay staring at each other if it doesn't work out...." Christie pulled out a bag of spring mix greens and a container of leftover Cajun red beans from the fridge and shut the door with his foot.

"What about David? Maybe your he-man farmer would like to go along."

The idea of David in Cancún provoked a wistful pain somewhere in the region of Christie's heart. "I wish. But I told you it's not like that. We're just friends."

"So? Friends can go to Cancún together. Friends can even end up getting frisky together. In Cancún."

"Yeah, not going to happen. Anyway, he can't leave the farm."

Christie heard Kyle sigh over the phone, and his voice

grew serious. "Okay, so just you, then. Please think about it? I'm worried about you, babe. It would be good for you to get away with us for a week, be around your people. I worry that you're getting attached to this straight farmer, and you'll end up hurt—physically or otherwise. You said you don't think he even realizes you're gay."

"David wouldn't hurt me," Christie said with conviction. "He's not the violent type."

"*Or otherwise.* He could still break your little heart."

Christie felt his stubborn streak raise its sharp-toothed head. "He can't hurt me if I have no illusions. And I don't."

"Yeah? Well, you should hear your voice when you talk about him. *Oh, David!*" Kyle mocked the words.

"Shut up, bitch."

Kyle laughed. "Seriously, why don't you check out some of the clubs around there? Or look on Grindr. I looked in your area the other day, and there were quite a few listings. Some cute ones too."

"Why the hell are you looking on Grindr, Kyle?"

"*For you*, Christie. I looked *for you*. Jesus, I'm not going to cheat on Billy." Kyle sounded defensive.

"You'd better not."

"I won't! We're talking about you, not me."

"Well, I'm not in the mood for a faceless fuck."

Don't I wish I were. He hadn't touched another person since Kyle's overdose in August. That was the longest he'd been celibate that he could remember. But he promised himself he was going to change his ways, and the idea of hooking up with a total stranger on Grindr when what he really wanted was David.... It felt all kinds of icky. And that should set off major alarm bells right there.

"Fine." Kyle changed the subject. "So how's it going getting the house ready to sell?"

"Slow." Between working, cooking, and spending way too much time over at David's farm, Christie hadn't made any progress toward finishing clearing his aunt's things or getting the house ready for sale.

"Think you'll be all done and back in the city by summer?" Kyle pushed.

"By summer? Sure." That sounded far enough away to Christie. He did need to get on with things. And he would after the holidays. "Hey, sweets, I need to get going. I have to get back to work. I have to start on a new campaign this afternoon, and I'm cooking tonight."

"Okay. But please promise me you'll try to get out and meet some gay men, all right? You're spending too much time with He-who-shall-not-be-touched."

God, if Kyle knew how much time he was actually spending with David, he'd have a fit. "Okay. I will!"

"Bye, brat! Call me soon."

Chapter 8

The first snow of the year arrived on Tuesday, November 19. David walked out of the farmhouse at 5:00 a.m. to find an inch already on the ground and thick, fat, fluffy wads falling heavily. The forecast was for six to eight inches, but it looked like that was going to be conservative. This was *snow*.

He felt inexplicably lighthearted about it. He loved snow as a kid, but as he got older, it became more of a burden than anything—plowing the drive, losing access to the back of the barn, freezing water pipes, worrying about the livestock getting mired in the stuff. But today... today he was in a good mood, and he was willing to concede it was magical.

Christie was supposed to come over to make authentic Italian pizzas tonight. David was looking forward to it. He'd start a fire in the woodstove in the kitchen later. It would feel cozy in the house with the fire inside and the snow outside. He mused about it as he went about his morning chores. He also thought about the chicken dumpling soup Christie had brought over the night before. It was so tasty. He had enough left over for another big bowl for lunch.

After he finished the morning milking, feeding, and watering, he went into his workshop in the barn to clean and repair some tools. People tended to think farmers had the winter off, but that was hardly the case. The growing season was nonstop work on the land, so the months of winter were spent trying to catch up on everything else. He needed to empty out and disinfect his milk tank, clear the lines, do maintenance on all the farm equipment, do any cleaning and organizing he'd put off, order seeds and supplies, catch up on bookkeeping, and a million other tasks.

He tried to repair a clogged blower, but he needed an itty-bitty Philips screwdriver, and all the ones on his worktable were too big. He had one in the farmhouse, but it was a long walk through the snow. In frustration he tried again to open the bottom drawer of the old worktable. The wooden monstrosity was built by his grandfather. It had a fantastically large work surface and built-in drawers along one side, like a desk. But the bottom drawer had been jammed for as long as David could remember. Like always, today it just wouldn't budge. There was probably some tool upright in there that was blocking the sliders. It was one of the many *someday* problems on the farm's never-ending list. It was depressing to think about how long that list was.

Frustrated, David gave up and set the blower aside. He picked up a pair of huge shears to sharpen instead.

At noon he left his workshop to head to the house for lunch, and he found the farm transformed. He shuffled through a good foot of drift crossing the yard. The snow was thick and fluffy and dry as a bone. Oh, this was good stuff, this snow. In a few days it would be soggy and icy and an absolute pain, but right now it was like a pillow from heaven.

He found the itty-bitty screwdriver in the junk drawer and put it in a pocket for later. Then he warmed up leftover chicken dumpling soup and a delicious nutty bread Christie had made that tasted purely wonderful smeared with apple butter. He ate at the small kitchen table, watching the snow continue to come down. The view was so thick with flakes it looked like the white Swiss dot curtains Susan put up in Amy's bedroom.

He had an urge to reach out to Christie. He debated with himself. He didn't want to get greedy or impinge on Christie's workday. But the idea of sharing this rare magical snow with someone—*with Christie*—was too appealing. He decided to call instead of text.

"Hey, David. What's up?" Christie sounded surprised to hear from him.

"Hey. You seeing the snow out there?"

"Yes! It's fantastic. I'm trying to get a rev done for my boss so I can go out and play in it." The joy in his voice made David's enthusiasm bubble higher.

"I was thinking the same thing. How do you feel about snowmobiles?"

"God yes! Where do you normally ride?"

"Around the farm, and there's a trail through the woods the locals use. Would be nice to get to it before dark. It's so pretty out there."

"Sounds perfect."

"Is three too early for you?"

"No, that works. I'll bring all the dinner stuff too and cook there afterward."

"Why don't I pick you up on the snowmobile? We can drop the food at the house before we head out. The farm lane drifts up pretty high because of the wind, so you'd struggle walking over here."

"Okay. Thanks. See you at three?"

"See you then."

The rest of the afternoon was all happy anticipation. David fixed the clogged blower and a few other tools, then texted Earl to make sure he'd be in as usual to do the evening milking. Earl was a retired farmer David had hired a few years ago. He came in three hours a day to do the second milking and muck stalls. He said he could make it fine despite the snow, which David was relieved to hear.

He went to the garage to check the snowmobiles. He filled the newer one up with gas and made sure it started. Then he brought in the cows and shut the pasture gate. The snow was getting high enough they'd possibly flounder. Plus, honestly, he wanted to be able to ride the snowmobile in the pasture without worrying about the herd.

He sent Christie a reminder to dress warm, took a shower, and got on his own snow clothes. He was at Christie's by three. The ride over there through the deep powder was everything he could have wished for. This was going to be a blast .

"Ready to go?" he asked when Christie opened the door.

Christie's cheeks were bright and his eyes sparkled. He looked as excited as David felt and was bundled up in jeans, boots, and various layers of fleece and wool. "Yeah, just let me grab the food and my parka."

They trudged out to the snowmobile. "I can put the food in the back." David lifted the top of the rear seat and placed the bag inside. "You can ride behind me back to the farm."

He felt a little strange saying it, but Christie grinned. "Sounds good to me."

David got on the snowmobile, and Christie put a leg over and sat behind him. The excitement David had been feeling about the snow all day peaked, tingles running up his legs. "Better hold on."

Christie scooted closer so his parka was up against David's back. He put his hands on David's hips. David started the snowmobile and backed out of the driveway. A moment later they were heading down the farm lane.

"Wow! You're right, this lane really drifts over!" Christie had to yell in David's ear to be heard over the engine.

David nodded. He didn't trust his voice to speak at the moment, and particularly not yell. Anyway, it was nice going down the lane between their houses in silence.

When they got to the farm, David stopped the snowmobile and turned it off so they could hear each other, but Christie made no move to get up.

"Think we need to put the food in the house?" David asked.

"It's probably just like being in the fridge where it's at now, right?"

"Yeah." David hesitated. Christie's hands were still on his hips. "I have another snowmobile if you want to drive one, but you'd have to follow me closely. I know where the potholes and branches and things are. You can just ride with me if you want."

Christie was silent for a moment. "I'm okay like this if you are."

David didn't mind at all. He started the engine again,

and they were off. He rode around the pasture for a while. It was ten acres and had some fun little hills and dips. Then he opened a gate and they headed down the slope to the woods, where he could pick up the local trail. When he got back on the snowmobile after closing the gate, Christie's hands didn't go back to his hips. Instead he put his arms around David's waist completely and shifted a little closer.

David rode through the snow, the dark branches of leafless trees on either side, and the orange and peach of sunset at the horizon, and he felt... incandescently happy. He couldn't remember the last time he had felt like this, like joy was a fossil fuel buried deep in his soul, and he had suddenly struck deep and hit a gusher. He felt vibrant and alive, wanting to be in this moment and nowhere else, wishing he could bottle it up and keep it forever.

Christie snuggled up closer behind David as if he were cold, chest pressed to back through layers of winter wear. He tightened his arms around David's waist, hands entwined under his ribs.

David knew he should probably turn and head back to the house. But he wanted to ride just a little while longer. It felt so good, Christie against him like that.

Too much, a worry niggled in his mind. *You like this too much.*

He pushed the thought away. Everyone needed human contact from time to time. He wasn't hurting anyone, certainly not Christie. Right now he was going to focus on the snow and on this feeling of happiness and not berate himself with ideas of right and wrong, appropriate and inappropriate. Or why he felt like he was soaring.

He put his gloved hand over Christie's and rode on.

That evening David nodded off in front of the woodstove while Christie watched the news. The homemade pizza had been delicious. He helped with the dough and Christie brought ingredients for two combinations—a Margarita pizza with various cheeses, and one with prosciutto ham and a long, pale-green pepper. The heat from the woodstove proved to be a little too soothing after the meal and being out in the snow for hours. When Christie nudged his leg with a knee and smiled down at him apologetically, David roused himself from his rocker, abashed. They bundled up again, and he drove Christie home on the snowmobile. The farm lane was even more drifted than it was when he picked Christie up.

"Guess we'll have to go the long way around on the roads 'til this lane clears a bit," David said when they arrived at Christie's driveway.

"That works, as long as they plow the streets."

"They'll be clear by midmorning," David assured him. The township was good like that. And David would make sure his own driveway was done early in case Christie wanted to come by.

Christie paused by the side of the snowmobile, hesitant. "Good night, David. I had a blast today. It was fun. It's always fun being with you."

There was an edge of something in his voice, but David didn't want to analyze it. "Yeah it was fun. Night, Christie." He revved the engine and pulled out.

River and Tonga were already asleep on the rug when David returned. They didn't even stir. He decided to call it a night and banked the fire in the woodstove. It was only ten, but he was full, content, and hideously sleepy. The dark and warmth of bed sounded good. He shut off the lights and went up.

He woke several hours later to sweaty sheets, tangled limbs, a hollow need, and a painfully aching erection. He'd been dreaming he was trapped in an avalanche of snow that fell on him from the roof of the barn. He'd been terrified at first, but then in his dream, someone was in the snow with him. *Christie.* They pushed and patted the snow with their hands until they formed a little room, like an igloo. It made perfect sense in the dream. Then Christie said they had to warm up to survive, and he pressed close, his back to David's front. He pulled David's arms around him like a blanket, and David wanted to save him, to warm him, but he was so turned on. He couldn't help but rut against the seat of Christie's jeans, *rutting, rutting.* And in the dream, Christie pushed back and moaned, working his hand between his own legs.

David woke rutting against the sheets, frustrated. He was too old to spend in his sleep, but he was close. He squeezed his eyes shut in the dark room and pushed his hands under the waffle-knit shirt he slept in, rubbed his skin, his nipples, with calloused hands before shoving them into his pajama bottoms.

Lord, it was months since he had an orgasm, and longer still since he was this hard and aching, since sex felt this good. He tried to reimmerse himself in the dream as he stroked, feeling the snow around him and Christie's body against his. It wasn't long before the pleasure peaked, sharp and bright, and he pumped seed into his flannel bottoms and all over his hand.

And then... then he was awake, empty, and ashamed. He turned on the bedside lamp and got up to clean himself off and change his pants. He couldn't look at himself in the bathroom mirror.

It was a sin. Touching himself was bad enough, but to think about *that* while he did it.

But it started as a dream, he reminded himself. He couldn't control his dreams. He'd had dreams about crazy sex things in the past, even one memorable dream-slash-nightmare about masturbating in a church pew during service through a hole in his pants, hoping not to be caught. That didn't mean he'd actually do something like that, in real life Christie was his friend. That was all it was.

That was all it could be.

ACT II:
GERMINATION

Chapter 9

Thanksgiving

David came in from the morning milking to find Amy in the kitchen in her robe. She was staring blearily at a large raw turkey sitting on the counter in a pan. She yawned.

"Hey. I told you you didn't have to get the turkey ready. My friend Christie is going to do that."

"It's almost seven thirty. I should at least start some stuffing, or the meal will be late."

David put a hand on her shoulder. She'd had a heavy week of nursing finals at school, she said, and she looked tired. He felt a heavy fondness for her trickle down his throat. He was happy to have his kids home, but he was nervous about today, if he were honest. "I told you he's a good cook. He's got plans for the stuffing."

He knew Amy didn't care much for food preparation, but like him, she had a strong sense of duty. It was just like her to worry about the meal. "Who is this guy again?"

David poured himself a cup of coffee. "He's Ruth Landon's nephew, our neighbor on the other side of the lane. He lives alone and likes to cook, so he's been sharing meals with me in exchange for grocery money. He's a nice guy."

"But why—"

He heard a car pull into the driveway. River, in his doggie bed, only shifted his eyes toward the back door, still in his morning snooze. But Tonga gave a happy yip and ran over there. His tail banged staccato on the wall near the door.

"That's him." David went out to help.

Christie got out of his car looking festive in his parka and a bright-red scarf.

"Happy Thanksgiving," Christie said cheerfully. "I brought lots of bags."

"I've got it." David went to the hatchback of Christie's car and opened it. He grabbed four of the fabric grocery bags. "Are you feeding an army?"

"You can't stint the holidays." Christie grabbed the final items from the back—a bag with what looked like straw inside and a Tupperware cake saver.

This close up David noticed the extra paleness of his face, everywhere but the two little flushed spots on his high cheekbones. His blue eyes were darker than usual too. Christie looked nervous.

David didn't blame him in the least, but he tried to be reassuring. "Thanks for coming today. It's nice to have you here."

"Thanks for inviting me even though your kids are home."

David cringed a little at Christie's usual bluntness. "Why wouldn't I? I'd like for you to meet them." It was true. He did have an itch to get Christie, Amy, and Joe in the same room, to try to reconcile the two halves of his life a little.

Was Christie a "half" of his life already? It sure felt that way. Their friendship had grown very important to him in a very short amount of time. But he was still a little terrified about this. Christie was so different from Amy and Joe. *He* was different when he was with Christie.

What would Amy and Joe make of it? What if they didn't understand? But his kids had their own lives. Why shouldn't he be allowed to have one too?

"Come on." He gave Christie a smile he hoped was encouraging and led the way into the house.

Amy stood in the kitchen with a clean turkey baster in one hand and the other grabbing the counter. She stared at Christie as they walked in, her mouth hanging open.

David and Christie put their armloads of bags and things on the counter.

"Amy, this is Christie. Christie, my daughter, Amy."

"Hi, Amy. I've heard a lot about you." Christie was polite and super smooth. Amy, however, was not.

"Oh." She was still staring. Then she blinked, looked down at her robe, tossed the turkey baster on the counter like it was hot, and blushed. "Oh, h-hi. Dad, you didn't tell me we were having company so early!"

"I just told you—"

"I have to get dressed! Wow, you brought a lot of food. Can I help? Just let me go get changed, and I'll help. Okay? I'll just be a minute. So don't worry about getting the turkey in. Be right back!"

Amy fled the room. David felt a little guilty. He told Amy Christie was coming over early to get the turkey in, but he should have reminded her this morning when she as half-asleep. She was obviously embarrassed to be seen in her nightclothes. Not the best way to introduce them.

Still, she seemed very enthusiastic and friendly.

"She's adorable," Christie said, unpacking the bags.

"Yeah. I mean, thanks." David frowned as he grabbed some butter and went to stick it in the fridge.

"Oh, you can leave that out. It's easier if it's softened."

"Okay." David stood there, fridge door open. It didn't occur to him Amy might find Christie cute. In retrospect he should have known. Christie was a very good-looking man, and closer to Amy's age than his. Did Christie find Amy attractive that way too? The idea of the two of them *dating* was horrible, gut-wrenching. He felt a little sick.

No, that would never happen. Amy dated Christian boys. And she surely wasn't Christie's type either. He probably dated sophisticated women in the city. David was getting upset over nothing. He must be more worried about this day than he realized.

Christie gently took the box of butter out of his hands. David blinked and looked up. He saw quiet grace in Christie's eyes.

"It'll be okay," Christie said softly. "You're having a lonely friend over for the holiday. No big deal, right?"

His tone was odd, as if there were more to it than that, as if he were making up a story that wasn't true. But that was the truth, wasn't it?

David took a deep breath. "Right. So what can I do to help?"

Christie looked at the coffee pot on the counter, which was nearly empty. "Can you make another pot of coffee? I'm dying for some. And there's a bag of muffins in my stuff. Maybe put those on a plate? You can leave them on the counter for people to nibble on for breakfast. I'll start the stuffing."

"I'm on it." David started another pot of coffee.

Amy came down a few minutes later, dressed in a long black skirt, boots, and a red sweater. Her hair was back in her usual bun, and her face was scrubbed clean. She smiled nervously. Christie was chopping celery and carrots on Susan's old cutting board.

"You're fast," Amy said. "Dad says you're quite the chef. So what's the plan?"

"Cornbread and sausage stuffing. I cooked the sausage last night. It's in that red container. You can sauté the onions if you'd like. The pan's hot."

Amy came around the counter and found the onions Christie must have chopped the night before. She put them in a pan that contained melted butter. "So Dad says you live in that house at the end of the lane?"

"Yes. My Aunt Ruth left it to me." *Chop, chop, chop.*

"That's nice. Do you work in this area?"

"I'm a graphic designer. I work from home."

"Oh cool! What sort of things do you do?"

Christie slid the chopped celery and bits of carrot into the pan with the onions, and David decided things were going okay. He could go get cleaned up. He said as much, and they both waved him off, so he went upstairs.

By the time he showered, changed into a nice shirt and pants, and made it back downstairs, Joe was awake. He was sitting at the kitchen counter with a cup of coffee and a muffin. He watched Christie stuff the bird from a mix in a big bowl while Amy stirred a pot on the stove.

"Morning, Joe. I guess you've met Christie Landon. He's Ruth Landon's nephew. You remember our neighbor Ruth. She passed last year, and Christie moved into her place."

"Amy already introduced us, Dad." Joe's tone was flat.

"Okay. Great." David wasn't sure what else to say. He took a muffin. "How are these?" he asked Joe, since he was eating one.

"Good," Joe said without much inflection. He took another big bite of his.

He was watching Christie, his face a neutral mask. But David sensed disapproval, and it caused a flush of irritation he swallowed down. Sometimes Joe reminded David of his father. He was built just like him—short at five eight, and stocky in that Germanic way. He had the same dark hair and thick, forward jaw. Joe was like his grandfather in other ways as well. He was deeply religious and had strong opinions of right and wrong.

"That stuffing looks so yummy. I can't wait to taste it." Amy was all smiles. "Doesn't it look good, Dad?"

"I'm sure it'll be great. I told you Christie is a wonderful cook."

Christie looked up at David and gave him a warm smile. "I just need to truss this up and we can get it in the oven. David, can you look in my bags and find a little pack of skewers?"

David looked and found the packet. He opened it and removed what looked like long straight pins with a loop on one end. He handed them to Christie, who used them to close up the skin at the turkey's cavity over the stuffing.

David took a muffin and had a bite while he watched. They had bran and oats and dried cherries and walnuts. So good.

"There! All set." Christie took the pan Amy was minding and poured a butter mixture over the bird. He picked up the roasting rack, and David hurried to open the oven door. Christie slid the turkey inside. "We'll need to baste every thirty minutes. Can you set the timer on the microwave, Amy?"

"Sure." Amy punched the numbers in on the microwave's timer function.

"Oh, almost forgot. I was going to put a little foil over the breast. David, can you grab some foil?"

David looked around the kitchen, trying to remember where Susan kept it.

"It's in the third drawer down next to the fridge," Christie said.

David found the foil and handed it over. Christie made a little tent and opened the oven to put it over the bird.

David went back to the counter to finish his muffin and found Joe staring at him with a frown.

"What?" David asked.

"How did you two get to know one another?" Joe asked, looking from David to Christie.

"Yeah, Dad," Amy said. "I was wondering too."

"Christie likes to cook, so we made a deal. I pay for half the groceries, and he does the cooking. It's been a real blessing. A real blessing." He said the last firmly, gave Christie a grateful look. He didn't want Joe's stiffness to put Christie off.

"That's wonderful, Dad." Amy gave Joe a glare. "I'm so glad you've been getting good meals and some company too. You spend so much time alone on this farm." She smiled at Christie. "So... what else is on the menu?"

Christie took his phone out of his pocket and looked at it, scrolled. "The cranberry salad is already made and in the fridge. We don't need to start the sweet potatoes yet."

Amy stepped closer to look over his shoulder, and Christie held the phone out so she could see it too. "Oh yum! I love roasted brussel sprouts."

Joe turned toward David. "So Dad, what's new here? Have you got the tractor running yet? How much did you get for the corn this year?"

It felt like an escape hatch to talk about something

ordinary, and also distract Joe, so David took it. He ended up taking Joe out to the barn to look at the tractor. Christie insisted they were fine and practically shooed them out. Probably he didn't feel any more comfortable around Joe than Joe felt around him.

When they got back from the barn, Christie had gone home to get something, Amy said. He returned a few hours later, and by then it was time to prep the last-minute dishes, and the kitchen turned into the equivalent of a speedway pit. Amy was Christie's sous chef, doing whatever task he set her to. David tried to help but mostly got in the way. Joe disappeared upstairs.

They sat down to eat early afternoon. Christie had made a centerpiece for the table with some straw from the barn, a pumpkin, candles, nuts, pomegranates, and leaves. It looked like a decoration from a magazine. And the meal! Even by Christie's normally perfectionist standards, he'd outdone himself. The turkey was golden brown all over and wonderfully moist. There were homemade rolls, sweet potatoes in a candied bourbon sauce, mashed garlic potatoes, orange balsamic roasted brussels sprouts, cornbread-sausage stuffing, and a chunky fresh cranberry dish with walnuts that was better than the goopy stuff Susan used to get out of a can. The gravy was so good it made David want to moan when Christie let him taste a little on a clean spoon in the kitchen.

When they were seated, Joe spoke up. "Do you mind if I say the blessing, Dad?"

"Go ahead, Joe."

They all took hands around the table. Christie was between David and Amy, so David held Christie's hand in his left and Joe's in his right. He shut his eyes.

"Our Heavenly Father, thank you for bringing us

together for this celebration of thanksgiving and for the bounty of food on our table."

Christie's hand was large, but he had soft skin. It was a little damp, probably from all the kitchen work. David swallowed a lump in his throat.

"When I think about the things we have to be especially grateful for this year, I think about our good fortune, Amy and me, to have been raised by a loving Christian mother and father. Even though Mom is in heaven with you now, Lord, I know she's looking over us and encouraging us, with love, to remain true to you and to the ways of Christ she established in our home."

"Yes, Lord," said Amy.

Christie squeezed David's hand a little. David swept his thumb across Christie's knuckles to reassure him. It was disconcerting to hold Christie's hand, made David both happy and deeply anxious at the same time, like he felt on the snowmobile.

"I think about the blessing of your church and your Word, which teaches us what is holy and what is sin, and helps us to reject the ways of the wicked, Lord. I think about the joy of *Christian* fellowship with those in the church. These friendships nurture our hearts as well as our immortal souls."

David was only half paying attention to Joe's blessing, but when Christie tried to pull away his hand, it sank in what Joe just said. It was a dig at them, to be sure.

"And Lord—"

"Amen," David said loudly. He dropped Christie and Joe's hands and opened his eyes. "Thank you, Joe," he said briskly.

Joe shot him a look but muttered, "Amen."

"Amen," said Amy.

"So who wants some of these sinfully delicious sweet potatoes?" Christie said a little too brightly.

Chapter 10

The meal turned out well, which topped Christie's own personal "list of things to be grateful for." He'd wanted to impress David's family. And they all commented on how good everything was, repeatedly. Even Joe grudgingly said the turkey was the best he'd ever had.

But Christie's appetite was hollow. He was full after a dozen bites, probably because his stomach was currently full of bitter acid.

He was hurt, and he didn't like the feeling. It was stupid. He'd told himself not to expect much from David's kids. He told himself before the day even began to just go with the flow, be a little mouse in the corner. It was nice David even included him, and this day wasn't about him. But it was hard. These were David's *children*, for God's sake. They were important in his life. And Christie was....

Christie was in way over his fucking head. He cared about David too much. It stung to sit in David's home and listen to Joe's reminders during prayer that it was *his mother* who belonged at this table, not Christie, that David belonged *to them*.

It was true, so why did it hurt? David was his friend, nothing more. He wasn't a husband, partner, or even boyfriend. *Friends.* But even that chaste relationship, apparently, was not something Joe Fisher approved of.

Amy was a sweetheart, but she was way more conservative than even the church women Christie grew up with. She'd explained while they were cooking that she had never cut her hair. Women in her church were *allowed* to, but her own mother never did, and Amy decided to wait until she was married in case her husband preferred it long. She was also a little more interested in Christie than was a good idea, but that awkwardness beat the hell out of Joe's reaction.

When David passed the gravy to Christie, he put a hand on Christie's upper arm and smiled briefly. Christie smiled back, but when he looked away, Joe was staring at him with cold eyes.

Christie poured gravy on his potatoes, his pulse hammering. That look! Joe knew. Joe knew he was gay. It had been a long, long time since Christie felt any anxiety about that, but he did now. It wasn't that he gave a shit what Joe thought, but he did care what he might say to David. Damn it. He should have made sure David knew he was gay a long time ago. At the start. Now it would seem like he'd been hiding it.

Joe and David talked about his classes. Joe was taking Old Testament law this semester, which made Christie want to chuck biscuits at his head. But Amy found it interesting.

"Why do they even have you study that? Jesus overturned so many of those old laws," she asked.

"Jesus said he came to *fulfill* the law, not destroy it," Joe rebutted.

"Yes, but we don't avoid shellfish or pork anymore,"

Amy countered. "He said 'turn the other cheek,' not 'eye for an eye.'"

"We need to understand the Bible in its entirety. It's our history, and it's the word of God."

"Isn't sharia law based on the Old Testament?" Christie put in innocently. "Stoning women who aren't virgins, that sort of thing?"

Joe smiled thinly. "'Sharia law' is Muslim. And it's based on the Quran, not the Bible." He used an instructional tone, like Christie was being ignorant. He'd missed the shade, then. Too bad.

"So! Buella's about to give birth," David put in quickly.

"Who?" Amy asked.

David blushed. "One of my herd. Thought it might happen this week while you all are here."

"That would be nice," Amy said. She turned to Christie. "Have you ever seen a calving? It's really interesting and, gosh, are calves cute when they're that little."

"No, but I'd like to see it. I asked David to text me when Buella goes into labor, no matter what time it is." He smiled at David, who smiled back.

"I've been giving Christie quite the farm education. He's been helping me out some."

"How is it that you have so much extra time on your hands?" Joe asked to Christie. "I thought Amy said you worked a job from home."

"Yes, Joe, I do. But I'm always happy to spend any spare time I have with your father." Christie dug the words in with a verbal heel, looking Joe steadily in the eyes.

David coughed. "Wow, this stuffing is delicious. Huh, Am?"

"Really good, Dad," Amy agreed, seemingly oblivious.

"What classes are you taking, Amy?" Christie asked cheerfully. "Your dad says you're in nursing?"

Amy's eyes lit up. "Yeah! It's hard, but I love it. This semester...."

She talked about her life at school for a bit, which was at least a neutral topic. But the tension at the table never lessened one iota, at least not for Christie. After the longest meal ever, probably in the history of mankind, it was finally time to clear the table. He popped up and took a load of plates to the sink. David came in after him.

"I don't want you washing a single dish," David insisted. "You and Amy spent hours in the kitchen today. Joe and I will do the dishes."

"Okay." Christie wasn't about to argue. He rubbed his forehead and lowered his voice. "I'm sorry that was awkward, David. I'm not very good at holding my tongue."

David looked behind him as if to make sure they were alone and stepped closer. "You were very patient. I'm sorry about Joe. I don't know what's gotten into him."

"It doesn't matter. Hey, if you guys are going to tackle the dishes, maybe I'll head out. I wanted to call some friends today, say Happy Thanksgiving."

"Sure. We'll box up all the leftovers, and I'll bring them over."

"No, you keep them. You've got a house full."

David looked determined. "I'll bring you over enough for several meals at least. Everyone likes turkey leftovers."

"Okay."

"Okay. Thank you for today. Really. It was the best Thanksgiving meal I've ever had, and I'm sure the kids appreciated it too."

David's voice was soft and sincere. Normally it was the sort of tone that would make Christie melt. But he was still raw and hurt inside. He shrugged. "Thank you for inviting me. It would have been depressing sitting at home alone."

There was an awkward moment standing close there in the kitchen. Christie wanted to touch David—give him a hug or even rest his head on David's shoulder for a moment of comfort. But they weren't like that. Why did it feel so strongly that they were? Why did Christie crave it like air?

David gazed at him, his hands clenched at his side.

"Okay, then. I'll just say good-bye." Christie slipped past David and stuck his head in the dining room. "Amy, Joe, I'm taking off. It was great to meet you both."

"Oh? So soon?" Amy stood up. "Well, bye, Christie. That meal was delicious!" She came over and gave him a carefully chaste little one-armed hug. "Thank you for cooking today and for making Dad eat decent food while we're away at school. It was so nice to meet you too!"

Joe stood up at his chair. "Yes, thank you for the good food. God bless."

David saw Christie to the door.

"Enjoy your time with your kids. See you Sunday, maybe?"

"We'll see. They leave Sunday morning. I'll text you."

Christie got into his car and drove down the Fisher driveway. He tried hard to dispel the feeling of disaster that loomed over him, the sense it would be the last time he ever visited David Fisher.

*   *   *

After Christie left David started scraping dishes, and Joe finished clearing the table.

Amy came bouncing into the kitchen. "I'm going to take River and Tonga for a walk."

"That's one way to get out of dishes," Joe complained, carrying in a load from the dining room.

"Hey, I helped cook! Dad said you guys were on dish patrol."

"It's okay, honey," David said. "Go ahead. The dogs could use a walk."

Christie had a habit of "dropping" things for them to gobble up. They adored him for it, but they were putting on weight.

Amy stuck out her tongue at Joe teasingly, but he barely responded. "Boy, you're such a grump this holiday."

Joe grabbed a dishtowel and swatted Amy's hip with it, grinning. "Am not. Go on if you're going. Shirker."

Appeased, Amy batted her eyelashes at Joe as if she were the bratty little sister instead of the older one. She took off with the dogs. For a few minutes, David scraped and rinsed dishes in peace, stacking them by the side of the sink to wash.

But Joe eventually spoke up. "So. How long has this been going on? This 'friendship' with Christie?"

There was a slight edge to his tone, but David ignored it. "I dunno. Since early October, I guess."

"How do you even know the guy?"

"I told you he's our neighbor. He's Ruth's nephew."

"The old lady who lived on the other side of the lane? It's not like we knew her all that well."

"I rent part of his field, so I had to talk to him about it. What exactly is the problem, Joe? You were rude to him, and there's no call for that, especially after he made that beautiful meal for us."

Joe huffed, taking a large pot to dry it. "It's pretty weird seeing someone like that in our home. And he seemed awfully comfortable here. Getting into the cupboard and fridge without even asking you. Knowing where Mom kept the aluminum foil.... If he's just cooking for you for pay, why doesn't he leave the food on the doorstep? Why is he eating at our table?"

Our table. As if Joe had a right to say what went on there even when he wasn't home. David's lips tightened along with the band of anger around his chest. "He lives alone, and I live alone. Why should we both eat alone?"

"Dad." Joe looked at David with worried brown eyes, hands on his hips. "You shouldn't be friends with that guy."

"Why not?"

"Because he's worldly. Liberal. I doubt he's even a Christian." Joe's tone was bitter.

"He was nothing but nice to you, Joe."

"Lord help me, Dad, you're so naive!" Joe was getting increasingly frustrated. He wrenched the damp dishcloth in his hands. "Fine! I'll just say it. It's as clear as day that Christie Landon is a *homosexual*, and that he's got the hots for you!"

"What?" David's pulse was thudding, and it wasn't because of the hot dishwater his hands were in. "That's not true. Why would you say something like that?"

Joe shook his head in disgust. "You haven't been out in the world much, so you don't know these things. But believe me, that guy is gay! Absolutely. Why do you think he's spending so much time over here? He wants to... to.... Geez, Dad. Wake up!"

"You don't know that he's... gay. But even if he is, that doesn't mean.... Two men can be friends without it having to be... that."

"Sure! But my male friends don't come over to my house and act like they know what's in every cupboard. They don't cook for me and set the table all fancy for me like a wife. What do you think Pastor Mitchell would say about you associating with a homosexual in your own home like that? What, every week? How often is he over here?"

David wasn't about to admit Christie was there pretty much every day. "We share the cost of meals! And he's an artist. He likes doing things up fancy like that. It's not—"

"Then why doesn't he just drop the meal off if you're 'sharing costs'? Why does he spend time working on the farm when he has his own job? Why does he *look* at you like that, Dad?" Joe practically spat with disgust.

David shook his head. He scrubbed hard at a crusted fork. His stomach physically hurt, and he felt light-headed. He worried he might lose his Thanksgiving dinner. "That's enough! This discussion is over, Joe."

Joe kept talking, but he softened his tone, sounded sympathetic. "I understand you desire company. Of course you do! So why not go to the men's fellowship at church? Or why not ask Mrs. Robeson over for dinner? Jessie told me she thinks the Lord wants you two to be married. We both think it's a good idea too. Mrs. Robeson would be a good wife for you."

David gawked at his son in disbelief. "You and Jessie Robeson discussed us? What is this, a Disney movie? How many times do I have to say it? I'm not interested in Evelyn Robeson!" David slammed his palm on the edge of the sink, hard.

Joe's eyes widened but a mean glint shone in them. "But you *are* interested in a good-looking gay man? Is that what you're saying?"

"Why do you keep saying he's gay? You don't know anything about Christie!"

"Geez, have you ever even met a gay man before? Holy

cow! No wonder people can take advantage of you. Seriously, Dad, he's *gay*. Ask him yourself if you don't believe me. He's a sinner, not someone you should be breaking bread with. Paul warned the Corinthians about associating with those who commit sexual sin. 'Do not be yoked together with unbelievers. For what do righteousness and wickedness have in common? Or what fellowship can light have with darkness?'"

David felt his blood pressure rise to dangerous levels. His stomach lurched and he tasted acid. He knew Joe wouldn't easily take to Christie. They were as different as night and day. But never in his wildest dreams did he anticipate this level of venom or Joe's assessment of the situation.

"Joseph Fisher, you had better stop talking," David said, his voice low and warning.

"I'm just trying to help you see what's going on."

"You don't *know* what's going on. You don't—" His voice cracked.

He wanted to say, "Christie Landon is my friend." He wanted to say, "You don't have any right to come home once in a blue moon and tell me what to do." He wanted to say, "You sure stuffed your face at lunch for someone who has so much against my sharing meals with Christie." He wanted to say a lot of things. But he was too choked up to summon words. His throat swelled shut with rage and with something else, something like shame that burned and bit and made him clammy and light-headed.

If he stayed in this room, he was going to do something he'd regret. He'd never wanted to hit Joe as much as he wanted to hit him right then. *The way my father beat me.* David promised himself he would never hit his kids. So he left the dishes halfway done, grabbed his coat, and stormed out of the house.

Chapter 11

"Oh my God, Kyle, it was a disaster!" Unshed tears thickened Christie's voice, but he ruthlessly swallowed them down. He promised himself years ago he never shed one more tear over a homophobic asshole or bully. He wasn't about to break that vow over Joe Fisher.

"Oh no! Baby, what happened?"

Christie flopped back on his bed, the phone pressed to his ear. "Well, the meal was *amazing*." It was important to acknowledge that. "But his son hated me on sight."

"Oh, honey!"

"His name's Joe, and he's going to be a minister. You should have heard his prayer at the table. It was all about how their mother was watching and how David should be friends with other *Christians* instead of with me."

"You're kidding!"

"His daughter Amy was nice, but I don't even think she shaves her legs! I didn't understand how conservative his church was. They're worse than the one I grew up in. I felt like I was in Utah or something."

Kyle listened to Christie rant on until he finally ran down.

"Aw, babe. I'm so sorry you had an awful Thanksgiving."

The words didn't sit quite right with Christie. "It wasn't *awful*."

He wanted to be with David today, and he wanted to make a nice dinner for his family, and he did. He couldn't completely regret it. But even besides Joe's rudeness, religious mania, and clear distaste for Christie, other things bothered him too. David was nice, but not as warm and funny as he'd been lately. It was clear he felt awkward, unsure how to treat Christie in front of his kids. And Amy was... not flirtatious exactly. She wasn't that kind of girl. But she was... hopeful? Interested? Appreciative? She wouldn't have viewed him like that if Christie was introduced as David's *partner* instead of a casual friend and neighbor.

There was the rub. He *wasn't* David's partner, and he never would be. The thing that was so painful about today was the divide between the way Christie had come to view himself in David's life and the truth when the harsh, glaring light of outsider perspective was cast on it. *Ugh.*

"I've been such an idiot," he whispered into the phone.

"Oh, Christie." Kyle sighed. "I hate to say it, but I told you so. You went and fell for this guy, and now you're paying for it."

"I hate this." Pressure clogged his chest and head again, and again Christie pushed it away. He wasn't going to cry over a man either. "I liked him *so much*, Kyle. So much."

He couldn't begin to understand the incredibly strong instinctual pull he'd felt for David from the start. How it could have been so wrong, yet felt so right?

"I know, babe." Kyle's voice was all sympathy. Christie

wished Kyle were here so he could hold him and pat his back and tell him it would be okay.

"I don't know what to do," Christie admitted, staring up at the ceiling. "I don't know how to go on after this."

"Yes, you do," Kyle said firmly. "This is hurting you, and I hate that. You need to cut David loose. Go out to a bar or go on Grindr and meet someone else, someone to help you forget. Tell David you can't cook for him anymore. Make up some excuse if you have to. Or... I know! Come stay with me and Billy for Christmas and New Year's. We'd love to see you. And that way you can get away for a few weeks and make that your clean break. We'll go out dancing. You need to remember how badass *fierce* Christie Landon is, and why *you're* the heartbreaker. Amiright? This David should be so lucky you'd even give him the time of day."

"Yes," Christie said. He did need to remember himself again. Be hot. Be shining. *Living well is the best revenge.*

Kyle was right; he had to stop hanging out with David. He was just getting more and more attached. He had to stop hurting himself like this.

But if he were going to check out, he would go out a *winner*, not with that meal with Joe as David's last memory of him. One more time, then, something special. He would make sure David Fisher knew exactly what he'd be missing.

*   *   *

Joe wouldn't come out to the barn. David knew this. Joe would finish the dishes, and when he was done, he'd flop in front of the TV. When Amy returned from her walk, she'd probably join him.

David wasn't worried about getting caught.

Nevertheless, when he went into his workroom in the barn, he padlocked the door from the inside just in case.

His secret was hidden so well no one would ever find it. It wouldn't be found until after he'd died and gone, maybe generations from now. Someday they'd tear down this barn and maybe put up condos. His secret would be dug up then. But there was nothing to identify him on or in the box, and by then, no one would have a clue who had lived here or when. No one would care.

It had been a while since he'd gotten the box out. The last time was probably six months before Susan died. But he found it right where it was supposed to be. Firewood was stored against the wall in neat piles. There was a loose board behind one such stack. He had to move logs to uncover it. And then once he thumbed aside a few nails and pushed the board open, he still had to hunt around with his hand in the dark space beyond. The box was stuck way to the left, where he could barely feel it. He found the small metal ring on the lid and pulled.

The box—an old metal correspondence box, probably from the Civil War—just fit between the boards. He wiggled it out. He sat on the concrete floor, legs wide, and put the box between his knees. Opened it.

There was pornography on the Internet; he knew that. He'd even dared Xtube once or twice. You could select "men" who liked "men" and everything. But he was always too paranoid to be able to relax while on the computer. For one thing their computer was in the family room, with no good door to bar the way. Untenable risk at any time of the day or night. Even once Susan was gone and the kids moved out, he hadn't felt comfortable there. He wasn't sure how to erase his history or electronic trail or whatever it was. He didn't trust what the porn sites might install on the computer, or if they might be able to get his name and address from his files somehow. Then, too, the family room had big windows that didn't have shades or curtains. Besides, he wanted to keep *this* out of his home. That way it wasn't real.

It wasn't real if no one knew.

He wasn't a homosexual. He'd never actually touched another man, never went down on his knees or put his penis into another man's mouth or ass, never admitted it to anyone, never said the words out loud. Therefore it was just an "idea," like daydreaming about being a sailor or something. It was still a sin to... to think about another man, to touch himself thinking about it. But he figured God might be sort of tolerant about it as long as he never acted on it with another person. What turned a man on was his own private business. Whatever else circumstance could deny you, it couldn't take away your thoughts. Not those.

He carefully removed the items from the box. Each one was so old and so generic it could never be tied to him, even if someone did find the box, even if *Joe* found it. He could deny he ever knew it existed.

His first magazine, gotten when he was just seventeen.

Hey, guess what? Someone dropped off a whole big box of porno. I was lucky to find it before my dad did.

Richard Klutz. His dad owned the town dump, and Richard was popular because of the weird shit he found and brought to school—toasters, radios, roller skates, all kinds of things that were still useful. But this was the best thing Richard ever found.

He told only the guys he thought were cool. David still remembered that day, gathered around the back of Richard's old Buick in the school parking lot, looking in the trunk. Guys grabbed magazines and stuffed them down their shirts, rolled them up and stuck them in pockets, exclaiming over the pictures but too nervous to linger long on school property. Getting seen by a teacher didn't bear thinking about. They'd probably get expelled.

This magazine was in the trunk that day too.

"What the hell?" someone had said, opening it up. "This is weird homo stuff."

"Hey, I didn't pack the box," Richard said defensively. "Not my fault what the perv was into. Take what you want, and I'll dump the rest. Don't want to be caught with it in my car."

"Bet you already took the best magazines," another guy complained.

"You know it," Richard smirked.

David took a girlie magazine and stuck it in a pocket. He said nothing, but he watched. He watched Richard gather up what was left—including that "homo" magazine—and stick it back in a torn cardboard box. He watched Richard drive around to the back of the school and heard the bang of the lid of one the bins back there. Richard drove away waving at them and grinning, like he'd pulled a fast one.

That night Christie slipped out of his room after his parents were in bed. He walked the five miles to school in the dark and searched the school trash bins with a flashlight until he found the magazine. He brought it home and hid it.

It frightened him, how much the magazine turned him on. Hard, jutting cocks, furry balls, nipples in hard, muscular chests. The feature spread starred a big man with a buzz cut and a young, slight-bodied brunet guy. David looked like neither of them. He was always solid and sturdy thanks to the farmwork, so he wasn't slight like the guy in the magazine—*like Christie*—but neither was he a big brutish muscle guy. That didn't stop him from being fascinated by the pictures of the two—of them kissing, or the young one on his knees with his mouth stuffed full, balls against his chin. There was a picture of the big guy spreading the younger guy's cheeks, showing a tight pink furl. Penetration. Ejaculation. Mouths contorted in simulated ecstasy.

He'd touched himself to these pictures so many times over the years he didn't even see the details anymore. The close-ups of penetration, or erect flesh, were just triggers for him now, like a real hard copper penny dropped in a wishing well, an extra visual stimulation to ground his own fantasies.

He'd had fantasies of nameless, faceless men all these years. *All these years.* Vague masturbatory play reels of some stranger coming to the farm and fucking David in the barn or sucking David hard or bending over, pants down, to present a hairy ass for the taking. Why would some guy just come into the barn like that? Well, why not? Fantasies, daydreams, didn't have to make any sense.

There were other things in the box too. There was a small vibrator, equally untraceable, an old jar of Vaseline, a book of naked men he bought in a sex shop off the freeway near Pittsburgh years ago, an old one that had probably been in the shop forever, undated. He paid cash, his pulse pounding stupidly. The clerk didn't even look him in the eye.

Over the years he looked at the box when he needed to, when it all became too much to bear—the responsibilities, the kids, the farm, money. Sometimes he used it to get himself aroused before going to Susan in their bed. Once he pushed inside her—always missionary position—he closed his eyes and thought of the images in the box. Susan liked sex when she was young, and she got offended if he didn't want to do it often. But after Joe was born, she only wanted it sporadically. And in the later years, not at all. It was a relief.

His deepest secret. Always his secret. For so many years.

He could have, he knew, looked for an actual man. It wasn't easy where he lived, but it wasn't impossible either. There were times when a guy looked at him a certain way—at the hardware store, gas station, even in church once or twice. If he'd wanted to, if he'd been brave or maybe stupid, he could have gone after it. He could have had sex with a stranger in a car or a rest stop bathroom. But that would make it real, wouldn't it? Real and sinful and tawdry too. He wasn't a pervert. He wasn't desperate, roaming around looking for someone to return his knowing glance, seeking anonymous sex. He wasn't—

Christie Landon is gay.

David packed the items back in the box and clutched it to his chest, breathing hard. Stupid. He'd known, he must have known. He just hadn't admitted it out loud in his own brain. Christie wasn't just "city." He wasn't merely "different," "softer," "attractive," "sophisticated," or "artistic."

He is a homosexual.

Oh God. Suddenly his view of their relationship shifted. It was like he'd been looking through a kaleidoscope and seeing this pretty abstract picture full of brilliant color and light, but undefined. And then with one rotation of the dial, the picture snapped into place, and it wasn't abstract at all; it was crystal clear.

He and Christie Landon weren't just friends. They were *dating.*

It was so obvious, in retrospect. All he had to do was imagine Christie was female. If Christie were a woman, even a woman as young and attractive as Christie was, it would have been obvious from that first Sunday when he came over to the farm and they ate Indian food together that there was an attraction there, the potential of more, unspoken expectations. David would have backed off right then, worried it was inappropriate with a woman that young.

But Christie wasn't a woman, and David hadn't backed off. He'd been in denial. He closed his eyes and shuddered at the self-revelation. He liked Christie *so much,* felt so drawn to his company. He could talk to Christie more easily than he'd ever talked to anyone in his life. He wanted Christie around as much as possible, had come up with excuses to spend even more time with him. He even dreamed about him in a sexual context, for God's sake. How had he not seen it? But he'd been in denial for so long his brain was stuck in its same old groove. It was like that old saying about the left hand not knowing what the right hand was doing. And maybe he'd not acknowledged it consciously because then... then he would have had to stop.

It was the secret part of himself he held in this box that was reaching out for Christie—the part of him that longed for a man's strength, body, cock, touch.

He was falling in love with Christie Landon, if he wasn't already there.

His body stirred now at the thought. He knew from the first moment he saw Christie that he was enormously attractive. David just hadn't finished the sentence: *To me. He's enormously attractive* to me. It wasn't like he had intentions all along of trying to get him into bed. And yet now that Joe had said the words out loud, picked at the scabs over his heart, David had to admit he'd been acting like a love-struck fool.

No wonder Joe got uptight. He probably reacted in such an ugly way not because of the way Christie looked at David, but because of the way *David* looked at *Christie.*

Oh Lord. Shame burned through him, and he shut his eyes.

Was he that obvious? Was he a pathetic closeted homosexual fixated on a beautiful young man? At least Christie was a young, beautiful *gay* man. It wasn't like David was drooling over a youth at Sunday school. But gay or not, Christie couldn't possibly be serious about his affections. Why would he want David? Christie was the essence of life and confidence, talent and charm. He was young and perfect in face and form. David was over-the-hill and led the life of a boring farmer with two grown children. It made no rational sense. At best David was a temporary stop-gap while Christie was staying at his aunt's. Maybe Christie *was* dallying, flirting with the old man. For David, though, it was earth-shatteringly serious—and dangerous.

He sat with that pain for long minutes, his eyes closed and his muscles physically aching from the heavy load of stress, the sense of failure, and humiliation.

But he finally realized, fool or not, he hadn't done anything irreversible, not yet. He hadn't tried to touch Christie. His golden rule of "only in my mind" was still unbroken, even if, in his heart, he had already committed that sin, already fallen for a man.

Lusted after him. His dream came back to shame him once again. The way he rutted against Christie in that impossible igloo, as impossible as their being together in real life. He wouldn't be pitiable. He wouldn't try to take advantage.

There was no way around it. He needed to distance himself from Christie Landon.

Chapter 12

David's resolve disintegrated the moment he stepped into Christie's house on Sunday evening and saw what Christie had done. He took in the scene with jarring, shocked flashes of comprehension. The little dining area in the kitchen of Ruth Landon's house had been transformed into a tropical paradise.

Christie had set up tall foam core panels showing blown-up photos of a beach scene all around the small kitchen table. The table itself was set in a large wooden tray that was filled with white sand. Exotic music played low, something with drums and the sounds of the ocean. There were paper lanterns that flickered with light, a tropical print tablecloth, and dishes heaped with rice, grilled pineapple, and fish. Christie had even changed the air itself. The thermostat had been cranked high, there was an artificial breeze blowing, probably from a fan somewhere, and the house smelled of the sea, tropical flowers, and delicious food.

David squeezed his eyes shut, overwhelmed. Holy cow. No one, *no one*, had ever done anything like this for him. Heck, no one had ever done more than bemusedly tolerate his interest in faraway places, much less taken him seriously, *listened*, and tried so very hard to give him something special.

Bora Bora.

"David?"

David swallowed and opened his eyes. Christie looked nervous. "Too much?" he asked with a self-deprecating laugh. "I told you I'm obsessive. When I get a creative vision, watch out."

"It's amazing," David managed, his voice rough.

"Cool. Well… um, we might as well eat before the food gets cold. You'll want to take your shoes and socks off before you step into the sand."

It was a practical consideration that somehow got David moving again. He noticed Christie's feet were bare. He had long, thin feet. David forced himself to look away. He took off his work boots, one at a time, and tucked his socks inside them without saying anything. He rolled up the cuffs of his jeans while he was at it. Somehow he managed to make it to his chair at the table. The fine sand felt cool against his bare toes. After he sat down, he dug them in, memorizing the sensation, his foolishness hidden by the cover of the table.

Christie sat down too, the color still high on his cheeks. He had never looked more beautiful. But there was something different about him, a studied reserve in his face. He didn't look David in the eyes. "So I made *poisson cru*, which is tuna marinated in lime and coconut, grilled vegetables, a Tahitian fruit pudding, sticky rice, and vanilla panna cotta for dessert."

"You… you shouldn't have… it's incredible." David's voice sounded gruff.

"Well." Christie looked up at him with an oddly fierce

look. "In lieu of plane tickets to Polynesia, it will have to do."

David looked at the table. He should start putting food on his plate, but he couldn't move. There were things bubbling up inside him—painful things, sharp things. He squeezed his eyes shut.

"David? Are you all right?"

David opened his eyes and looked at Christie. He couldn't possibly speak the words, but it must have shown on his face because Christie's expression grew shuttered, a cold blankness coming over him. When he spoke his voice had a callous edge.

"It's fine. I already know what you're going to say. I wanted to make this meal for you because I wanted to thank you for your friendship. It's meant a lot to me. But I won't be able to keep doing this, you see. I need to go visit my friend Kyle in New York for a few weeks, and I have a new brand campaign that's going to have me swamped. So I won't have time to cook."

Ever, that's what he was saying. Christie didn't want to be friends anymore. And even though David had planned to say much the same thing, his chest lurched horribly at the blunt words. *No. Please, no.*

He couldn't reply, so he nodded just once, his mouth twisted tight.

"It was Joe, right?" Christie's face was strained. He spoke with great care, eyes on his plate. "He told you I was a fag."

"You didn't—you never mentioned...."

Christie shrugged with an expression that said he couldn't care less. "Where I'm from people just *know*. At the start I didn't think about having to *tell* you, or that I...." His voice faltered, then picked up again, strong and bitter.

He raised his gaze to David's, defiant. "Frankly it's no one's goddamn business. Do you go around announcing that you like women? But I'm sorry if you feel shocked or something. You don't have to stay. I get it."

There was an out: Christie was holding open the door and even getting angry so David had an excuse to coast through that exit easily, guiltlessly.

But instead Christie's words swept David up and washed him the other way. Why did he think for one second it would be a good idea to distance himself from Christie? He suddenly never felt surer about anything than he did at that moment—he could not give Christie up. If he walked out that door and never saw Christie again, he might as well die. Because life wasn't worth much before Christie appeared, and it would be worse having had this and lost it. The mere thought ripped his guts out. *You're trying to scare me away because Joe hurt you. But I don't care. I won't let you.*

He unclenched his fists and picked up his fork and knife. "This looks great. I like fish." Stupid, banal words, but they were all he could muster.

He cut off a piece of the delicate whitefish. A knife wasn't even needed; it flaked easily under his fork. He managed to give Christie a small smile before putting the morsel in his mouth. It melted on his tongue, tasting of lime and heat and of places he'd dreamed of many times.

Christie's blue eyes watched him warily. "Going for the macho stoic response, huh? Shall we just not talk about it?"

David blinked at him. He knew Christie was just lashing out, but the words hit home. He wasn't *ignoring* it. Maybe he did ignore things, or rather, silently put up with them. Maybe that *was* his weakness. But that wasn't what he was doing now. He was… he was just deciding he wasn't going to let it come between them.

"By the way, it wasn't my nefarious plan to seduce you, if that's what Joe is worried about," Christie went on, his words still bitter. "Yes, you're a very attractive man. And yes, I'm gayer than a box of rainbow stickers. But I know you're straight, and believe it or not, I have no trouble finding men. I don't need to steal my kicks from a guy who's not interested."

David's fork clattered to the plate, loudly. His emotions roared up, too much to handle. It was all too much—what Christie had done for him in arranging this whole special meal, Joe's disgusted accusations, his own fear and guilt and wanting. But mostly he couldn't stand the hurt that radiated through Christie. He couldn't bear that Christie felt rejected.

Before David could think twice, he made a noise like a growl, lunged forward, grabbed Christie's face with both hands, and crushed their lips together.

There was an absolute tempest inside him. It felt like a class-five hurricane, raging and howling and sending bits and pieces of long-standing walls flying. It wasn't a kiss so much as a statement, a moment of rebellion, an act of desperation, or maybe one of solidarity. His mouth was closed and hard. But after tensing below him for a moment, Christie relaxed, softening into him.

David's stomach flipped over and, contrarily, the storm inside him eased. Christie's mouth felt very warm and plush. A sort of peace came over David, and he sighed. He pulled back enough to rest his forehead against Christie's. His eyes felt welded shut, like they'd never open again. He could feel Christie's breath on his face.

"Oh my God, David," Christie said with quiet shock. "How long have you had that bottled up inside you?"

David's insides quivered with either silent laughter or silent sobs. "A long time. Forever, I guess."

He gently disentangled himself and sat back in his chair. "Sorry. I didn't mean to.... I just wanted you to know that I don't care what Joe said, and I don't judge you. I'm the last person to judge anyone. I don't want to stop being friends. Okay?"

Christie watched him with a sad expression. "Okay."

"Okay." David picked up his knife and fork.

They ate quietly for a while. David had lost his appetite in the swamp of emotions, but it slowly reawakened as his blood cooled and the flavors tempted his tongue. The sticky rice was wonderful, especially when paired with a little of the whitefish and mango salsa. There were even little black seeds sprinkled over the sticky rice.

The black seeds were such a pretty touch. Christie paid attention to small details like that. He had so much energy and so much heart, and he found such joy in creating. He was the opposite of lazy. He would never, for example, have a drawer that had been jammed for twenty years. David admired that tremendously. Maybe part of it was Christie's age. He wasn't old enough to have had his spirit crushed yet. Then again, maybe Christie never would be crushed. He stood up for himself. He knew what he wanted. He wasn't ashamed, not of being gay or anything else. What different lives they'd led.

He shot Christie a look. Christie was watching him with thoughtful curiosity, as if he were seeing David in a new way. And that was pretty terrifying. "When you lived in New York, your friends, the people you worked with...."

"Knew I was gay? Of course. Most of my friends were gay too. It's not a big deal there."

"There are still hate crimes. Right? I see them on the news."

"Yes. But most people are fine with it. You can't live your life worried about what some assholes think." Christie frowned. "I mean, I know it's not that simple in a small town like this."

It wasn't simple in David's life, not at all. Most everyone he knew was Mennonite, and it was considered a grave sin in their doctrine. But he didn't want to think about his reality right now. He wanted to hear something new. "Tell me what it was like in New York."

So Christie talked. He told David about his best friend, Kyle, and how he'd just gotten married to another man at city hall. He talked about some of his other friends and how they all dressed up for the gay pride parade each year. He talked about the clubs in New York and the dancing. He admitted he'd drunk too much and needed a change.

It was the first time he'd talked in such detail about his life in the city, and now David knew why. It all sounded foreign to him—interesting and sophisticated but also shallow. Wasn't there someone special to Christie? Someone who was more than a friend or a one-night stand? His descriptions of the small apartment he lived in were grudging and dismissive, like he hadn't spent much time there. David was too much of a homebody to thrive in a life like that, even if... even if he were younger and free and... and a lot of other things he would never be.

"It was brave of you to come here alone," David said over panna cotta and coffee.

Christie shrugged. "Like I said, I needed a break from the city, and I had to deal with Aunt Ruth's things....

Besides, lack of courage has never been my problem. More like too little self-preservation instinct. It's gotten me in trouble a time or two."

Silence fell, and by the time David finished the last bite of his dessert, there was a new tension in the air. Christie shifted in his seat, moving his legs toward David. His knee rested lightly against David's thigh.

David knew he should move away, but he couldn't manage it. The press of Christie's knee started currents moving inside him that had been still for a long time. It felt sexier, somehow, then the kiss they shared, maybe because David was in pure shock through most of that.

Dear Lord, I kissed Christie Landon.

"I can help clean up," David said nervously. He started to pick up his plate, but Christie grabbed his wrist, keeping him from getting up.

"You can talk to me, David," Christie said quietly.

"I.... Yes."

You're one of the only people I've ever been able to talk to. Even so David wasn't sure he could talk about being gay. Not yet. He had to figure things out on his own first. He felt like he should make something clear. "I know...," he started haltingly. "I don't expect.... I know I'm way too old for you. But I very much appreciate being your friend."

Christie stared at him, his pupils large and black. He softened his grip and moved his thumb, just once, along David's wrist. "I keep telling you forty-one is not old. And I find you seriously hot. You have no idea."

"Hot?"

"Hot." Christie nodded adamantly. "You'd be dishy anywhere, even in New York."

David pulled his hand away so he could run it though his hair, nervously. "Thanks. I.... Hmmm." He didn't believe that, but it he was grateful if Christie really thought so.

He got up and started clearing the table.

They worked together to take all the dishes over to the sink. They had to walk in and out of the large sand flat Christie made, and it was weird for his feet to go from sand to linoleum and back again. It felt like his life, actually. Being with Christie was like stepping into the sand—exotic, interesting, almost a fantasy. Then the linoleum came, the everyday, ordinary, inescapable reality of his life that underlay it all.

Walking between the two was damned messy.

"I'll do the dishes later," Christie said when the table was clear.

"I can help."

"No, really. I'm so not in the mood to do them right now."

Christie's voice was warm and low. It made those eddies stir up again in David's stomach and groin. "Okay."

He stood in the kitchen with his hands stuffed in the front pockets of his jeans. "Thank you for going to all this trouble. The meal was delicious too. I'll never forget it."

"It was my pleasure."

With a determined look, Christie linked his arm through David's and walked him toward the door. When they got there, Christie took David's coat from the rack and held it out for him, much like David did for Christie all those weeks ago. David let himself be helped into it. Christie seemed anxious to get rid of him, which stung a little. But the meal was over, after all, and maybe they could both use some space after what they'd talked about.

Christie tugged the sides of David's coat closed, his

mouth set in a firm line. He was so close. "There's something I want to say."

David took a shaky breath. "Go ahead."

Christie raised his eyes to look at him. They were unusually dark and deep, almost the turquoise of the sea in Bora Bora. "I like you, David. A lot. I don't want to lose our friendship, no matter what. I know this is complicated for you. I get it. But if you want more, I would like that. I would really, *really* like that."

He closed the distance between them, slid both arms up around David's neck, and kissed him.

David's eyes slid shut and his knees went weak. He couldn't summon an ounce of resistance. His hands slipped around Christie as if they knew what to do. His mind blanked out and he let it. Just this once he wanted to *feel* without questions or self-recrimination. This time the kiss wasn't a shock, and he was very aware he was kissing a man. He reveled in the texture of Christie's lips and was more than ready to open for Christie's tongue. David savored the taste of coconut and spice, man and sin. He kissed back with everything he had, drawing hungrily on Christie's tongue and tilting his head to seal them together more tightly.

Lord, it felt so sexy. Kissing Christie was as good as his food, as surprising as his conversation, as luminous as his eyes. Want pushed through David with the suddenness and strength of a heart attack. Oh. Oh Lord. He never imagined he would feel lust like this, powerful and raw and bound up somehow with love and admiration and hope. Had he ever felt anything so good with another person in his arms? No, never.

If this was wrong, David would go to hell gladly because

nothing ever fed his soul like this. He almost sobbed at the thought of how long he'd denied himself this pleasure.

Christie pulled back, breaking the kiss and staring at him, breathing hard. "Right. I thought that might be pretty damn tempting. I.... We should take this slowly. I think?" He sounded doubtful.

"Yes," David agreed. He didn't want to take things slowly. He wanted all of Christie *now*. But another few breaths brought a clearer head and waves of nervousness and even a little guilt. Christie was right. He didn't want to blunder into this and regret it in the morning—or have Christie regret it. He still had to come to terms with acting on his desires in the flesh with the idea that he wouldn't be taking advantage of Christie—or vice versa. David reluctantly let go, his arms falling to his sides.

Christie gave a rueful smile. "Text me when you want to do dinner again. Okay?"

"I could pick up food tomorrow. Italian?" David offered. He didn't want Christie to feel like he had to cook all the time, but he didn't want to skip seeing him either.

Christie thought about it, then nodded. "That sounds good."

"Okay. I'll see you tomorrow."

"Good night." With a wistful look, Christie opened the door, and David walked through it.

As he walked down the dark lane back to his house through the crusty remains of the last snowfall, David wanted to shout for joy. He wanted to store this moment, and this feeling, in a bottle like a magic tonic. He wanted to spin like a child and praise a god who probably wasn't all that thrilled with the development.

This. Somehow *this* incredible thing had come into his life when he'd given up hoping for anything exciting to ever happen again. And he couldn't find it in himself to be even the least bit sorry.

Chapter 13

Christie floated through the dishes and through shoving the foam core panels back into the garage. Dismantling the sand box, he decided, could wait until morning. It was far too practical a task, and he didn't want to kill his buzz.

David is gay. Closeted, yes, but still gay.

And we kissed. He was passionate and trembling. Oh good God.

Crazy ideas flew through Christie's mind. Fantasies about a kitchen that was *theirs*, cuddling on the couch, and trips together to far-off places. Fantasies that involved words like "marriage" and "forever." It was crazy. Before David came over, Christie was determined to end it. Now, dear God above, he was utterly, devastatingly smitten.

He adored David's solid, masculine presence, how real he was, how competent at working with his hands, how mature and grounded and dependable. He loved the gentleness and seriousness inside that all-he-man frame. Now that the door had been opened to having David romantically, to belonging to him and having David be his, it was like life shoved Christie right off the edge of the pool into the deep end. Hard. He wanted *it all*. The entire white fucking picket fence.

Shit, it was terrifying.

He poured himself a glass of red wine and decided to take a bath. He needed some assisted daydream time. He added some muscle-soothing bath salts, ran the water hot, and climbed in. His aunt's tub was the kind with a shower overhead and sliding plastic doors in lieu of a shower curtain. He shut the doors so the steam would build up and sank against the back until his chin was just above the water and his long legs were bent, his knees rising like the peaks on the Polynesian beach panels he made.

Maybe you'd like to take a walk after dinner? Climb some hills? He thought absurdly. He could picture David's large, rough hands on his knees, sliding downward....

No. Jerking off in the tub was all well and good, but it wouldn't solve anything. He needed to *think*.

Christie knew they could have ended up in bed tonight if he'd encouraged it. But he knew instinctively it would be a mistake. Not a huge mistake, probably, but a mistake nonetheless. When David came to his bed, Christie wanted him to do so soberly, having had plenty of time to think about what he was doing, to *choose* it without the temptation of a hard dick pressing against him addling his brain. Because ultimately it was David's life that was going to have to shatter and be rebuilt for this. If he chose Christie, it would have consequences. He had to make that decision for himself.

Christie snorted at his thoughts. When did he get so responsible? But it wasn't just about David, not really. It was self-preservation. If David came to him of his own free will, having fully considered the fallout, then he'd be strong enough to stay. Christie wouldn't end up being shoved away later in a fit of fear and denial. Or at least he could hope not.

Did Christie honestly want this? He did. God, he did. It wouldn't be easy. This wasn't like meeting some nice guy in the city, someone unencumbered and openly gay. But then Christie would never have met someone like David in the city.

Had David ever been with a man? Christie was pretty sure he hadn't. In fact, he'd married young, so he'd probably only ever had sex with his wife. It was hard to even imagine being gay and confined to a life like that. God, the things Christie wanted to show him! The things he wanted to make David feel. He shuddered in the warm water.

But even if David wanted him, wanted a relationship, there were so many barriers in the way. *Joe*, for one. Christie couldn't begin to imagine being a stepdad to Joe Fisher. God help him. He might as well just stick his head in an oven right now. And Amy. How would she take the news her dad was gay and dating the cute young neighbor? Probably not well. Then there was the area they lived in. David couldn't just up and leave his farm. How would people take it if Christie moved in with David, if they were a couple? And did Christie seriously want to stay in Lancaster County? A temporary respite from the city was one thing, but permanently?

That line of thought should put him off—a million miles off, in fact. But all Christie had to do was picture David's face, close his eyes, and remember how easily they talked over meals, how he kissed Christie at the kitchen table, all grief and longing, how he was so ready, passionate at the doorway, and the list of why-nots melted away like the salt crystals in his bathwater.

Things would take the shape they were going to take. There was no point anticipating exactly what the trouble would be, though undoubtedly there'd be some. The real question was this: was Christie prepared to fight for David?

Yeah. *Fuck* yeah, he was. David deserved happy, and Christie deserved David. And a big "fuck you" to anyone who thought otherwise.

*   *   *

David lay in bed that night, unable to sleep. Christie had kissed him. *I like you, David. A lot.*

He had a hard time believing it, but apparently it was true. He supposed it should have been obvious. Like Joe said, why else would Christie spend so much time with him?

For the same reason I want to spend all my time with him. There's something between us, something that defies all logic but is strong nonetheless.

It suddenly occurred to him he hadn't said anything back after Christie's confession. He barely said good night. Good Lord. It was so long since he dated or courted anyone, since he had to think about these things. Feeling like an idiot, he went downstairs to fetch his phone and brought it back up to the bedroom. He sat up against his headboard in the dark and sent a text.

I like you too.

He sent it. Then he added *A lot* and sent that too.

Christie's reply chimed in the dark. He sent a smiley and the line *I know this is new for you. Don't worry, we can take it as slow as you want.*

David huffed. He was a grown man. He was married for twenty years and fathered two children. He didn't need to be coddled. Yet he remembered the wave of nerves and guilt he felt when Christie kissed him. There been heat, certainly. Fantastic heat. But there was that other too, toward the end. He wondered if Christie sensed it. Was that why he pulled away?

David considered it. Christie said David could talk to him. How strange to be able to talk about this with someone. Finally he typed, *It is new. I've only ever had photographs. Of men.*

The phone was silent for a long while, so long David started to second-guess himself. He shouldn't have admitted that. It sounded so lame. And the implication was he'd *touched* himself to those photos. Oh Lord. Did Christie think he was pathetic?

Just as he started to panic, his phone chimed. The text message came up. *Photos like this?* There was a picture attached. Heart in his throat, David hit it with his thumb to bring it up.

A soft noise escaped his lips. *Dear Lord in heaven.*

The photo was of Christie, or at least the part of him from his waist to his upper thighs. It looked like he was lying on his bed. He wore soft pajama bottoms in plain blue, and *he was erect.* The material of his pj's did little to disguise the shape of his hard member. Christie had his palm on his hip as if to frame the photo's central feature. But no framing was necessary to draw David's eye. He stared and stared. Christie's cock under the thin material looked long and heavy. The head tapered a little, was smaller than his width at his biggest point, as if made to *insert.*

Oh my God.

He couldn't believe Christie sent that. Had he thought Christie was brave? The man was *fearless.*

The photo sent a primal physical reaction coursing through David. It chased away any thoughts of guilt or sin and left only want and an aching arousal. David closed his eyes and breathed. When he could finally type again, he sent: *You have no idea what you do to me.*

Show me, Christie replied.

David's face burned with embarrassment. He didn't dare take a photo like that. Did he? But Christie went first. In a way it was easier like this, with Christie in another place. David didn't feel as self-conscious as he would have in person.

He thought about trying to take a photo like Christie's, showing his erection under pj's. But David's bottoms were thicker and plaid. It would be hard to make anything out except a tent. He stripped them off and tried a few options, hardly able to believe he was doing this. He chose one in which his palm was mostly over his erection but the shaft peeked out along the side. He took the photo close up, which looked a little obscene, but he sent it anyway, his mouth dry.

Christie's reply came a moment later. *God, I am so hard right now. This is what I want to do to you.*

David held his breath and tapped the photo. It was a picture of Christie's mouth and throat. He had his head tilted back, light blond hair caressing his neck, and he had two long fingers inserted between his lips. His lips were pursed and his cheeks hollowed. He was sucking his fingers.

David groaned and spread his legs. He'd never had... that, not really. He tried to guide Susan's head down a few times when they were newly married. But she didn't like it, and he couldn't remember what it felt like for the few seconds she tried to please him. He'd looked at the pictures of that act so many times in his secret stash, trying to imagine the sensation.

Christie wants to do that. To me.

He was rigid and throbbing at the idea, at the image of Christie's mouth and throat. He had to give himself a few strokes. Every inch of his body felt sensitive, crying out for touch, for Christie. Every cell craved him. It would be easy to orgasm just looking at those two photographs. But he made himself slow down, massage himself lightly with two fingers and type a reply.

Never thought I could feel like this. You're so beautiful. Show me more.

Christie's reply was quick. OK. *Show me more too.*

There was a pause while Christie, David hoped, took photos. David was so lost in a haze of lust he didn't think about reciprocating until his phone dinged again, and he realized he should have been taking a picture of his own.

But when he opened what Christie had sent, the thought flew from his head.

Christie had removed his pj bottoms and was completely bare. The photo was taken from between his spread and raised knees. He was still lying on his back, and the image showed the curve of his buttocks, a tight, hairless sac, and the fat root of his erection. The angle was exactly what David would see if he were lying between Christie's thighs.

He groaned. A delicious, shuddering throb started in his cock and ran through him from head to toe. Christie shaved down there. David had never seen that done, but he loved it. He loved the idea of how smooth Christie would feel, to his fingers, to his mouth, could imagine the clean smell of him. And if he spread Christie's thighs a little more with his hands, tilted him up a bit, the secret part of him would be revealed, a forbidden entrance. It was forbidden, but not by Christie because Christie was brave.

Christie would open himself up, give himself entirely, dare anything.

David squeezed his cock with his fist, trying to hold back the tide, but it was no use. The squeeze felt too good, the image before him stuck too deeply into his most sexual urges. He couldn't help squeezing again, rhythmically, two, three times, four, and then he was coming. He tried to keep his eyes open as it washed over him, intense yet with a tinge of hollowness, like listening to a recording of a loved one instead of being with them. He wanted, oh, he wanted.

He waited out the frantic beating of his heart. When he looked down his cock was just starting to soften and pearly drops painted his stomach. *Christie.* He wanted to give Christie something to edge him over too. Without letting himself reconsider, he took a photo of his stomach with its satiated cock and evidence of bliss. He sent it.

He got up and went to the bathroom to clean himself off. When he returned there was a new photo waiting. It showed Christie's fist, tight around the head of his cock with white ejaculate all over his thumb and wrist. David made a sympathetic noise in his throat and his spent member gave a weak little pulse.

Christie had managed to hide most of his cock in the photo, though, and when David thumbed back through the previous pictures, he couldn't fully see it either. Christie was teasing him. He was holding back something that David would only get to see in person.

He smiled and typed in a single word. *Soon.*

Chapter 14

Christie waited for four days. He could hardly believe his own fortitude. He'd always been a "dessert first" kind of guy. But... he kept his hands to himself and waited.

The day after their Polynesian meal—and subsequent phone sex—Christie thought maybe he should give David some space and not join him for dinner that night. Possibly he was being a coward. He worried David might be experiencing some guilt, and Christie didn't think he could handle seeing that.

It had been good, though. God! Christie had never had phone sex before, but knowing it was David on the other end of the texts and photos—David, the handsome, shy man he'd been secretly lusting after for months—made it one of the most erotic experiences of Christie's life.

He could feel David's need behind every word, was turned on by the way David fully committed to it, took photos of himself in a show of trust and desire, the way Christie's photos sent him over the edge so quickly.... Christie woke that night dreaming about it, and he looked at the photos and came again, and again that next morning too.

But however much he enjoyed it, he was still a little

worried David might suffer a guilt backlash. He texted David at noon.

Do you need some time to yourself tonight? I can cook tomorrow.

But David's reply was quick and to the point.

No. Would like to see you. I'll get the food.

Right, then. Tonight it was.

Christie managed to get in a decent day's work. The diary clients loved his campaign, and he was now at the stage of adding in new features they'd requested to their website design. His boss also asked him to review the work of a younger designer and offer suggestions. When dark fell—it came early this time of year—he put on his snow boots and walked over to David's.

The wind was frigid in the lane between the two properties with no corn to block the way and a bed of icy stuff on the ground. It reminded Christie that December was only a day away. He wondered if David would like to help him decorate Aunt Ruth's little house. It would be the first time Christie had a home of his own at Christmastime.

But that reminded him that Amy and Joe would probably be back again for Christmas. He was so not ready mentally to go there. He arrived at the farm with cold hands, what he guessed was a red nose, and a case of the nerves.

"It feels like it could snow," he said as David let him into the warm house.

"It could, if we had any moisture in the air, but there's not even a chance of it 'til next week."

"You're like my own private weatherman," Christie teased, forcing good humor.

David gave him a sheepish look. "I get the farmer's forecast on my phone."

"Ah. A secret kept from us city types. I get it."

David laughed a genuine laugh, and then it felt easy between them. Christie's worry David would be weird appeared to be ill-founded. He was perhaps a little more awkward than usual, but not in a bad way. He already had the table set, so they unpacked the take-out bag and loaded up plates without any fanfare. They talked about the things they usually talked about at first—Christie's work, the farm. They didn't talk about being gay or about what they'd done the night before.

David made no move to touch Christie throughout the meal, but there was something new about him all the same. There was a softer look in his eyes, and he let his gaze linger. It wasn't lustful, but it was *appreciative*. Openly so. He gazed at Christie's neck with a small smile for at least a full minute, as though he were watching a particularly nice sunset.

Only now did Christie realize how much David stopped himself from looking before, the way his eyes would only touch on Christie briefly. It was heady having David look at him like that, like he was desirable, beautiful. It was such an extremely *fond* look. It felt... it felt like a date, even with take-out Italian and not a single candle on the table.

They cleaned up the plates together at the sink, David washing and Christie drying. When they were done, David hesitated over the empty sink, swallowed nervously.

Don't push him, Christie. Let him lead.

"I'd like you to be honest," David said. "Are you genuinely attracted to me? If it's just pity or curiosity, or because you're bored out here in the sticks, then I'd prefer it if we stay friends. Sex... it means something to me."

That hurt a little, as if sex meant nothing to Christie. But he supposed he'd deserved that opinion in the past. He leaned back against the counter and folded his arms. "David, I've never been as attracted to *anyone* as I am to you—physically, emotionally, sexually...."

David looked up at him with an expression like disbelief. He opened and closed his mouth before he got words out. "Me too."

Christie smiled. "Your pace. Okay?"

David blushed a little and nodded. "Yeah, I—thanks."

"How about I make dinner on Thursday? I still need to try that toffee pudding, so I was thinking British."

"That sounds great."

"Okay, then." It made Christie stupidly happy just to have a for-sure future date set.

"Unless you need some space," David added quickly.

"Nope. You?"

"No."

"Okay."

"Okay." David walked Christie to the door but made no move to kiss him again. So Christie said good night and went home. He didn't even notice the wind in the lane this time.

On Thursday he made shepherd's pie, fresh steamed peas with mint, and toffee pudding. On Friday night they had a lovely sausage and bean stew with whole-grain cornbread made with yogurt. They didn't touch or kiss, but they both did a lot of looking and so much smiling Christie's face hurt.

It felt like a slow courtship dance to Christie, and it was driving him fucking bonkers. The photos on his phone were all well and good, but he craved the real thing. If

David didn't make a move soon, Christie would attack him out of sheer sexual frustration.

*   *   *

On Saturday morning David was pleased when Christie came over to get in some heavy lifting. David was mucking out stalls, and he tried to give Christie an easier task, but Christie insisted on helping. Temperatures had been below freezing overnight, and the icy straw-and-waste material was heavy on the shovels and heavier still in the wheelbarrow. They both ended up drenched in sweat.

"So... tomorrow's Sunday," Christie said as they spread clean straw in the emptied stall.

"Sunday always comes the day after Saturday around here. Maybe it's different in New York."

Christie rolled his eyes, but he smiled. "Smartass. I was just wondering if you've got plans for tomorrow? Church-type plans? Or kids-home-from-college-type plans? You said you go to church sometimes."

"No plans." David wondered what Christie had in mind. Whatever it was, he was probably going to say yes. He already wanted to.

Christie wiped his face with his sweatshirt, pulling up his shirt hem to do it and revealing a flat stomach with a fine trace of golden hair below his belly button. It sent a thrill of longing singing through David's blood. It was a calculated move, he was pretty sure. But Christie spoke innocently. "Well, I thought it might be nice to go somewhere. How long can you be away from the farm? Could you manage six hours?"

"I have to milk in the morning, but I can call Earl to see if he'd come over for the second round, even though it's a Sunday. Six hours shouldn't a problem. What did you have in mind?"

"Can I surprise you?" Christie's eyes were hopeful and his smile irresistible.

"I guess we'll see about that. What would I have to wear to this 'surprise'?"

Christie tilted his head, considering it. "Something clean and comfortable. Jeans and a nicer long-sleeved shirt or sweater. Or khakis. It doesn't have to be fancy."

"I can manage that." David wondered if he could iron a shirt without burning it. It was years since he'd bothered. *A surprise.* He smiled to himself. He liked surprises.

Christie's eyes were warm. "Thanks for trusting me. I think you'll really like it."

"Of course I trust you." *I let you see me, naked, over the phone.*

He knew Christie was waiting on him to make a move, to touch him *in the flesh* instead of hiding behind a phone. He wanted to, God knew he did, but it never felt like the right time. They'd been having dinner at the farm, and it was awkward in the house. The ghosts of his past life were too thick there. He couldn't quite cross through those layers of habit to take his male lover into his arms. And he still struggled with his own guilt and sense of self, though not nearly enough to make him want to stop seeing Christie.

"We're going out of town, then?" he asked.

Christie looked mysterious. "You'll see. But it'll be someplace new for both of us. Sound all right?"

"Sounds like an adventure."

On Sunday David woke early, too anxious to sleep. He

was done with his morning chores by six. He showered with more care than usual and spent way too much time ironing a shirt. He chose a blue Oxford dress shirt Susan once got him for Christmas. It matched Christie's eyes. He realized it did no good if his shirt matched someone *else's* eyes, but he kept being drawn back to it, and in the end, he wore the damn shirt. He hurriedly ate a bowl of cereal. At the agreed-upon time of 8:00 a.m., he knocked on Christie's door.

"Morning." Christie was all ready to go in his black ski jacket and a blue sweater. He looked young and gorgeous standing in the doorway, and David felt a lump in his throat.

"Want to take my truck?" he offered.

"Sure. But we only need to drive about a mile."

"A mile?" There wasn't a whole lot within a mile, and David felt a nudge of disappointment.

"To the train station," Christie explained. "We'll be back by three. Okay?"

"Sure." David's excitement moved up a notch.

The Amtrak station in town was no more than a platform. David parked in the small parking lot. He got out and waited for Christie to choose a side. If he took the small footbridge to the other side of the tracks, they'd be headed toward Philly and New York City. If he stayed on this side, Harrisburg. Christie headed for the footbridge.

On the train they settled into two seats. Christie insisted David take the window, and the train pulled away from the station.

"Philadelphia?" David guessed, looking at Christie's pleased smile. It would be hard to do New York City in only six hours.

"Yes. When was the last time you were there?"

David had to think about it. "Amy had a choir competition there in tenth grade. So that would have been about six years ago."

It wasn't a good memory. Joe had stayed home and Amy went on the school bus, so it was just him and Susan who drove to the city. It was before her cancer was been diagnosed, but she hadn't been feeling well and complained the whole time. The traffic made her nervous and she didn't like crowds. It was a stressful day.

Christie looked at him with surprise. "That's sad. I hear Philly's a great city."

"Well, the farm."

"I get it. So... what do you know about New Zealand?"

Christie's eyes were bright and he looked as excited as a kid at Christmas. He must miss the city, David thought.

"Um... New Zealand. It has famous national parks and hiking trails. People go there from all over just for that. There's one called the Milford Track and another called Te Araroa, which is over eighteen hundred miles, like our Appalachian Trail." *Nat Geo* had an article on Te Araroa, with stunning pictures of craggy mountains and coastline views.

"Really? I didn't know that. What else?"

"It's near Australia."

Christie raised an eyebrow. "Is that it?"

"The indigenous people are the Maori. They've integrated with the contemporary culture to a high degree compared to other countries."

Christie smiled a secretive smile and looked out the window. "Sounds interesting."

They arrived at the Amtrak station in Philly an hour

later. Christie led them through the huge lobby area and outside to a line of taxis.

"The Philadelphia Art Museum," he told the driver.

David was open to the idea, though he wasn't all that interested in old paintings. Honestly doing anything at all with Christie in Philadelphia sounded like a grand time. He watched out the window as the taxi made its way through the city. It felt different being here this time. He felt like he did on that trip to Washington DC. It was a little intimidating with all the people and cars and the maze of buildings, but exciting too, and full of possibilities. He looked over to find Christie watching him. Christie's hand was loosely fisted on the seat between them, and David had the urge to take it. He didn't, but he smiled. "This is fun."

"You haven't seen anything yet," Christie promised.

The art museum opened at ten, and they were a little early, so they walked around the grounds. It was situated in a park on a high point overlooking the river. It was a beautiful place, even on a cloudy winter day. They found a gazebo with a view the Schuylkill River and watched a tourist boat putt putt on by.

David felt alive and happy, just to be someplace new. The fact he was with Christie made everything feel more... hopeful, like he was a different person and anything was possible. That feeling intensified when he noticed a gay couple in their twenties walking down a path nearby. They were holding hands as if it were the most natural thing in the world. He caught himself staring and looked away.

"Thanks for bringing me here," he told Christie.

"You can't thank me until the end of the day. It still might suck in the end."

"But I already know I like it. Just this is great."

Christie shook his head. "You're too easy. Come on. They should be open by now."

It turned out the museum was hosting a special exhibit on Maori Culture. It was *fantastic*. There was a section on dress with woven skirts of all designs arranged on poles in front of photos of Maori wearing them. There were baskets and wood carvings, paintings, weapons, and boats. There was even a real life-sized shrine, a triangular structure with a tall pointed roof that was covered in wood carvings. David hadn't learned that much about the Maori from *Nat Geo*, and he read the displays with interest. Christie seemed engaged too. They pointed things out to each other as they noticed them. Christie loved the wood carvings in particular, and said he wanted to try sketching some animals in that style when he got home.

As they wandered through the halls, Christie drew closer until they were brushing shoulders. David saw the gay couple again, walking through the exhibit. They were still holding hands. They seemed to be completely unconcerned, and no one was yelling at them or even watching them.

What would it be like to hold Christie's hand here? *This is my boyfriend, lover, husband. Isn't he beautiful? He's good too. He's smart and productive and generous and so sexy.* The idea made his chest swell with both anxiety and pride. Was he too old a dog to learn new tricks? Could he belong in a world this modern?

It wasn't all that hard to imagine being a different person *here*, in a swanky museum in Philadelphia, surrounded by exotic things. But he didn't live here. He'd been born and beaten and bred on a farm, taught to be one thing—an upright churchgoing farmer. Could he remain in that same web and still break free? Was that even possible? Did he have the courage?

Would "courage" even cut it?

He noticed Christie watching the couple too, but as soon as he realized David was looking at him, he turned to the exhibit in front of them and commented on it.

Christie, David reminded himself, was "out" in New York City for years. He'd probably held hands with a man in public before, had probably done way more than that. He had to find David's reticence frustrating, backward, and parochial, if not personally insulting.

The thought of disappointing Christie made something hot and sour surge inside David. And he realized, standing in the middle of the Maori exhibit, he had to shit or get off the pot. He'd been playing around with the idea he could *date* Christie in his own head for the past few days, in the relative isolation of his own property, without fully committing to it one way or the other.

Daydreaming never solved anything.

If he wanted to be with Christie in real life, to *deserve* that, he had to be prepared to acknowledge his feelings. That was only fair.

Well. The Philadelphia Art Museum was as good a place as any to start. No one knew him here. He could practice being brave. He took a deep breath and put his shoulders back. He tugged Christie's hand gently from the pocket of his coat and entwined their fingers.

Christie glanced at him from under his lashes, his eyes soft. "You don't have to do this."

"I want to," David said, and he meant it. "Come on." He pulled Christie to the next display.

They spent over three hours at the museum, then walked back to the Amtrak station. On the way they stopped and had sushi. David could take or leave raw fish, but the teriyaki and California rolls were good. Mostly he was happy to finally be able to take Christie to a nice meal out.

"So you'd never want to live in a city like this?" Christie asked as they ate.

David looked out the window at the busy sidewalk, trying to find an honest answer. "I don't think I'd mind. I can see it would be exciting. It's hard for me to imagine, though. I've only ever lived on the farm."

"You've never lived anywhere else? Even for a few months?"

David shook his head. "I thought about going to college, but then my dad died. It's probably for the best. I was never that good at school."

"Are you kidding? You're a factoid machine! I swear you have every *National Geographic* ever printed memorized."

David smiled, pleased. "I can learn things when I'm truly interested in them, but I always hated tests. I was terrible at math and English."

"God, math!" Christie shuddered. "Why do you think I went to art school?"

"Because you're incredibly talented."

Christie's eyes sparkled. "Did you ever think about a different career, maybe when you were little? Like... I don't know, a pilot? An archaeologist? You'd be so good at something like that, anything with history or geography."

His praise sounded sincere. David moved some vegetables around on his plate. Had he thought about it? A million times. He'd thought about selling the farm a million times. But thinking and doing were two different-colored horses. "You never felt like you had to do things because people expected it? Not even, I don't know, God?"

Christie thought about it, his face serious. "I guess we all do. I mean, I don't want to hurt other people. I want to be a good person. I want to do good work. I don't like lying or stealing and all that. But there's a difference between doing what *you* think is right and doing what other people tell you to just because they say so. I mean, are you going to allow your life to be defined by a two-thousand-year-old book or by other people's opinions? Or are you going to listen to your own heart? Do you know what I mean?"

David looked at him for a long moment. He wished he was as wise as Christie when he was eighteen. Maybe his life would have been different. Though of course he could never regret having Amy and Joe.

"I suppose I do." He ate a few pieces of sushi. "The farm has always been there. There's always work to be done. I'm my own boss. I'm good at it. I'm doing something productive in society—raising food. I was able to be around when my kids were young...." He shrugged. "If I wanted to do something else, I'd have to pay to go to school for it, and then what if I couldn't find a job? Plus what would happen to the farm?"

Christie looked thoughtful. "I can see where the farm life would be good for raising kids. Sorry, I didn't mean to be critical. I know it's an important job. I just wondered if you ever wanted something else."

David swallowed. He'd wanted a lot of other things over the years. But right now only one of them felt important. "I want you," he said quietly.

Christie's eyes grew dark, his expression soft. His Adam's apple bobbed as he swallowed. "I want you too."

They finished their dinner in silence.

Chapter 15

Christie had hoped taking David out of his environment might grease the wheels on their relationship, ease whatever clog was preventing David from acting on their mutually admitted attraction. But he was still surprised to be quite so right.

Not only was David enthusiastic company on their trip to Philly, but he was attentive. Like, *boyfriend* attentive. Once he worked up the nerve to take Christie's hand, there was rarely a moment for the rest of the day when he wasn't touching Christie somewhere—placing gentle fingers on the small of Christie's back as they went through a door, resting a hand on his arm, or standing close enough to brush against each other if they weren't actually holding hands. At the restaurant he pressed his thigh into Christie's the whole meal.

Christie thought a trip to the city might help David move forward, but what he didn't reckon on was it would make *him* move forward too, or rather, make him fall another devastating dozen feet on his own slack line above the abyss.

It was one thing to imagine being with David on the farm. That had the tinge of pure fantasy. It was another to be out with David in a real city with David all handsome and glowing and interesting and treating him like he was something beautiful and fascinating. How the hell was he supposed to handle that? To not want that *forever*?

The mood was somber when they got on the train to go home. Their relationship had become a lot more real in just the past few hours. They stayed longer than Christie had planned, and it was four by the time they got on the train. The car they were in was almost deserted, and the sun set not long into the ride. That left them in a compartment with only dim running lights and not a soul visible from their seats.

They sat side by side, silent in a contented way. David had his hands in his coat pockets. But when Christie leaned against his shoulder, he shifted to put his arm around Christie and pull him close. They were nearly the same height while seated, and Christie laid his head on David's shoulder. And then he couldn't resist the temptation to tilt up his chin and nose along the ruddy skin of David's neck. He smelled like the crisp winter air of the city, with earthy, salty base notes. Christie took a little taste with a soft, openmouthed kiss, skimming his tongue over the barest trace of stubble on David's neck.

In an instant the mood shifted. What was relaxed and contented, introspective, and even a little weary flared into molten heat. David tensed, his breath hitching. He titled his head to the side, inviting Christie's exploration. What could he do but oblige?

He let his lips travel up and down the corded muscle. His eyelashes brushed David's jawline and the tip of his tongue made a wet trail that raised gooseflesh. He brushed aside the collar of David's shirt and sucked just above his collarbone, rhythmically.

David made a low noise and pulled Christie tighter to his neck with the hand that was wrapped around his shoulder. He shifted his hips restlessly in his seat. Christie managed a glance down and saw a magnificent bulge visible under the denim.

Oh God. Christie was filled with suffocating desire. Tingles of heat washed from the top of his head to the tips of his toes, which he curled in his shoes.

Now, his body demanded. *Want you right now.*

He placed his hand on David's jaw to urge his chin down and met David's lips.

This kiss wasn't hard and tight like their first kiss at the table, or tentatively passionate like their second kiss at the door. No, this was all lush, sensual greed, laving tongues and hitched breath. It was heaven. David pulled him tighter so they were practically chest to chest, his tongue perfectly slick and urgent in Christie's mouth. Christie put a hand on David's thigh, squeezed, and let it drift higher. He wanted to feel David so badly he thought he might die.

He'd just brushed the warm, rigid bulge with the palm of his hand when David hissed and pulled away from the kiss. He grabbed Christie's hand. Which, fair enough, Christie hadn't been about to stop touching.

"We're on the *train*," David whispered in a wrecked voice, as if Christie had somehow forgotten.

Christie chuckled. "You don't say. You know they have really big bathrooms on these Amtraks."

He reached out his fingers again for nirvana, but David held his wrist and moved over to the far side of his seat. His expression was fierce. "I want you in a *bed*, Christie Landon. This is important to me."

Part of his insistence, Christie knew, was a plea for

mercy. Because if Christie pushed, tempted, touched, he could have David, right there on the train. And God, Christie wanted that. But it would be incredibly selfish.

It was not only *their* first time, he reminded himself, but David's first time with a man, or with anyone other than his late wife. And he deserved all the care, attention to detail, and romance Christie could bring to it. Or at least a damned bed.

Christie took a few breaths, trying to fight his urge for *here, now, more,* and drew away his hands. He sat back in his seat and looked at the ceiling. "You're going to kill me. Literally. I have no blood left in my brain. Possibly the opposite of a stroke could happen. Would that be fainting? Yes, I might faint."

"We'll be home soon. You can't possibly want this more than I do."

Christie turned his head to argue the point, but then he took a good look at David. He was staring out the window at the dark, arms folded hard over his chest, and there was a sheen of dampness on his brow. He was flushed and tense and looked like a loud noise would have him plastered on the ceiling.

Yeah, he was dying for it too.

Christie stood up. "Right. I'm going to go get us both a cup of coffee in the café car because I want you wide, wide awake later. Possibly all night." With a smirk he moved down the aisle. They both could use a little space.

*　　*　　*

For the rest of the train ride, David said very little and tried to hold on tight to what he was feeling. He didn't care about consequences, didn't care about religion or philosophy or his late father or what the Bible said. The only thing he cared about was the hunger that had opened up inside him, a glorious hunger that was like a deep, primal maw. It was more absolute and undeniable than anything he'd ever felt in his life.

That kind of need was precious. He didn't want to lose it before they got somewhere he could do something about it. But occasionally a thread of an actual thought would run through his brain. He was about to be with *a man.* Christie wanted him. They wanted each other. Christie was real, flesh and blood, with a real cock, which David would be able to touch, suck, rub.... It was a sharp, glittering reality and was blade edged with need and worked through with faint, lingering traces of nerves.

When they finally pulled into the train station, he and Christie hurried off the train and got into David's truck. He drove the short distance to Christie's house, clasping Christie's hand firmly on the console between their seats. They didn't discuss where or when, but David needed it to be Christie's house, at least tonight. He didn't want to open the doors to memory that would be unavoidable in his own bedroom.

They pulled into the driveway and David turned off the truck. He looked at Christie, hoping to God for an invitation.

Christie bit at his bottom lip. "Do you need to get back to the farm to take care of the animals? You could come back later, if you want."

"The animals are fine. Earl knew to feed and water them."

"Thank God! Come in, then." They got out of the truck, and Christie opened the front door of his house with a key. The door barely shut behind them before Christie turned and was in David's arms.

They kissed awkwardly, both of them trying to struggle out of their coats at the same time. On some level David heard Christie's shoes hit the floor, but he could only focus on the heat of the kiss. And then Christie was pressing him against the door, tangling his denim-clad legs with David's.

David hands found Christie's back and he slipped them under the waistband of his jeans. It was loose, as if he'd already unbuttoned them. He slid his palms down, under the elastic band of what felt like boxers, smoothing over the bare skin of Christie's flank. His ass was small and firmly rounded. David dragged his fingers down until he felt the lightly furred muscles of Christie's thighs, the lovely curve where legs met buttocks. He caressed that curve.

With Christie's tongue in his mouth, their erections grinding together, and his hands cupping Christie's ass, it was almost perfect. It was almost enough. But David's jeans were binding, and his hard flesh pressed painfully against his zipper as Christie thrust against him.

He pushed off the door. "Bedroom," he murmured against Christie's mouth. He stepped them backward, even as his hands were working on their own agenda. He pushed Christie's pants and briefs off his hips. They made it as far as the hallway when he felt the top of Christie's bare thighs and the slap of his freed erection. He couldn't resist moving his hand around to *feel* and, dear God, the shaft was hot and rigid in his hand. His fingertips encountered the soft, smooth sac underneath, and *oh*.

His knees threatened to give out right there. He wanted to sink down, wherever they were, and see, smell, *taste*. But Christie had a destination in mind. He broke their kiss and pulled David insistently the rest of the way to the bedroom. His pants were around his thighs, so he shuffled adorably. It should have been amusing, but with Christie's shirttails playing peekaboo with his erection, it was sexy as all get-out.

Christie's cock was on the big side, as large as it looked in the photograph with the blue pajamas. Maybe it looked especially large because his hips were so slight. It was red and fully erect. The rounded purple head peeked from between his shirttails. David couldn't keep his eyes off it.

When they reached the bed, Christie let go of David's hands to kick off his pants, pull the socks off his feet, and his shirt over his head. David watched the reveal and hoped he wasn't going to hyperventilate.

Christie truly desired him. His eyes were dark blue with huge pupils. His fair skin was flushed pink on his cheeks and chest. And he looked *so hard*. His tip was wet and glistening with precome.

"Can I undress you?" Christie asked, his voice lower than usual.

Only then did David realize he should have been stripping too. Half-dazed, he reached with trembling fingers for the buttons of his shirt, but Christie pushed his hands gently aside. He unbuttoned David's blue shirt from the top down, resisting when David leaned in for a kiss, as if to say: *Not yet. I don't want to have to stop again.*

Christie pushed the shirt from his shoulders, squeezing the muscles there. Then he slid those hands to David's waist, teasing the dark hair under his navel with his thumbs, opening his belt, and slipping cool fingers under the waistband to pop the button.

For the second time, David's knees felt weak. He closed his eyes to try to regain some composure. He felt like he was burning up and shaking with chills at the same time.

This was ridiculous. He wasn't a teenager. But everything about this felt different, new, overwhelming. He'd wanted it so bad for so long, even longer than he'd admitted to himself. He never expected this to happen, certainly not with a man who was as beautiful as Christie, not with a man he loved.

He felt Christie gently unzip and pull down his pants, skimming his artists' hands over David's hip bones. Something warm and wet nudged his cock. His eyes flew open to find Christie on his knees. He kissed David's tip and let it trail wetly along his cheek. Christie looked up at him, his blue eyes lit with a dangerous spark.

"Okay?" Christie asked. He gave the head of David's cock a little lick.

"Oh dear Lord." David leaned down, reaching for the nightstand before he fell over. "Yeah. Yes. I—just let me get on the bed."

He kicked off his shoes and pants in a furious rush and half fell, half sat on the edge of the bed. Because dear Lord, if Christie was going to do *that*.

He leaned back on his hands as Christie shuffled toward him on his knees playfully. His thighs fell open and Christie moved between them, all tight chest and pink glowing skin.

David breathed hard through his nose, grasped the bedspread beneath his fingers. "You don't have to," he whispered as Christie steadied the base of his cock, pointing it toward his mouth.

"Oh, there's *nothing* I want more," Christie said wickedly. Then he proved that he meant it.

The word "worship" came to mind, along with "perfect," and "incredible," and "oh good heavens." Christie licked David's shaft teasingly, then rolled his balls in one hand and sucked them. David had never even dared imagine *that*. It both tickled and caused an electric pulse to run up his cock and tighten it, like a drawstring. Christie ran the tip of his tongue under the head and suckled the tip like a lollipop. All the time he looked like he was savoring a great meal, completely lost in the sensual art of it. He only looked up at David's eyes now and then, his gaze muted, like he was in another world.

When he took David in to the root and started drawing on him in a rhythm, David couldn't watch anymore. He flopped onto his back with a loud groan. *Another minute. I'll let him go on another minute.* He didn't want to come yet. *Now? Ever?* But it felt so damn good. It was the best thing he'd ever felt in his life, the friction teasing and yet enough to ramp him up fast. Christie's sucks and pulls drew him tighter and tighter until it felt like he might contract into a blissful nothing. His body reacted like he was twenty, his cock twitching and throbbing. He felt himself release a pulse of precome into Christie's mouth.

Christie moaned as if he loved the taste. He rubbed the broad flat of his tongue firmly up and down the underside of David's cock. Its smooth-rough surface took him to the edge of an impending explosion in seconds.

"Stop!" he sat up and pushed Christie back.

Christie looked up at him with a smirk. "Close?"

David nodded. "Not yet. I—c'mere."

He took Christie's arms and pulled him up on onto the bed, scooting back himself until Christie was lying fully on top of him. They kissed deeply, and he ran his hands up and down Christie's body, from his shoulder blades to his thighs and everywhere he could reach. Christie was vocal, soft moans vibrating in his throat. Soon enough David felt compelled to roll them over and get on top. He covered

Christie and linked their hands, pulling Christie's arms over his head.

He paused to look down into Christie's eyes.

His lover. He felt too much. His chest was so tight he almost worried he was having a heart attack.

Christie stared up at him and put one calf over the back of David's leg, raised his hips a little. "Do you want to fuck me?" he asked, looking almost shy.

Yes. No. Lord, David did want to do that. He wanted everything. He nodded, unable to say it out loud.

"Me too. I've thought about it. Fantasized. Let me up for just a second."

David rolled off Christie so he could reach the bedside table. He brought out a bottle of lube and a condom. David swallowed and took the condom, put it on. His hands trembled.

"We need to open me up first. Bet they didn't show you that in the porn."

David shook his head. His brain cleared a little with the break in contact even though his erection still throbbed, painfully hard.

Christie opened the cap on the lube. "Give me your hand."

David held out his palm, and Christie put a dab of lube in it, spread a line up his middle finger. "Start with one. It's been a while since I bottomed." He lay down on his back and spread his legs.

The sight of him like that reminded David of the photograph Christie sent him. He had to close his eyes for a moment to control his surge of lust, back it off so he didn't come before he could even get inside. Breathing out, he opened his eyes and found Christie had pulled back one thigh, revealing a pink furl. David reached out to touch it lightly, allowing the lube to run over it.

Christie hissed in a breath and pulled his leg up higher, tilted his hips. Did that really feel good? It apparently did. As David rubbed there and then slowly pushed inside, Christie's breath grew ragged and his erection redder. A line of clear fluid eased from the head to pool on his belly. Christie's eyes were locked on David's face. He was so open and vulnerable. If he could be that trusting, David could too. He stared back, looking away only long enough to add another finger and watch, with fascination, as Christie's tight body accepted them, drew him in. He felt the muscles relax as he thrust, able to go a little deeper every time. It was just like Christie said; David was opening him up. Only the opening was happening in David too, in some organ just below his heart, maybe where his daydreams lived.

"Want you now," Christie said, his voice fierce. He pulled on David's arm, making him withdraw his fingers.

Hell yes. He wanted to be inside Christie now, felt like maybe he always had been inside Christie and never understood it. He moved over Christie's body, his arms holding him up. Christie wrapped his calves around David's hips, and he moved his hand down to guide David into place. And then David's instinct took over, and he was pressing in, *breaching*.

It was tight and hot, slick and soft all at the same time. There was friction, resistance, and Christie's rim squeezed tight at the base of David's cock. But Christie urged him forward with his heels, and David pushed all the way in until he couldn't go any farther. He ground in place to make sure, taking in the sensation of Christie's smooth balls against the root of his own , loving it. He had to stop for a moment to keep from ending it too soon. He collapsed onto Christie's chest, put his face into his neck, and breathed deep, sucked the skin there.

Christie stroked his back for a moment, but soon he was wiggling and thrusting lightly with his hips. "Please, David. Need you."

"I'm here." He rose back up on his arms and started to move, at first just with his hips. But soon he was making love to Christie with his whole body. Propped on one elbow, he used the other hand to sweep Christie's side and chest, work at his nipple. He thrust so hard and deep Christie had to brace them against the headboard with one hand.

Perfect, sexy, beautiful.

How was it possible David never felt more like a man than he did right now, making love to another man? He loved the tight grip of Christie's body, the way he could feel his testicles on every thrust, the hard length that bounced on Christie's stomach as he moved, the low, masculine cries coming from Christie's mouth.

I love Christie. Period.

He was close, so close. He moved his hand down to grasp Christie's erection. The angle was awkward, but his hips did most of the work, shifting Christie in and out of his fist. Christie canted his hips a little more. "There! Right there! Oh God, don't stop. Don't stop!"

David didn't stop. He moved faster, squeezed Christie's cock a little tighter. Christie grunted a series of "ohs!" and then stilled, his whole body contracting and his eyes rolling up in his head. His come shot out in great bursts, hitting his chin and clavicle. David groaned and started to come too, trying to hang on as Christie's body clamped down and nearly forced him out.

When he finally rolled off to the side, he was laughing, a pure, delighted sound.

"What's so funny?" Christie asked, sounding dazed.

"That was incredible." David pulled off the condom and placed it down by the bed.

"Right?" Christie chuckled.

"Your body is amazing. I never.... It was so tight you nearly pushed me out at the end."

"Contractions. God, I came so hard." Christie rolled toward him and rested his chin on David's chest. "Okay?"

David wasn't sure what he meant at first, but then he realized; he meant cuddling. David put his arm around Christie and pulled him close. "Always."

David held Christie as he dozed. He couldn't stop marveling at him—his eyelashes, his jaw, which was growing rough with end-of-day stubble, the masculine body, the soft cock, still so appealing, lying limp on his thigh. David did not regret this. There was no second-guessing, no guilt. For the first time in his life, he'd taken something he truly wanted for himself.

Maybe someday in the weeks and months and years to come, when Christie was no longer there, maybe the memory of this feeling would shrink enough to make room for self-recrimination. But right now being with Christie was like hot sunlight. And when you were in the sunlight, it was hard to imagine the darkness.

Chapter 16

Pastor Mitchell came by on a Wednesday morning in the middle of December. He brought a Bundt cake his wife had made. "A little Christmas cheer," he said when he handed it over.

David was patching a drainpipe outside the barn. He put down the tools and took the cake. "Thank you, Pastor." He didn't want to linger with the man. He knew he had a rebuking to look forward to for missing so much church. But Pastor Mitchell had visited Susan often when she was sick. David didn't want to be rude. "Would you like a cup for coffee?"

"That would be very nice, thank you."

They went inside. There was a small Christmas tree in the kitchen by the window. Christie helped David put it up a few days ago. The farm's kitchen was where they spent most of their evenings, and Christie was enthusiastic about celebrating Christmas this year. He "oohed" and "aahed" over the boxes of old Christmas ornaments, many from when David was a kid.

David blinked at the tree momentarily, reminded strongly of Christie. Then he made some instant coffee—the sooner to get the minister in and out. He took the two cups over to the table.

"I see you're all ready to celebrate the birth of our Lord," Pastor Mitchell said, taking the coffee cup. He'd been the local Mennonite church's minister for the past twenty years at least. He was in his sixties and had a large family of his own. He was kindhearted but could be quite dogmatic. David admired him but didn't particularly like him.

"More or less. I don't like to make a huge fuss, especially now that the kids are grown."

Pastor Mitchell nodded. "Well, I hope you'll attend church for the next few weeks. The Christmas services aren't to be missed."

He waited expectantly for an answer. David had to decide if he was going to simply evade the issue or be honest. But Pastor Mitchell had driven all the way out here; he deserved better than to be lied to. And David suddenly found he did want to talk about it. "I'm not sure when I'll be coming back. I guess I have some issues with church doctrine these days."

Pastor Mitchell's face grew grave. "I'm so sorry to hear that, David. Will you speak with me about it?"

David fiddled with the arm of the chair. Maybe he should have considered how to word it before he'd started this discussion, but it was too late now. He exhaled a sigh. "I always had issue with certain things, but I went to church for Susan's sake, and for the kids. Now I find my doubts are first and foremost in my mind."

"What is it that you doubt, David? Do you believe in God?"

"Yes. But I don't believe God rejects whole groups of people because they're... they're Buddhist or Muslim or... or homosexual." His *Nat Geos* had taken him to many countries and exposed him to many faiths. It always bothered him how the Mennonite church was so ready to dismiss those billions of people because they weren't born-again Christians. He had a hard time believing an all-knowing God would be that limited in interest and scope.

Pastor Mitchell blinked, as if surprised by David's answer, but he nodded in acknowledgment. "How God judges an individual is up to God at the moment they meet their maker. It's not up to us."

"That's not what I hear from the pulpit."

Pastor Mitchell held up a hand. "*However,* that doesn't excuse us from living according to the scriptures to our best and fullest ability. It's my job to help people understand what the scriptures say. And according to the scripture, those who don't accept Jesus Christ cannot enter heaven. And sodomy.... Sodomy is a sin, David."

David closed his eyes, anger burning in his throat. Yeah, this was only going to get him all upset, and he didn't need that today. He should just thank the pastor for coming and show him to the door.

"Tell me exactly what it is that troubles you," Pastor Mitchell urged, his voice kind.

Maybe it was the anger, but David found the words. "I've raised two kids and a whole lot of animals, and one thing I've learned is that all creatures are born with their own personality. You can nudge it this way and that a little, train their behavior through repetition, reward, or fear, but you can't change their fundamental nature."

Pastor Mitchell leaned forward, his eyes intense. "Sin may be part of our fundamental nature because of Eve's original sin, but we have free will. We can choose God."

David shook his head. "Who we desire is part of our fundamental nature. Why would God allow a person to be born with a nature they have to fight or deny their entire lives?"

Pastor Mitchell frowned. "I don't know that I agree that homosexuality is instilled in a man from birth. But even if that's the case, a righteous man can choose not to indulge it. A person might be born with a propensity for gambling or alcohol, but it's possible to fight it, with God's help."

"It's not the same thing as drinking or gambling!" David was getting frustrated. "I can't believe God wants us to go through life without love. Our church allows even ministers to marry, have a family. And *you're* supposed to have dedicated your whole life to God." David's pulse was pounding in his neck. He'd never argued with anyone from the church before. But he couldn't seem to hold it back now. He clenched his fists on his thighs.

Pastor Mitchell looked thoughtful. He stared out the window for a moment, as if deep in thought. "David, is this because of your neighbor? The one who's homosexual? Joe mentioned to me that you've been sharing meals with this man."

"Joe told you?" David was shocked and more than a little irritated.

Pastor Mitchell raised his hands in a soothing gesture. "He came to service last Sunday, and I asked about you. I've been worried about you since you haven't been attending church. Joe confided in me that he was concerned for you himself. He mentioned this neighbor, that's all."

David pursed his lips. It wasn't Joe's place to be discussing him with Pastor Mitchell. "Jesus befriended tax collectors and prostitutes. He said, 'Let those who are without sin cast the first stone.' I never got the impression we were only supposed to talk to other Christians."

"Not at all! We're to be a light in the world. But he also told Mary Magdalene to *go and sin no more*. David." Pastor Mitchell looked at him pityingly. "I don't believe we should reject homosexuals, but they need to give up their sin and repent. If they persist in their lifestyle, then fellowship with them is problematic."

"By 'sin no more' you mean they're supposed to live the rest of their life celibate or force themselves to have carnal relations with a woman they don't desire."

Pastor Mitchell sighed. "God gives each person their own challenges to overcome. If they do, they will be blessed and find peace. Yes, that is what I believe."

It made sense the way Pastor Mitchell put it, but David knew, from years of pain, it wasn't like that. He could feel the truth deep inside him now, rigid as his spine. He was barely alive all those years he lived a so-called righteous life. He hadn't found peace. He'd been nearly suicidal.

"Well. Thank you for coming by," David said. There was no point in arguing further.

But Pastor Mitchell didn't get up. He sighed and shook his head. "You wouldn't be the first to fall away over this issue, David. Homosexuality. Gay marriage. Sometimes it feels like it's tearing our country, and our church, apart." He eyed David with deep concern. "Can I ask if this is purely a theological issue for you, son? Or is it a personal one? Will you pray with me about it?"

David knew what the pastor was asking. But he wasn't about to give him an answer. He stood up. "You can pray for me if you like, Pastor, but right now, I need to get back to work."

Pastor Mitchell took the hint, but when they got to the door, he turned, his face serious. "David, I've known your family for a lot of years, and I know the Fishers were bedrocks of our church long before I got there. You should know that you are an example—to your children, even though they're grown, and to your community. Whatever you're wrestling with, you need the church now more than ever. Please come to services. And consider allowing me to counsel you. I want to help. I can come back another time if it's more convenient."

"I'll think about it," David conceded. He reached out his hand and the pastor shook it.

"God be with you, brother."

*　　*　　*

Christie spent more and more time with David over the next few weeks. They'd been drawn together before, but that felt like nothing compared to the magnetic pull between them now that they were lovers. The word "greedy" came to Christie's mind. Fierce Christie. *Greedy* Christie. He was greedy for every moment of time he could get with David. And if he wasn't finagling some way for them to be together, David was.

They ran together three mornings a week. On the mornings they didn't run together, Christie went over to the farm with David first thing in the morning to get in an hour of physical labor before he started his desk job at home. They texted each other throughout the day, had dinner together every night, and most evenings, David slept at Christie's house. He'd walk back to the farm after helping Christie clean up dishes. He'd do his evening chores, then come back to spend the night.

Christie had always been fond of Aunt Ruth's little bedroom. He splurged when he first arrived on a midnight-blue comforter with cream trim, cream pillows, and high-thread-count blue sheets. But now that David was in his bed at night, it finally felt like his own room, like a little oasis they'd carved out for the two of them.

Christie tried to savor this first heady bloom of love without worrying about the future, and he could tell David was trying to do the same. They didn't talk about it. It was too fragile and new, like a beautiful soap bubble. Maybe because they were friends first, now that they were intimate, now that Christie was allowed to touch David, kiss him, and take him to bed, his emotions were already at "ten."

David was unlike any man Christie had ever been with. Most guys Christie's age were so self-centered. David was the opposite of that. He was honorable, family-centered, home-centered. He was humble—almost too much so. And he was curious, still impressed by the world. Best of all he touched Christie like he was always amazed he could do it, couldn't believe Christie was real. He touched Christie as if he loved him.

But they didn't say the words. They were only together about a week when David raised the issue of the holidays. They were lying in bed together at Christie's house, watching snow fall outside the window.

"Amy and Joe are coming home for Christmas. My mom and Aunt Gladys are coming up from Florida too." His eyes were fixed on the snow, but his brow was furrowed into a frown as if he wasn't sure how Christie would take the news.

Christie wasn't surprised, but it felt shitty all the same. He tried to view it practically. No way was he ready for a repeat of Thanksgiving. "That'll be nice for you. I'm thinking about going to New York for a week. Kyle and Billy invited me to stay with them."

"You could see all your old friends. You must miss the

city terribly." David turned his head to look at Christie. There was a note of doubt in his voice, like maybe he was worried Christie would decide he liked it so much he'd just stay.

"Yes, but I'll be back." Christie played with David's thick hair. He liked to rub his thumb over the bits of gray at his temples. They were thicker, coarser, like literal silver threads.

The idea of being away from David at Christmas sucked, but they'd been lovers for such a short time. It was way too early to expect David to out himself to his entire family. That battle would come eventually, perhaps, but not yet. If they were still going strong in the New Year, maybe they could tell his kids in the spring or something.

"I think that's probably for the best," David admitted reluctantly. "But I'll miss you. Won't be much of a fun Christmas."

"Me too. But we can text."

David smiled slyly. "Yeah. You're pretty good at that. But if you send me any naked pictures, give me a warning so I don't open them at the Christmas table."

And like that their plans for the holidays were set.

One night in mid-December, they were having a dinner of Cajun catfish, coleslaw, and hush puppies when David asked, "I was wondering if you'd mind sleeping at my place tonight?"

It was the first time he'd suggested anything of the sort. Christie was surprised. "Sure. What's up?"

"Buella's close to her time. I'm thinking it might be tonight, so I'd like to be where I can keep an eye on her.

And I know you wanted to see it. It's possible she'll give birth in the middle of the night."

"Absolutely. I don't want to miss it."

David gave him an indulgent smile. "Well, I'll try to make sure you don't."

After dinner David helped Christie clear the table and then sat back down in his chair and pulled Christie into his lap for a snuggle. He often did things like that for no discernible reason other than the fact it was possible.

Christie enjoyed the contact, breathing into David's neck. As usual when they touched, his brain released all sorts of ridiculously warm and fuzzy feelings. It was addictive. "Were you this affectionate with Susan?" He knew he shouldn't ask, but he needed to know.

David shook his head. "Once Amy was born, we had a more functional relationship."

"Was it like this with her at first?"

David hesitated. "No. It was never like this." He rubbed his chin against Christie's hair. "We met at church. I told you I inherited my dad's farm at eighteen. It was a big responsibility. My mom encouraged me to find a nice girl and get married. At that age I was in a hurry to be an adult, a man. I was trying to do all the right things. And she was a nice girl. Pretty. And I... I guess I was running away from what I really wanted."

"Did you love her?"

"Yes. Not like this, but in a different way. She was a good woman. She deserved better than me. But I think she was content with the house and the kids, her friends at church, her ladies' group, her crafts."

Christie couldn't imagine living life for twenty-some years with a wife. "Do you think maybe you're bisexual?"

he asked, stroking David's neck. "I mean, when you were with her sexually, was it something you enjoyed?"

David's hands froze on Christie's back, and he grew tense. Christie knew David had a hard time criticizing anyone in his family. Probably he didn't want to say anything disrespectful about his deceased wife.

"It's okay. You don't have to—"

"I'm not interested in women like that. If I'm honest it was always more of a duty than anything else. The sex part. I had to imagine other things when it was going on."

"Close your eyes and think of England?"

David huffed a laugh, relaxing a little. "Englishmen, maybe." He shook his head. "I'm ashamed to admit it. It sounds so coldhearted and unfair to her."

"You're just being honest."

But the subject put David in a down mood. He gently pushed Christie off, and they got busy doing dishes. Later on Christie packed a few things for overnight, and they walked to David's farm across the dark winter lane.

Christie brushed his teeth in David's bathroom and put on the oversized T-shirt he liked to sleep in during the winter months. It felt strange when he walked into David's bedroom. It was a big room with distinctly cutesy decor à la Susan. The walls were painted a pale mint green, and the bedspread had big roses on it with lacy frills on the pillows. David was standing by the window, and he ruffled a hand through his hair as if the situation were awkward for him too.

He pointed to a walkie-talkie on the bedside table. "I've got the baby monitor on in the barn, but chances are she won't make a lot of noise. I'm setting my phone alarm so I can check on her every few hours in the night. Sorry if I disrupt your sleep."

"No way, I'm excited about this! I just hope we don't miss it."

They got into David's bed. Christie knew the sheets must have been washed many times since Susan died, but he still sensed her presence, and it made him shrivel in more ways than one. David leaned over to give Christie a close-mouthed kiss and pulled away again, apparently feeling the same. "'Night, Christie."

It would be the first night since they'd gotten together that they didn't make love. Christie felt a little pang about that, even though he totally understood why. "Good night, David."

David cupped his cheek and gazed into his eyes in silent apology.

"It's okay," Christie said. "It'll get easier."

David nodded. "Good night."

Christie slept well, even though the bed was softer than he was used to and he was in a new place. He didn't hear David get up and go out to the barn to check on Buella. When he woke up, there was light flooding the room, and his phone said it was almost eight o'clock.

He got up, brushed his teeth, washed his face and hands, put his clothes on, and went downstairs to find David. When he reached the kitchen, David was just coming in the back door. He looked tired. Poor guy had probably been up and down all night.

"I didn't miss it, did I?" Christie asked.

"No, she just started. You've got a little time yet if you want to have a cup of coffee."

There was a full pot on the counter, so Christie poured

himself a cup. "I want to go see. Feels like waiting around should be part of it. Like an expecting dad."

David smiled indulgently. "All right." He poured himself another cup of coffee too, and they put on their coats and took their cups with them out to the barn.

Chapter 17

David had seen so many animals born on the farm it should have been old hat by now. Yet there was something about seeing a new being emerge from the womb, or even an egg, that never failed to invoke curiosity, wonder, and a hint of fear lest things not go well. He'd seen stillbirths before, and they were unsettling. It simply seemed wrong that nature could put so much effort into forming a creature from nothing, and yet fail to breathe in the last important component: life.

Having Christie there for Buella's calving made David more excited and anxious than usual. He wanted things to go well for Christie's sake. When they got to Buella's stall, he let them inside. She was standing stock-still and panting by the trough. She had mucus and gunk coming from her vulva, sign of an imminent birth.

"Wow," Christie said quietly. "Well, okay, then."

The surprise in his voice made David smile. "You've honestly never seen a live birth of any kind?"

"I know, right? How sheltered are we these days? But no. We had a dog when I was a kid, but we neutered her. No puppies for us. I can't even remember seeing one on TV."

"Well, come here and feel her side."

David had Christie feel Buella's bulging flank. Her muscles were rigid and the body of the calf was large. Christie's eyes widened as the calf moved. "How long will it take?"

"It depends. It can be fast or it can be slow. Feels to me like the calf's in a good position, though."

"Is it super painful for her like it is for women?"

"It's not as bad for cows. At least most of the time the mother doesn't seem that stressed about it, and it doesn't take hours like it can for a woman." Unless it was a bad birthing, of course. But David didn't want to jinx it.

Christie took it on himself to pet Buella and keep her calm. She accepted the touch, preoccupied with what was going on with her body, her eyes glassy and focused on the beat of some internal drummer. She would move around quickly for brief spurts and then stand still again, panting.

It was no more than an hour before something began to emerge from her vulva.

"Look." David pointed at the bit of brown.

"What is that? A nose?"

"The tip of a hoof. When the calf's in the right position, it comes out front legs first, and its head is resting on its knees. We'll see a few inches of leg before we see the head."

Once the calf was in the birth canal, it went quickly. Buella strained and soon two full hoofs were visible, side by side, then more of the legs. Finally a perfect little face appeared, eyes closed behind the gooey coating of the amniotic sack.

"Oh wow!" Christie was enthralled. He stared at the little face. "That's a calf!"

David chuckled. "Funny how that works."

"That's *crazy!*" Christie was very excited, and that made David smile like a loon.

"It's just nature."

"So what do we do? Do we need to pull it out or...?"

"It's best to let it happen at its own pace. But you can catch the calf if you want so it doesn't hit the floor. It won't hurt it to fall, but you can ease its way down."

"Awesome."

Christie took this duty very seriously. He stayed right by the calf as more of it emerged. He even held on to the front legs, not pulling on them, but just supporting the weight. The full head appeared, then the shoulders.

"Its face is so perfect, but it doesn't look awake," he said quietly. "It's alive, right?"

"It'll wake up once it's out." But David felt the calf's throat just to be sure. Its heartbeat was steady.

"So we're about to see if it's a boy or a girl," Christie commented happily.

"Yup."

He loved Christie's shining face, the light in his eyes. He loved being able to give this experience to him. But as soon as he thought that, David was reminded of other births.

He was in the room when both Amy and Joe were born. The thought made his stomach clench with anxiety, reminding him of Susan and the entire life he'd had with her. That life felt like it had happened to someone else. Christie would never have that experience—watching his child be born. And even if he did maybe have a baby with a surrogate someday, David probably wouldn't be there to see it.

"It's coming!" Christie said.

The remainder of the calf suddenly slipped from Buella in a gush. Christie carefully lowered it to the floor. It was on the large side for a newborn since Buella had run a little late, but it was perfectly formed.

Buella turned and began licking the calf at once, clearing it of sticky fluid. After a few moments, the calf opened its eyes and lifted its head.

"It's okay!" Christie exclaimed. "Oh my God! I just saw a calf being born!"

David grinned. "Yup."

"And it's a girl! Look!"

David grabbed a box of wet wipes from the windowsill and handed some to Christie. He cleaned his hands as Buella licked the calf. The newborn was looking around as if entirely bewildered to find itself in a barn. It seemed content to just hang out in a tangled lump on the floor, but Buella was having none of it. She insistently nudged the calf to get up. Being a mother seemed to bring out the bossy streak in most animals.

Christie tossed the soiled wet wipes and then put his arm around David, rested his head on David's shoulder. They watched the calf struggle to its feet, fall, and struggle again until at last it was standing.

"This is amazing. Thanks for sharing it with me," Christie said.

David kissed his blond hair. "Glad it worked out."

"It's just beautiful. This whole thing."

David knew what Christie meant. The morning light was streaming in through the windows of the open half door of the stall. The straw was thick and clean. The barn interior always had had oodles of rustic charm, and there was a happy new mother cow and her newborn calf. It was the kind of moment you wanted to linger on, to remember. Life could dole out a lot of manure, so you had to weigh the good stuff like gold.

"There are things I'd miss about the farm if I left," David said without thinking about it.

"Is that something you've thought about? Leaving the farm?" Christie asked with surprise.

David nodded. He pulled Christie closer, and Christie tightened the arm around his waist. "I've thought about it. But I wouldn't get so much for it that I could retire in luxury. I'd have to find another line of work."

"But if it's paid off. You'd probably at least get enough to support you for a few years if you wanted to go to school. Hell, you don't even need to get a degree. You can fix anything. In a place like New York, a handyman who's actually reliable and can fix stuff is like the holy grail."

"I don't want to be a handyman. I'm not that good with people, and I'd rather use my brain." *For once.* He didn't say it. Christie looked like he wanted to argue, but he swallowed the words.

So far Christie had never pushed him, and David appreciated that. But he knew Christie wouldn't stick around forever if he remained in the closet. *In the closet.* Geez, it seemed like only yesterday he couldn't even admit to himself he was gay. Now he was officially "closeted." The weight of Christie in his arms reminded him why he was more than willing to cop to it. If Christie was the prize, he'd admit to being the damned tooth fairy.

Christie turned so he could put both arms around David's neck. "But you could sell the farm if you wanted to? I mean, it's yours all free and clear?"

"On the deed, yes. But it's Amy and Joe's heritage too."

"Do either one of them want to be a farmer?"

"No. But they're still young."

Christie frowned. "Listen, I appreciate that you're a

great dad and all…. But you need to think about yourself too."

"Thinking of himself" had been a foreign concept for most of his life. He never had that luxury when there were mouths to feed and bills to pay. But now? He had more freedom now than he'd had since he was eighteen. Heck, this thing with Christie wouldn't have happened if that weren't the case.

"Maybe so. And I need to think about you too," David added. Holding Christie like this, it was a growing conviction. The crack he'd created in his world was ever widening. He couldn't imagine giving this up, going back to his previously lonely existence, back into denying himself. And yet he had no idea how to reconcile this… love affair… with the life he'd lived for so many years.

"I know what you mean, though," Christie pulled back a little so he could look at David's face. "There are things I'll miss about this place too, when I go back to the city."

"Me, I hope."

Christie stared at him. "That's not what I meant. I don't want to have to miss you. It's not inevitable, is it?"

David's heart gave a weighty thump. Leave it to Christie to be blunt. He touched Christie's cheek. "No. Not inevitable on my end."

Christie's face softened. "You're the end that matters. Because I'm all in."

David huffed a laugh. He couldn't resist drawing Christie in tighter, hands on Christie's back. He kissed Christie's forehead and let his mouth rest there.

"I'm the end that matters? You're the one who's young and beautiful." *Successful, generous, amazing.* "You could do a lot better than a grizzled old man like me."

Christie shook his head. "Forty-one is not old! And I've

been out there. I've sown probably almost as many wild oats figuratively as you have literally." He laughed sadly. "I know a good thing when I have it. And you know how stubborn I can be."

"Be stubborn," David urged. *Be stubborn for me, Christie. Be stubborn for both of us.*

Christie pressed tighter, kissed his neck. David sighed, letting his head fall to the side. He smiled at himself—already horny and feeling deprived because they hadn't had sex the night before. He'd gone for months between orgasms before. But everything about Christie aroused him. He couldn't get enough.

He looked toward the door, thinking about scooting Christie in that direction and back to the house. Something moved in the window. Startled, David pushed Christie back.

"What is it?" Christie asked.

"I thought I saw someone." David hesitated, a sense of cold dread washing through him. He was sure he'd seen a face at the window.

"Do you want to go see?" Christie suggested nervously.

Right. No point standing here like a fool. Making his legs move, David went over to the door and left the stall. He didn't see anyone outside the barn, but he thought he heard the slam of a car door.

The dairy man wasn't due until later that morning. Earl? But Earl never showed up before three. David walked quickly around the side of the barn and then past the old pump house. By the time he got to a clear view of the yard, he was too late to see who was there, but he heard the sound of a car driving fast down the driveway on the other side of the house.

Please, God, let it have been the FedEx or UPS man. Maybe

there would be a package at the back door. Maybe the guy was looking for a signature or something.

David walked up to the house, Christie trailing behind him. On the porch stoop was a large platter covered with foil. Definitely not FedEx or UPS.

He lifted the foil and saw it was a platter of Christmas cookies. They were in a decorative ceramic dish shaped like a Christmas tree, but the dish was cracked down the middle, and some of the cookies were broken too. Whoever left it had dropped it on the stoop, either accidentally or angrily, or in too much of a hurry.

His heart pounding, he picked up a piece of cookie and tasted it. Way too much flour and not enough sugar. *Evelyn Robeson?*

"Is everything all right?" Christie came up behind him. "What happened?"

David looked up at him. "She must have seen us."

"She who? It wasn't Amy, was it?"

"No." David sighed. "A woman from our church."

"I'm sorry, David." Christie looked worried.

"It's not your fault." *I shouldn't have been holding you, kissing you in the barn in broad daylight.*

"Is there anything I can do?"

The moment felt wretched, almost as bad as when Joe was there. David hated the way he felt—fearful, ashamed, and guilty. And he didn't like the look on Christie's face—worried and unhappy. This wasn't Christie's problem.

"It's fine." He stood up and brushed off his hands. "Maybe it's for the best. She's been trying to suggest she and I should date, and I wasn't interested."

Would Evelyn hold her tongue? That was the real problem. Would she tell people at church what she'd seen?

If she did there was a good chance Amy and Joe would hear about it. Maybe she'd be too embarrassed to talk about it, though. And what had she seen other than a hug? Maybe she'd misinterpret it.

But the broken platter didn't bode well.

"I should go home and get to work. It's after ten," Christie said in a worried voice. "Thanks for letting me see the birth, David. It was amazing. And I'm so sorry about this." He waved at the cookie platter.

"It's all right. I'll see you tonight. At your place?"

Christie nodded and managed a smile. "Okay. Have a good day."

But nothing felt quite right as Christie walked away.

ACT III: THE REAPING

Chapter 18

God, Christie hated being in New York for Christmas.

No, that wasn't true. He *loved* being in New York for Christmas. It was being in New York without David he hated. It felt like someone had surgically removed half his ribs, so he was walking around unsupported internally. They also took all of his sense of humor while they were at it, excised that sucker with an X-Acto knife.

Kyle did his best, blond bundle of holiday bliss that he was. They went shopping at Macy's, Tiffany's, and all the best holiday stores. They walked around Rockefeller Center and Central Park. They went to a midnight off-Broadway production of *Scrooge*. But all the wonderful tastes and sights, the cheerful times with his friends.... He wanted to share those with David. Without him there it all felt pointless. Christie tried not to let that show. He didn't want to be a downer.

He was glad to see Kyle and Billy seemed happy. They argued now and then because Kyle was opinionated and Billy was no pushover, but they were also affectionate nearly all the time and seemed to have slipped into hardcore coupledom—finishing each other's sentences, dividing up household chores with the grace of a well-oiled machine, and still having enthusiastic sex, if the noises that came from their bedroom at night was any indication.

Christie and David did those things too. But the difference was Kyle and Billy were permanent. They were secure. They were in a place Christie could only dream about.

It was pretty much impossible for him to lie on the couch in his mounds of bedding and not think about David. To be fair he thought about David all day, but at night in particular, with the sounds of Kyle and Billy making love in the next room, his brain wanted to take the long view.

He wondered if he would still be with David when next Christmas rolled around. And if so if they'd be in a painful long-distance relationship, or if he'd still be at his aunt's house or what. He couldn't imagine himself spending a family Christmas at the farm. It was hard to see himself ever fitting into the family unit that included David, Amy, and Joe. And that was upsetting and depressing as hell. It triggered a lot of his deepest insecurities. Christie had been raised that a family was a mama, a poppa, and the kids. There was no place in that picture for the gay boy.

They went to The Boiler Room on Christmas Eve. Kyle was all excited about seeing their old friends. But it felt flat, like watching an old movie you'd seen way too many times before. Nothing about The Boiler Room had changed, including the regulars who commented on, bitched about, or tried to get a quickie from the fresh newbies. But *Christie* had changed. He couldn't believe he'd spent so much of his life there, all of his twenties, in fact. He'd so much rather be spending a quiet evening with David, cooking dinner, cuddling on the couch with their books, or watching a movie, spending long hours exploring each other's bodies.

To make it worse, he had to fend off quite a few advances. Every time he said no he thought about how much of himself he'd given away all those years. This was a life he definitely didn't want to return to. But if things with David didn't work out, he could see himself getting sucked back into this because... what else was there, really?

He *knew* he and David were incredibly important to each other, that they had a singularly unique connection. They had from the start. But he also knew David had some very difficult decisions to make.

He spent most of that evening at The Boiler Room texting David on his phone. Kyle got annoyed with him and dragged him outside for some "fresh air."

"Jesus, Christie, I've never seen you like this," Kyle bitched. "You're pining more than our goddamned Christmas tree."

That made Christie laugh. "Sorry. I'm trying not to be pathetic, believe me."

"Look, I'm glad you've met someone, but I'm worried about you."

"I'm worried too. What if I can't hang on to it this time, Kyle? The one time when I desperately want to. When I *have* to."

Kyle pouted sympathetically and gave Christie a hug. "If you guys are meant to be together, you will be. He'll do the right thing. And if he doesn't, then it never would have worked out and he doesn't deserve you. No matter what you'll be okay, Christie. You always have been, and you always will be."

Christie didn't like the sound of that. Yes, he was a

survivor, but surviving without David didn't sound like much fun.

"I really want to meet this guy," Kyle put in, a little threateningly. "See if he's worth all this trouble."

Christie smiled. "Maybe you and Billy can take the train over for the weekend sometime this winter."

"That would be great. Now put away the damned phone, come back inside, and dance with me. Let's show them we're still fierce, Christie."

And so they did.

David's mother was not happy with him. "It's Christmas Eve, David! Even if you haven't been going to church regular, you should go this one night to be with your family. Goodness sake. You should be celebrating the birth of Jesus and giving thanks to God for a good year."

His mother, now eighty-two, was the sort who wouldn't miss church on Sunday unless she was lying in bed with an infectious disease and a fever of a hundred and three. She never let him miss it either when he was growing up.

"I'm not going tonight," David said firmly, and not for the first time. "I'm waiting on a call."

"From who?" His mother sounded completely bewildered.

"Yeah, Dad. From who?" Amy came into the kitchen dressed for the Christmas Eve service. She had on her best green dress and wore a bright-red headband and scarf.

"You look lovely, Am." He kissed her cheek.

"Thanks, Dad. Who are you expecting a phone call from?" Her eyes were mischievous. "Is it the same mysterious someone who's been texting you? And has you off your appetite and smiling to yourself this entire vacation? When do we get to meet her?"

She was teasing him. Amy didn't actually know anything, but she was closer to the mark than she knew.

"I don't have any news to share with you at this time," David said pointedly.

"Does that mean you will soon?"

"Amy, there is no news."

Amy's expression grew worried. "Then is everything okay? Is there a problem with the farm? Or are you sick? You haven't been yourself, Dad."

It hurt to hear her concern. It hurt to know he was going to upend her world in a serious way sometime soon.

"Everything's fine."

"You *should* remarry," his mother put in. "A farmer has to have a hardworking wife."

"That's true," added his Aunt Gladys. "You're still a young man, David."

"Yes, thank you. I'll bear it in mind."

It was the same advice he heard from his mother when he was eighteen. He tried to sound lighthearted to ease Amy's worry, but inside he was anything but. If he and Christie were to stay together, he'd have to tell them all someday soon, and the idea was gut-wrenching. He didn't look forward to the disappointment from his mother, but Amy.... Amy's disappointment would be a lot harder to take. She'd always looked up to him. A father needed to be a hero to his little girl.

"So. Where's Joe?" he asked to change the subject.

"Here." Joe came into the kitchen dressed in his gray pinstripe suit, white shirt, and a red tie.

"Is Amanda going to be at the service?" David asked.

"Of course, with her family." He looked David up and

down, taking in his jeans and red flannel shirt. "You'd better get dressed, Dad, or we'll be late."

"I'm staying home. You can drive my car. It's more comfortable for the ladies." He handed Joe the keys.

Joe frowned at him. "It's Christmas Eve, Dad. Come on. Just throw on some better pants."

"I'm not going, Joe."

Geez, how many times did he have to repeat himself? It would be easier to just give in and go. The Christmas Eve services were mostly singing and a short sermon. It wouldn't kill him to attend. But he'd feel like a hypocrite if he went. And he had no interest in seeing Evelyn Robeson or Pastor Mitchell, for that matter. *Can I ask if this is purely a theological issue for you, son? Will you pray with me about it?*

He had a sense of unease, a claustrophobic tension, like a cell door somewhere had slammed shut. Already things were getting complicated, and he hadn't even told anyone yet. Even trying to maintain a pleasant demeanor this holiday was difficult—he missed Christie so much. He couldn't see how people did this—lived two lives. It was certainly not something he was adept at. He'd be lucky if he could survive even a few more months of it.

He swallowed it all down. "I'll still be up when you get back. Have a good time. Mom, let me help you out to the car."

He opened the back door and took her elbow. She fell so easily these days. He helped her walk to the garage. And finally, finally he got them all into the car. He waved as Joe drove off.

As soon as they were gone, David went up to his bedroom and checked his phone. There was nothing new from Christie, and when he sent off a short query, there was no reply.

Christie was at a club called the Boiler Room, he'd texted earlier. The fact he was not replying now made David feel all kinds of anxious. It wasn't that he didn't trust Christie; it was their situation he didn't trust. He had no hold on Christie Landon.

He knew from the things Christie said that he'd "partied" often at The Boiler Room, that there was dancing, drinking, and frequently casual sex. Why wouldn't Christie indulge since he was visiting with his old friends?

The idea of Christie having sex with a stranger in a bathroom, maybe right this very minute, was awful. It made him want to throw up. Christie deserved to be worshipped and loved, not casually used. But what upset David more was the idea Christie might meet someone nice, someone available and *out,* and not come back. Or he'd come home and look at David differently, no longer *care.* There had to be a lot of guys in New York who were younger, handsome, and didn't carry all of David's baggage.

Ugh. He hated feeling so jealous and insecure.

He still hadn't heard from Christie by the time the gang returned from church. So he was not in the best of moods as he went to help his mother out of the car. It was after one in the morning, and his mom and Aunt Gladys went straight to bed. Joe followed after giving David a worried look and a "good night." He would definitely be bringing up the subject of church attendance later, David could tell.

He fixed himself another cup of herbal tea, and Amy lingered with him, so he made her one too. They sat at the counter and sipped the hot, minty liquid.

"Dad, what did you do to Mrs. Robeson?" she asked in a worried voice.

"Me? Not a thing."

"At church tonight she was very... weird. I said hello to her after the service, and she about bit my head off. She started talking about sin and about men being led into wickedness—about evil liquor and the ways of the flesh. She was really worked up about something."

David froze, his worst fears realized. Evelyn knew. And she hadn't misread what she saw in the barn as friendship either.

"She has no call to be talking to you like that. If she has an issue, she should be talking to me."

"But why was she mad? Did something happen between you two?"

"Nothing ever happened between me and Evelyn, though not for her lack of trying. I suspect she's got some sour grapes. Now go on and get to bed, honey. Tomorrow is Christmas, and Joe will have us up early."

"That's not right of her to be vindictive just because you don't like her romantically," Amy grumbled. But she kissed his cheek, wished him a worried good night, and went to bed.

David stayed up, still waiting for a text from Christie. But the problem of Evelyn Robeson preyed on his mind. The "evil liquor" was obviously her late husband, Luther. But "ways of the flesh"? That was his sin, all right.

He wasn't ashamed of what he was doing with Christie. But he was embarrassed about Evelyn in particular knowing about it. He felt sorry for her; she was so earnest in putting herself out there to him. But she'd find someone else, another man in the church, one who truly was "righteous." And that would be best for everyone. The question was: who would she tell in the meantime? And how much trouble would she cause?

It was just another reminder he was lying to a lot of people, and if he was caught out it was his own fault. After the New Year, he told himself. If Christie still felt the same after he had his trip to New York—*please, God, let him feel the same*—if he still wanted a relationship, then David would have to work out some plans. He had to figure out how the heck any of this was going to work. He had to come clean.

God, he missed Christie. Right now he just wanted to be alone with him and hold him tight, to let all the worry go for a little while. He wanted the holidays to be over.

He was lying in bed awake at 2:00 a.m. when his phone pinged.

Back from TBR. Miss you. Hope you had a nice Christmas Eve.

David picked up his phone and called.

"Hey," he said quietly when Christie answered.

"Hey! What are you doing still up?"

"My mom and the kids when to a midnight service, so I stayed up waiting for them to get home."

"You didn't go?"

"Nah. How was your night?" God, it felt so reassuring to hear the warmth in Christie's voice.

Christie sighed. "It was fine. Kyle and Billy and I danced a lot. He made me put the phone away. That's why I didn't text for a while. But I missed you. I kept wondering what you'd make of the place."

David closed his eyes and swallowed the golf ball-sized lump of relief in his throat. "It was a pretty boring night here." "Boring" wasn't the word for it, but Christie didn't need to hear about his drama.

They chatted for a while about how both of their Christmas Days were shaping up. Kyle and Billy were having family over to their apartment for a meal, so Christie would be helping to cook. David's group would hang out at the farm with a meal Amy and his mom would prepare, and probably watch Christmas movies on DVD later on. But the conversation soon turned intimate again.

"It's eight whole days until I come home," Christie said. "I'm not sure I can make it."

David felt exactly the same way. "Can you come back early? It wouldn't cost that much to change your ticket, would it?"

"No. But Amy and Joe don't leave 'til the second. Right?"

This was so damn hard. "Right. But they're going to a church supper for New Year's Eve, so I'll be home alone."

"Really?" Christie sounded hopeful.

"I know you'd have a lot more fun in New York, though. Were you planning to go to Times Square? I always see that on TV. Looks like fun."

"Kyle and Billy are planning to go, yeah. But God, it's such a zoo! The crowds are crazy and the subway is a nightmare. Maybe I should just come home."

David's chest grew so heavy he could hardly expand his lungs to breathe. "It's up to you. I'm sure you'll have fun if you stay. I can't offer you much more than a quiet New Year's Eve at your place."

"Sounds perfect to me."

Christie's voice was low and sensual, and it made David's throat close up and heat gather in his belly. "Yeah?"

"I could move the TV into the bedroom so we could watch the countdown while we cuddle under the covers. Naked."

Possibly the restriction occurring in the upper part of

his body had to do with the fact all his blood was rushing south. The heavy blanket on his bed poked up obscenely. He got up and locked his bedroom door, phone to his ear. Then he crawled back into bed and shoved a hand down his boxers.

"I can't think of a better way to celebrate a new year," he said, his voiced ragged.

"God! Just the idea is making me so hard."

"Me too."

"Are you alone? Can you touch yourself for me?"

"Locked in my bedroom. You?"

"On the couch, but Kyle and Billy never come out once they're in bed. I'm holding myself now, imagining it's you in my hand."

David groaned. "*Christie.*"

"Just hold it and squeeze for me. God, I love your dick. Want to be with you so bad right now."

Christie was breathing hard. He didn't talk that much during sex—David didn't either, for that matter. So hearing him say such dirty words out loud was hot, incredibly so. David squeezed as instructed, and it felt amazing. He was already so aroused. His body had adjusted to having a lot of sex lately, and it felt like Christie had been gone much longer than four days. The relief of knowing Christie was having sex with *him* tonight, over the phone instead of with someone else at the club, added to his arousal too.

"Miss you. Miss your hands, your mouth, your ass." David could hardly believe his own daring as he spoke the words.

"Miss you lying on me, your arms, the taste of you on my tongue. God, I'm stroking fast now. I can't help it. Pump for me. Pretend you're fucking me."

David did, listening to the faint sounds of skin on skin and Christie's breathy gasps over the phone. It was only seconds before he cried out softly, an orgasm churning in his balls and erupting onto his stomach. It felt wonderful, especially as he heard Christie come on the other end of the line. But when it was done, he felt bereft. There was no Christie there to hold, only himself in an empty room, a room he shared for twenty-odd years with Susan. It felt a little sordid.

Put that away. Be with him *right now.*

"That was good, but much better in person," he said.

Christie laughed. "I would hope so. Otherwise you could just date a sex chat line."

David smiled. "No worries there."

"So... should I come home for New Year's Eve? I could take the train back that day."

David hesitated. "I'd love to see you. But if you want to stay, that's fine too."

"No, I'll come home. If you're sure you can get away 'til midnight?"

If Christie were coming home, David would find a way to be with him, and that was that. But it shouldn't be a problem. The New Year's Eve service at their church was lengthy. They always had a potluck meal, foot washing, and then a service that lead up to midnight and ended with brotherly hugs and a prayer for blessings in the New Year. Unless something happened and one of them got sick, Amy and Joe would both go to that.

"I can get away."

"Perfect." Christie sounded warm, satisfied, and pleased. "I'll text you tomorrow. Okay?"

"'Night... Christie." David nearly said "love." But it was too soon for that.

"Hey, look at the time. It's Christmas. Merry Christmas, David Fisher."

"Merry Christmas, Mr. Landon."

David hung up the phone and found his earlier tension and worry had eased from his body completely. He fell asleep almost at once.

Chapter 19

When the morning of New Year's Eve finally arrived, David was so impatient to see Christie that the morning passed like a slow drip on a leaky faucet. He decided he needed a distraction and roped Joe into helping him replace some broken windowpanes out in the barn. It was a cold, gray day, with the promise of more snow that night. David was praying the weather wouldn't be bad enough to delay Christie's train or keep Joe and Amy home from church.

"So you're really not going to church tonight for New Year's Eve?" Joe asked as David pried the wooden frame off the window with a flat-head screwdriver.

"No, Joe. Not tonight."

Joe's face darkened and he seemed to be gathering himself to speak. David knew he couldn't avoid the lecture, so he gritted his teeth.

"We're all worried about you. Gran too. Why aren't you going to church anymore? Have you lost faith in God? Is it because of mom's passing? You know she wouldn't want this."

"It's not because of your mother's passing."

"Then what is it?"

The frame came up with a not-good splintering sound. David removed it carefully and set it on the ground. "Look, Joe, all my life I went to that church because it's what my folks wanted, then what your mother wanted, and what was right for you kids. I'm just... taking some time to figure out what's right for me. Can you understand that?"

Joe frowned. "But faith in God isn't something that should wax and wane with the seasons. Whatever you're going through, spending more time in prayer and with the support of other Christians will help."

"I don't care to argue about it, Joe," David said more firmly.

Joe picked up the new glass plate and David had him hold it in place so he could put the frame back over it. He should replace the entire window. The wood was old and starting to rot. It was another task for the never-ending list of "someday" chores.

"If you won't discuss it with me, you should at least talk to Pastor Mitchell."

"Look, Joe. I respect your beliefs, and I support your decision to go into the ministry. Please try to respect my beliefs as well."

"What beliefs?" Joe asked, sounding bewildered.

David barked a laugh. "When I've figured it out, I'll let you know."

They worked in silence for a while. Then Joe spoke up, his tone studiously neutral. "Are you still spending time with that neighbor, Christie Landon?"

David set some new nails and the wood of the frame cracked a little more, but it held. He sighed. "Yes. And I don't care to debate that either. You've already made your opinion clear."

Joe grunted something vaguely affirmative, but he didn't look any less worried about it.

Amy and Joe left for church at 6:00 p.m. By then Christie had texted he was on the train, and David was ready to crawl out of his skin with anticipation. He just had time to shower before he hopped in the truck and went to pick up Christie at the train station.

When he saw that blond head come off the train and that tall, lean form in a black parka and tight jeans, it was all David could do not to grab him and kiss him right there on the platform. Instead he took Christie's suitcase from his hand to have something useful to do, and led the way to the truck. Neither of them said anything as they drove the short distance to Christie's house. Their eyes said it all.

When they were inside, they stood and stared at each other for a long moment without touching.

"It's *pathetic* how much I missed you," Christie said.

"I know. It felt like my guts were ripped out."

Christie took a deep breath as though David's words had struck him hard. "This is crazy."

David knew what he meant: *It's crazy how intense this is, how much we feel after such a short time.*

"Yes, but I wouldn't trade it."

"Me neither."

Their coats came flying off. They ended up on the couch, wrapped around each other, still fully clothed. It wasn't about lust, not right away. There was a thirst that could only be sated by holding each other tight, and with kisses that were long, silent communications. *I'm here now. Nothing's changed. We're okay.*

But after a while, David's hands worked themselves into the back of Christie's jeans, and the bare curve of his ass was instantly arousing. *Want you now.* He kissed Christie harder, started to roll on top of him, but Christie pushed away. "Wait. There's something I want to show you."

He got up and brought over a black bag he'd carried with him off the train. He unzipped it and started bringing things out. There were a half-dozen takeaway containers and brown parcels. "This is from my all-time favorite deli in New York. I got one of their world-famous Reubens and an egg salad sandwich, all deconstructed so the bread didn't get soggy. And I got some of their best salads too. I thought maybe we could have a picnic in bed."

"That was very thoughtful."

"Well, I figured since I couldn't take you to New York, I'd bring New York to you."

"You need to let me pay for all that."

"No, this is my Christmas present to you," Christie insisted. "Well, one of them, anyway." He winked and took a bottle from the bag. "I also got us some champagne. I know you don't normally drink, but maybe you could have a little since it's New Year's Eve?"

"I'll try it." Why not? It wasn't like he was exactly full of moral principle these days.

"I also downloaded a couple of new movies to my laptop. So maybe we could crawl into bed, set up my laptop, and have dinner there. When it gets close to midnight, we can switch over to the countdown on TV."

Christie looked so excited about it, excited to be with David doing something so simple when he could have been in Times Square tonight.

Love flared up inside David so intensely that he could barely contain himself from blurting out the words. Christie always planned fun things and took pride in giving David interesting experiences, not to mention pure comfort and joy. He treated David like he mattered, like he was a precious relationship Christie wanted to court and feed. No one had ever treated him that way before in his life. He could fall in love with Christie for his kindness and generosity alone, but the packaging was pretty sweet too.

"Can I help set things up?" David asked.

"Yeah. I wouldn't mind taking a quick shower, if you want to take everything into the bedroom?"

"I'm on it."

They watched the first movie while having their New York deli-style meal. Christie chose *Taxi Driver* because it was set in Manhattan. David had never seen it, of course. The violence was a little horrifying, but he loved the New York-ness of the characters and all the shots of the city.

They took a break after the film and cleared away the food. When they got back to the bedroom, David very pointedly stripped off his shirt and pants. He was wearing only a pair of Christie's gray boxer briefs that got mixed up in David's things and wound up going through his laundry. He tried them on at home first and didn't think he looked too shabby in them for an old man.

Christie apparently felt the same way. He stared at David for a moment, then tugged off his own shirt and pj bottoms. They both climbed into bed and met in the middle, all cold sheets and warm intentions. They kissed deeply. Christie felt long and lean against David's body. The brush of his nipples was electrifying.

David needed to do something special for Christie. He wanted to show him how much he appreciated that he'd come home early, how much he'd missed him, how grateful he was for Christie's thoughtfulness in bringing him a taste of the city. *How much I love him.*

He rolled Christie onto his back and shoved the covers

out of the way. He moved down his body with hot, sucking kisses. He savored the shower-fresh taste of Christie's skin. Christie drew up his knees, gasping, as David nuzzled his belly. He was a little ticklish there. David parted those knees with a hand and slid between them. He kissed the inside of his thighs, the warm, humid crease of where legs met groin, and the smooth-wrinkled skin of his testicles. He loved that Christie shaved, was so soft and accessible to his tongue. He teased along Christie's perineum and crack until Christie was squirming with pleasure. He all but dragged David's head with both hands to where he wanted it. Smiling, David took Christie's shaft in deep.

He loved having oral sex with Christie. It was pretty much his favorite thing, though fucking him was damned good too. Having Christie in his mouth still felt new and dirty, and could get him close to his own orgasm in short order. There was no getting away from the fact that Christie was a man when his thick cock was dragging over David's tongue—years of fantasy made flesh.

David sucked enthusiastically, breaking every so often to lick Christie's balls and nuzzle his shaft. It wasn't long before Christie's muscular thighs began to tremble and his hands grew restless in David's hair. "God, that's so good," Christie gasped. "But I don't want to come yet."

"Mmmm." David was reluctant to release the treasure in his mouth, but he did. He let Christie pull him up into a wet, probing kiss. He was so aroused by now that his skin was almost unbearably sensitive as it pressed along the length of Christie's body.

David shivered and pulled back to speak. "I was wondering... how would you feel about being on top tonight?"

It was something they'd discussed. David had wanted to try it, but they hadn't yet; it worked so well the other way around.

David was staring down into Christie's face on the pillow as his blue eyes went a shade darker with desire. "Would you like that?" His tone was low and throaty, sexy. He ground his prick up into David's stomach as if offering it for David's use.

"Yes," David managed to croak.

"Then baby, I'm going to fuck your brains out."

The words, lewd and sinful, sent all kinds of thrills chasing around David's body. He suddenly felt weak and light-headed with desire. He allowed Christie to maneuver him onto his stomach on the bed. Christie grabbed some lube and a condom from the bedside table and spread David's legs apart with his knees. He was a little rough, which was thrilling. *Yeah, just like that.*

David had never played with himself there; he'd never dared. And Christie had done only a little teasing with a fingertip and tongue so far. So it was rather startling when he swirled lube around David's rim and then slowly sank one long finger inside.

David grabbed a pillow and bit into it.

"Okay?" Christie asked.

David nodded, not trusting his voice. It felt foreign and strange and kinky.

Christie didn't hesitate. He stroked David inside, finding some sensitive spot that made butterflies erupt in his stomach and his prick ache like cold-numb fingers. David bit the pillow harder and couldn't stop his hips from hiking upward. Being invaded was a weird sensation, not so pleasurable on the conscious side, but somehow his body reacted like Christie had lit a fuse.

The pressure in his ass increased: maybe more fingers. Christie rubbed in circles at something inside him. "How does that feel?"

Like my head's going to blow off. The sensation was more tightening pressure than anything, drawing up his balls and making him feel a knife edge he didn't entirely understand. It wasn't exactly like a pending orgasm, but it felt similar. "Good," he managed.

Christie hummed contentedly and pulled out. As strange as being invaded had felt, being empty now felt all kinds of wrong.

"Christie...."

"Hold on. I've got you."

Christie's voice was rough, wrecked. A moment later he was back, one hand on David's hip, soothing. "Lift up."

It should have been an embarrassing position, but David was too far gone to care. He raised his hips up, going onto his knees and giving Christie access. There was the feeling of a blunt head at his entrance, and then Christie was pushing in.

David felt the condom and the lube. He felt his skin stretch and burn. But mostly he felt Christie, Christie's prick, hard and warm and living, taking him as if David were an animal. Being fucked was one of his darkest fantasies, the deepest place he went to in his psyche when he'd pleasured himself alone in the barn, and only rarely even there. And it was happening in real life right now.

He cried out and buried his face in the pillow. His hands went back to grab Christie's thighs, hanging on.

"Okay?" Christie asked again, the word sounding forced from his throat.

"Don't stop," David managed. "Do it hard."

Christie grabbed David's ribs. He pulled out and jabbed

back in, as fast as the tightness of David's body would allow, and again. There was the feeling of more drizzled lube, more push and pull, and soon he'd loosened enough to allow Christie to slam into him with force. He slid his large palms up to grab either side of David's neck so he was crouched over David's back. He held David in place with his hands as he jackknifed his hips in and out, over and over, hitting something deep inside.

It was nothing like David had thought it'd be, but then, he wasn't really thinking anymore at all. He was being ruined, being burned to the ground as if by a foreign army, a stronger force. There was tension, a little pain, and a slow pleasure that insisted and demanded, growing and taking over his groin. He surrendered to it, cheek against the pillow, eyes rolled back in his head, used and taken. He didn't have to worry about Amy or Joe or how Christie felt or the farm chores or any of it. He wasn't even David Fisher anymore.

Christie slowed his hips, ground them in circles, and sped up again. His breathing grew raspier, faster, pained. "God, I'm close."

David knew he should touch himself; that's what Christie's meant. But he couldn't. His hands had somehow transferred to grasp the pillow, and he couldn't move. So Christie took care of that too. He moved one hand to palm the back of David's neck by itself, holding him down, and slid the other under his belly and grasped his erection. David was startled to feel how hard he was when Christie wrapped his hand around him. Whatever Christie was doing to that spot inside him, it triggered him in ways he'd never felt before.

The friction of Christie's hand caused heat to bloom almost instantly. It blossomed like a flower of fire in his groin. Pleasure shot up his spine and down his legs, and he was coming, coming *so hard*. It was so powerful his mind blanked out.

When David was aware of himself again, he was on his side and Christie was next to him. He opened his eyes to stare into blue ones. Christie grinned. "You're going to be so sore tomorrow. Sorry about that."

"Don't care," David said. He'd been sore and hurt for far less appealing causes.

Christie's grin faded. "God. That was—"

From the front of the house came the sound of someone banging on the door.

Chapter 20

Christie put on his sweatpants and went to get the door. David had a sinking feeling, but he held out hope until he heard the front door open and the caustic bite of a familiar voice.

"Where's my father?" It was Joe. He called out louder. "Dad?"

He heard Christie mumble something like "He's not here."

But Joe's voice got stronger, calling out. "Dad! I know you're here. Your truck's out front. Come out and talk to us!" Angry. Joe's voice was so angry.

David felt sick. A heavy resignation stole over him like he'd been injected with icy novocaine. This so wasn't the way he wanted it to happen, to be caught out like a naughty schoolboy. But the moment was here, and he wasn't about to let Christie deal with it alone or try to lie for his sake.

David got out of bed. "Joe, I'll be out in a minute." He used his "do it now" voice. He picked up his jeans and tugged them on, one eye on the bedroom door. If that boy dared to come in here.... But Joe didn't come into the bedroom. David buttoned up his shirt and tucked it in.

His feet were bare, but there wasn't much he could do about that with his shoes by the front door. So he went out into the living room to face the music.

Christie was standing in the middle of the room, arms folded across his bare chest and his face shuttered. His eyes found David's. They were dark and troubled, apologetic. Joe and Amy stood near the open front door.

Amy looked bewildered and a little scared, her eyes big and round. But Joe—Joe knew exactly what he'd interrupted. He had his fists clenched, and there were angry tears in his eyes.

"I can't believe this, Dad. How could you?"

"Joe, Amy—you two go on home. I'll be there in a minute," David said with a calm he didn't feel.

Amy spoke up. "We decided to come home early so we could be together at midnight, but you weren't there. Joe saw your truck over here. I don't understand, Dad. What's going on?"

"I said go on home now."

Joe turned on Christie. "You did this! This is your fault. My dad is not a homo!"

Something clicked on Amy's face, and her hand flew to her mouth. She looked between David and Christie with horror. David was starting to feel more pissed off than embarrassed. Christie shouldn't have to deal with this.

"Joe, that's enough out of you! You two turn around and walk back out that door. I will be back at the farm in five minutes, and we'll discuss it. Go now."

"Damn right!" Joe spat out, giving in to a rare curse word. "I don't want to be in his house. It makes me feel dirty."

"Joe, I said now!"

"*Daddy.*" Amy's voice was pleading and there were tears in her eyes.

He softened his voice. "Go on, Am. I'll be right there."

"David, you don't have to do this by yourself," Christie insisted. He was ramrod straight, his face flushed red with anger. "This is my business too. You can discuss it here."

"No, it isn't your business!" Joe shouted. "You are not part of this family!"

David shut his eyes, feeling like he was getting it from all directions. Now Christie was mad too. Not that he didn't have a right to be.

"Daddy?"

David opened his eyes and forced his voice to be level. "Christie, I need to discuss this with Amy and Joe alone first. Okay? I'll call you later."

Christie didn't look convinced, but he didn't argue. His expression was still dark with worry and with defiance too. His eyes flashed daggers at Joe. God help them all if he ever left Christie and Joe alone in the same room.

This was a disaster.

Back at the farm, Amy and Joe were waiting for David by the door. They filed in the house without talking. Joe's every body movement was one of suppressed frustration. He shut the back door too hard and all but flung himself into a chair at the kitchen table, texting on his damned phone. Amy looked hurt. Her face was pale and drawn. She sat in a chair at the kitchen table with Joe and stared into space.

Dear Lord, this is it. This is the moment I lose my kids forever.

This was what he'd feared and avoided his whole life. But now that it was here, he found he couldn't regret what he'd done. Couldn't regret Christie. Some of the heaviest chains that bound him all his life had fallen off, and he wouldn't put them back on, no matter what the consequences were.

He put his coat on the back of his chair, went to the fridge and poured three glasses of apple juice, and carried them over to the table, trying to present a calmer facade than was real. He prayed silently for wisdom and guidance in this conversation, but he had no confidence God was listening.

As soon as he sat down, Joe put his phone away and began. "How could you let that happen? *Why?* Why would you... I mean... a *man*, Dad. He's a man!"

"Be quiet, Joe."

"No, I don't think so! Not this time!"

David felt a sour spike of anger. "*Yes.* Shut it. I have something to say, and I'd appreciate it if you'd be quiet enough to let me speak in my own dang house."

"Please talk, Daddy." Amy straightened her spine, and she looked at him with troubled eyes. "I want to hear what you have to say. Joe, just let Dad talk."

Joe shook his head and slouched down in his chair, but he didn't argue further. He didn't look like he was in a receptive mood, but that was just too damn bad.

David looked down at his hands on the table. The words were so hard. So, so hard. It felt like vipers were crawling their way up his throat. "I guess... I guess I was born with an attraction to men. I've spent most of my life fighting it."

"What?" Joe burst out. "That's crap! This is all about that Christie guy. Just because he's young and—"

"Joseph Fisher, I am talking!"

"Just be quiet, Joe. Daddy, go on."

David silently gritted his teeth. "I tried to do the right

thing. Your grandad was not an easy man. And the church said it was a sin."

"It *is* a sin," Joe put in.

David ignored him. "I did love your mother, in my way. We were young when we got married, you guys know that. I did the best I could for her."

"If you've been doing so well all these years, why screw it up now?" Joe demanded.

David gave Joe a disbelieving look. "Because, *Joe*, I'm too young to sit around this farm waiting to die. And because...." He swallowed. "Because I'm in love with Christie Landon."

There was absolute silence at the table. Joe's mouth fell open and his complexion went a grayish red. Amy looked just as stunned, but after a moment, she blinked and shook her head, as if in denial. "Is this... I mean, are you *sure*? He's so young and.... How long have you been seeing him?" She sounded so doubtful.

David nodded tersely, even while his insides tumbled with stress. "He's thirty years old. And yes, I'm sure."

Her brow furrowed. "But he's.... I mean, does he feel the same way? Are you sure he's not just messing with you?"

"Of course he's messing with him!" Joe shouted. "He's going to move back to the city, and that will be the end of that. And you're going to be left to face the fallout, Dad. With the church. With... with your family. What is Gran going to say, huh? Or Amanda and her family? Is anyone going to want to do business with the farm? Have you thought about that at all? This isn't only about you, Dad. You're going to totally ruin things for Amy and me too! And what about mom's memory?"

David lost it. It was too much. To go from the heights he experienced tonight, seeing Christie again, holding him, what they did in bed, to *this*, this accusation and imposed shame and... and *pure selfishness.*

Something inside him snapped. There was an old china teapot that sat in the middle of the kitchen table with the salt and pepper shakers. Susan had kept it there for years. Now it was the closest missile at hand. David stood up abruptly, his chair falling over. He picked up the china teapot and threw it at the back wall where it smashed into a thousand pieces.

"Daddy!" Amy shouted, outraged. "That was Mom's!"

David couldn't care less. He looked around and grabbed the next thing at hand, a picture of a farm scene on the wall. He tore it off its hook and threw it at the wall too. It cracked and fell.

"Dad!"

It wasn't enough, not nearly. He took a step and opened the nearest cupboard door. Inside were glass mason jars Susan had used for canning, dozens of them. He grabbed some with both hands and started lobbing them at the back wall with all his might like a baseball pitcher. *Crash. Crash. Crash.*

He had no idea what he was doing, all he knew was he was filled with rage, sadness, bitterness.... There was *so much anger* inside him, and it had to come out. Better the dishes than Joe or, God forbid, the shotgun he kept up in the bedroom, the one he sometimes imagined aiming at his own head. *Crash.*

He heard himself shouting, but he was barely aware of forming the words. "Your mother's memory? Really? I'm supposed to stay locked up in this house forever for *your mother's memory?* Did it ever occur to you that I want a life too?" *Crash.*

Amy and Joe retreated to the kitchen doorway, as far from him as they could get. *Crash.*

"Do this, David, do that! Go to the store! Feed the cows! Do the milking! Get married! Put money in the bank! Stop daydreaming! Go to church! Marry Evelyn Robeson! I'm sick of it!" *Crash.*

"What about me? You get to go to college! You get a life! You get someone to pay your way!" *Crash.* "Am I just supposed to sit down and shut up and do what everyone else wants *my entire life?*" *Crash.* "I wanted something for me. I reached out for something just *for me*, for once in my life!" *Crash.*

Amy's sobs broke through the haze in his mind. He turned to see her crying in the doorway, her hands over her mouth. Big, bone-deep sobs choked out of her throat. Joe, next to her, was pale and shaken like he was terrified of his own father. And suddenly, as if he'd been slapped, the anger drained out of him. He felt exhausted and like a total bully. He'd scared his kids.

"I'm sorry," David whispered. "I shouldn't have...." He found he still had a mason jar in one hand. He put it on the counter, grabbed his coat from the floor, and went out the back door.

Chapter 21

After David left with his kids, Christie slumped against the front door, forehead pressed to the wood. He heard the angry slamming of car doors, heard Joe pull away with squealing tires, and the reversing of David's truck from the driveway. Then they were gone, and it was silent.

Christie heaved in deep breaths, trying to calm his racing heart. *That* had not been good, not good at all. He felt nauseous.

You knew this day was coming. There was no avoiding it.

Yes, but why, for God's sake, did it have to happen like that? On New Year's Eve, yet? With Joe and Amy arriving like a crashing freight train into *his* home and their private time together? He figured David would have to tell his kids eventually, maybe sit them down for a quiet conversation at his house. And maybe once they were done screaming, Christie would be slowly introduced. Not like this. This was *the worst*.

Yes, possibly one of the worst moments of his entire life, if not *the* worst.

Something hot stung his cheeks. Tears. Goddamn it. He punched the door. He didn't care about himself. Those two could be disgusted all they wanted with him. He didn't want to care what they thought, but David cared. They were his *children*. He didn't deserve to be treated like that, to be yelled at and slut shamed.

How would David handle it? What if this was too much? What if the ruts of his life ran too deep after all? *I think it's for the best if we stop seeing each other.* David would avoid his eyes when he said it. Maybe he'd give up, live the rest of his life married to some church lady or alone.

"No!" Christie said it out loud and pushed back from the door. "Hell no!"

David was *his*. He made David happy, and David made him happy, and everyone else could go take a long run off a short pier. But... it wasn't his battle to fight. It was David's. All Christie could do was hope he was strong enough to fight it and be ready to comfort and support him as soon as he could.

He paced in the living room, looked at the clock. It was twelve fifteen. They'd missed New Year's entirely. Great.

He grabbed his phone and hesitated. Kyle would be partying in Times Square. But it was after the golden hour, so maybe he was on his way home.... He sent a text. It was only a matter of minutes before his phone rang. Caller ID said *Kyle*.

"What's up?" Kyle sounded worried, and his voice was raised over background noise.

"Oh God, Kyle! I'm so sorry to bother you. But something terrible happened."

"It's fine. We're just making our way to the subway. Tell me."

Christie described what had happened, his voice alternating between hard and angry and quivering.

"Oh, babe, I'm so sorry!" Kyle cooed. "That *sucks ass*. And on New Year's Eve too!"

"I'm... I'm so scared," Christie admitted. He dropped onto the couch and pulled the afghan around him. His hands and feet were icy, and he was shivering. It had little to do with the temperature in the house or the fact he still wore nothing but sweatpants.

"Oh, sweetie!"

"What if he dumps me, Kyle? I don't think I can take it."

"If he does, then he would have skipped out sooner or later. You know that, babe. No one can walk out of a closet for someone else. He has to do that all on his own."

"I know," Christie whispered.

"Besides, if he lets you go, he's a total idiot."

"No, he's a good man. That's what worries me. He's such a good man. What if he decides to sacrifice his own happiness for his kids? Or what if they convince him it's a sin and he repents or something?"

"Christie, listen to me. If he really loves you and he's not a total pussy, he will stand up for you and tell his kids to mind their own business. If he doesn't, he's not worth it."

In his heart Christie knew that was true. He also knew David was not a pushover and they had an incredibly strong connection. Tonight was incredible before they were interrupted. He had to have faith in his boyfriend.

"It's fine," Christie said, taking a deep breath. "I'm just freaking out right now. I'm sure David won't change his mind. I just feel so bad for him. It's not fair."

"I know it's not fair," Kyle agreed sadly. "But it must be weird for them, right? Like suddenly their dad is gay? And they have to feel sort of betrayed and weird about their mom and everything. Maybe it just needs to sink in, and they'll come around. All the news reports say the younger generation is more open-minded, even in churches."

"That's true." Christie remembered Joe's face. He didn't

think Joe would ever come around. Amy? Maybe. At least she seemed like a sweet person.

Who had a little crush on you. Yeah, that didn't help.

There was a sharp knock on the door. Christie's heart leapt and he sat up. "I think David's back. I've got to go."

"Oh good! Text me later and let me know you're okay?"

"I will. Thanks for the talk. I love you so much!"

"I love you too, babe! Mwaaa!"

Christie hung up and tossed the phone on the couch next to him. He was walking toward the door with a smile when something smashed through the front window. Glass flew, something stung Christie's cheek, and the world tilted on its axis.

Christie stood frozen in the middle of the living room, staring at the large rock and smattering of glass on the living room rug. And then the front door was kicked in.

Three strangers walked into Christie's house. He didn't recognize any of their faces, but he knew why they were there. They were young, rough, and their faces radiated hate. They were bullies, *gay bashers.*

He spun and dived for his phone. He had to call 911. But the phone was kicked from his hand with a steel-toed boot. His fingers screamed in pain and the phone went flying into the wall. He heard it crack.

That's my new iPhone, motherfuckers!

He momentarily considered running for the back door. But he probably couldn't outrun all three of them, not without a head start. Instead he stood tall, crossed his arms over his chest, ignored the agony in his fingers, and glared at the strangers.

They were drunk. He could smell it on them and see

it on their faces. God knew Christie had seen enough drunks in the bars. The one on the left, the tallest one, was skinny but mean looking with a red beard, acne, and a Stones sweatshirt. His fists were clenched. The guy on the right was overweight, snub-nosed, and sneering. Under a brown coat he had an orange sweatshirt with deer antlers on the front. He held a baseball bat. The guy in the middle had long, curly dark hair, floppy lips over gnarly teeth, and he wore a dark-blue parka vest over a black hoodie. He held a knife in his right hand.

Fear skittered down Christie's spine. *Shit.*

"What do you want?" His voice was steady.

"You're the gay boy," said the one with the knife. "Moving here, waving your fairy ass around, corrupting people."

"Goddamn fags," said the redhead.

The one with the bat just raised it menacingly. "We hate fags. You all deserve to burn."

"Get out of my house," Christie said coolly. "Or maybe you like the idea of going to jail for the rest of your pathetic hick lives?" He knew he was in trouble. Bad trouble. But he couldn't seem to keep his mouth shut.

"The only person going anywhere is *you*," said the one with the knife. "You're going to move back to wherever faggy place you came from, like *tomorrow*. David Fisher doesn't want you here. Nobody wants your gay ass here. Get the fuck out of town while you can still move, or you'll be sorry."

"*If* you can still move after we're done with you," said the one with the baseball bat.

This was definitely about David, then. Were they friends of Joe's? Maybe they were just trying to scare him. Please, God, let them just be trying to scare him. *Say,*

"Fine." Say, "Sure, I'll leave." Then call the police once they're gone. Placate them, Christie. Come on.

But Christie suddenly wasn't afraid; he was pissed. Deep, dark, bile-sour anger boiled up inside him. He'd been through too much tonight, and these assholes were in his *house.*

"I will fucking see whoever I want to see," he spat out. "So fuck. You."

"Bad answer," said the guy with the knife, his voice shaky with rage.

"Let's see how you feel after this!" said Orange Sweatshirt.

The first blow was from the bat. Christie saw it coming and tried to dodge to the left around the couch, but it came in fast and hard, and it struck his elbow. The pain was immediate and excruciating. He was sure it was broken or at least cracked.

He fell onto the couch, clutching his elbow. Despite the pain he somehow scrambled over the back cushions. He had to reach the kitchen door, get out. He was a strong runner. If he could only get out into the open air, get a little space between them.

He made it a few steps into the kitchen before someone tackled him, wrapping around his hips and sending him off his feet. He landed on the linoleum, hitting his hurt elbow again. He screamed. Broken—something in his arm was definitely broken. He kicked his legs furiously and tried to crawl forward toward the door.

"Get off me! I'll kill you! Get off!"

Hands dragged him backward, the linoleum skittered under the outstretched fingers of his good hand. A fist punched his back, hard. Someone kicked his leg. He felt the blows, but they were nothing compared to the white-hot fire in his elbow.

"You will leave town, you little fag! We'll fucking *make* you! Say it! Say you'll leave!"

He was pushed over onto his back. All the hands on him felt filthy, dirty, obscene. The guy who had the knife punched him in the face. It hurt but the angle was awkward. Christie lashed out with his good hand, hitting anything he could find. He was still screaming, apparently. A hand covered his mouth and he bit it, hard.

"I will fucking kill you!" someone screamed. It sounded a lot like his own voice.

He was punched in the face. Again. Again. Pain seared in his ribs as a boot landed. It became agonizing just drawing breath.

I will fucking kill you. I will.... He continued to fight as hard as he could. As hard as he could, the ball-less bastards, fucking limp dicked rednecks, even while part of his brain went offline from shock and pain, shutting itself away from the scene like it was closing the door on a pantomime.

He could die tonight, end up one of those gay-bashing martyrs, a face on a poster.

God, that would kill David.

Not from these three losers. They aren't smart enough to end me.

The room was silent. He opened his eyes. Darkness danced in dots on the edge of his vision like a shadow-people version of *The Nutcracker*. He was alone in the house. And he was alive.

He tried to speak and bubbles came out. He didn't have to wipe them to know they'd be bloody. He could barely draw breath.

They meant to scare me, not kill me. You went a bit too far, you fucking idiots.

He was badly hurt. Badly. Hurt. Broken arm. Broken ribs, likely. Maybe a punctured lung. He could barely expand his chest around a stabbing pain, and his nose was probably broken too, swollen shut and throbbing. Air was now the most precious commodity on earth.

Phone. Call 911. Do it. Move, goddamn it.

He managed, hissing in agony, to crawl into the living room. Phone. Where was his phone? Oh yeah, it had hit the wall.

He found the phone. It took a long time. He might have passed out as he crawled around looking for it, more than once.

The phone was dead. His bloody, crooked fingers hit the On button again and again, but the screen remained cracked and dark. He had never turned on the land line, so his cell phone was all he had.

God, please help me, I don't want to die, he thought.

David, he thought.

Then he thought no more.

Chapter 22

David jogged out to the barn. It was dark and frigid—hell, it had to be past midnight by now. *Happy New Year's Eve.* He turned on the lights and made his way to his workshop. He shut the door but didn't lock it. If Amy or Joe needed him....

He couldn't lock the door against them. A father never stopped wanting to be there for his kids, even when they just pissed him off more than he'd ever been pissed off in his entire life.

But now he just felt defeated. He sat down on the stool at his workbench and slumped, face in his hands. What the hell was he going to do?

But he already knew—it was a horrible, vile, crawling sensation in his gut, like Satan emerging from the pit. His eyes stung. He blinked them rapidly.

Maybe he should break it off with Christie. Life just wasn't going to let him be. If he continued with this course, every single thing in his life would be set against him. As angry as Joe made him, he had a point. No one could take the farm from him, of course, but if he lived openly with Christie here, his neighbors would probably be shocked and many of them would avoid him. It was a conservative area. All the support he had from the Mennonite community and his church would be gone. Amy and Joe and his mother would probably also be estranged. He might not have trouble with the dairy company who took his milk or the co-op where he sold his crops, but he wasn't positive about that. And even if he could take all of that hostility himself, was it fair to expect Christie—lively, confident Christie—to be subjected to that too? On the other hand, if he sold the farm, what then? He'd be a nobody with no career, no friends, no family. Would Christie want him then?

It was all too much to bear, *too much*. He felt as hollow and blasted out as a railroad tunnel. He needed to write a letter. He needed to. He searched around the workshop and found a pen but no paper.

He had to write a letter to... to whom? To Christie saying good-bye? To Joe laying down the law? To God asking "why me?" An editorial to the local paper ranting about injustice? David wasn't even sure what he was going to put down in writing, only that he needed to. Why couldn't he find a goddamn piece of paper?

He searched the workroom, then out in the feeding aisle and milking stalls area. Why didn't he keep a notebook out here? What the hell was wrong with him? Even the back of a damn blank receipt would do.

He went back into the workshop, looked in the top drawer of the worktable, then the second one, and then he tugged on the bottom one, just in case it had mysteriously come unstuck at some point. But it didn't budge. Another problem he'd never gotten around to dealing with.

"Oh for heaven's sake!" he shouted out loud.

Angrily he picked up an ax by the woodpile and brought it down with all his might on the handle of the bottom drawer. The steel handle flew off with a pop and there was a crack from inside. The drawer came open a little. David tossed the ax away and pulled it all the way out. A thick magazine was on the top and it was bent and twisted. It had been jammed in the rollers, and that's why the drawer was stuck. David pulled it free.

He was about to toss it on the worktable when he really looked at it.

On the torn cover was a naked man. David paused, blinking at the magazine. He flipped some pages. It was a male porn magazine, but he'd never seen it before in his life. He looked at it more closely. It was old, older than his own stash. Based on the haircuts and typeset, it looked like it was maybe from the sixties. Inside were lots of black-and-white or garishly colored muscle men with erections and a few feature photo spreads of men with men.

Realization struck and he dropped the magazine. It hit the floor.

Oh God. Oh good Lord! That drawer had been stuck since... since....

It was his father's magazine. He knew it without a shred of doubt. His father was homosexual too, or at least fantasized about men now and then. Had he ever acted on it? Maybe, maybe not. But he worked so hard on the farm and rarely left, so he couldn't have had very much of a life outside his marriage. And then he dropped dead in the fields without warning. He didn't have the opportunity to get rid of the magazine. It was jammed in that drawer all these years.

Daydreaming never did one chore for you, or got you anything but misery.

His father. No wonder he as such a miserable man, so

stoic and unhappy. He dropped dead at fifty-eight, his heart just giving out. So much work. So much misery.

For the first time that long, awful night, David felt his eyes prickle with heat. He hadn't cried over the bliss he felt with Christie nor the rage he felt with Joe. But the thought of his father's unhappiness unmanned him. If only his father had talked to him. If only they'd been able to talk to each other.

He breathed long and deep, fighting the pressure in his chest. When it eased and his mind cleared a little, he found he was no longer confused or angry. He knew what the right thing was to do. And he felt at peace about it. Yes. Yes.

Thank you, God.

He tossed the magazine in the trash and left the barn.

David walked down the lane to Christie's house. It had started to snow and the air was frigid, but he didn't care. All the way there, he kept rehearsing what he wanted to say in his head.

I don't care what anyone says, I want us to be together.

Say you want that too.

I'll sell the farm. We can go wherever you like.

Say you'll still want me if I do.

I love you, Christie. I love you so much it feels like every cell in my body is infected with it. You're the best thing that ever happened to me.

Say you love me too.

The lights were still on in Christie's house, so he was awake. David jogged the last bit, but when he got to the front door, he found it slightly ajar. That was strange. Nobody kept a door open any longer than absolutely necessary in temperatures like these. The first thought that crossed his mind was Christie was leaving. He was packing up his car or something. Anxiety tripped in his chest.

Then David pushed the door open and saw him.

Christie was lying unconscious on the floor, holding his phone. He was only recognizable because of his blond mop of hair, his sweatpants, and long, thin feet. His face was swollen beyond recognition and his body was covered with blood and bruises. One elbow was purple and puffy.

"Christie!" David dropped to his knees by the body. He went to pull Christie's head into his lap before he realized he shouldn't move him. He could have spinal injuries. Christie was breathing, the passage of air through his mouth ragging and *wheezing* with a slight whistle. Oh Lord. His lungs. Something was wrong with his lungs.

"Baby, can you hear me?"

Christie didn't move. David took the phone from his hand, choking back his horror, but the phone was dead. Frustrated, he tossed it away and was relieved to find his own phone in his coat pocket. *Thank God.*

David had the local ambulance service on speed dial from when Susan was ill. He called it now, gave the address, and relayed the situation in a panicked voice to the dispatcher. She assured them they would be there as soon as possible. He hung up and dialed Amy. Another blessing—she picked up.

"Dad?" She sounded sleepy.

"Amy, I'm at Christie's. He's been badly hurt! Bring our medical kit over and hurry!"

"What—?"

"*Hurry!*"

He dropped the phone and leaned over the love of his

life, trying to see if there was anything he could do. "I'm here, Christie. I called for an ambulance, so hold on. Can you hear me? I love you so much. Please don't leave me."

Christie didn't open his eyes. One looked swollen shut, but the other pale eyelid remained closed all on its own. His breathing was so labored the sound of it rattled like death. "Oh God, what can I do?"

Christie's hands were both bloodied. It looked like he fought so hard! One appeared to have some broken fingers. David took the less-damaged hand gently in his own. "Christie, I'm here." David kissed his bloodied knuckles. "I love you so much. Please hang in there. Please don't leave me."

There was the sound of tires braking fast outside, but when the door burst open, it was Amy and Joe, still in their pajamas.

"Oh no!" Amy gasped in horror.

"Dad, what happened?" demanded Joe.

David was still kneeling at Christie's side, Christie's hand in his. He shot daggers at his son. "You don't know? Did you do this?"

"What, me? Of course not!" Joe looked shocked.

"Then who did?"

Amy knelt on the other side of Christie and opened their red first-aid kit. "Dad! We need to focus on Christie right now."

Of course. Of course they did. But damn if he didn't want to kill whoever did this.

"He's not breathing right," David said, his voice shaky.

"I know." Amy's eyes swept over Christie's bare chest and ribs, where patterns of purple were starting to fill in around dark-red puffy scrapes. "It's probably a collapsed lung. It looks like he was kicked hard in the ribs."

"Oh my Lord."

"It's okay, Dad. A collapsed lung doesn't have to be fatal. The doctors can fix it. I'm—" she stopped, as if she didn't want to say more.

"What?"

"Uh, I'm more worried about internal bleeding, like if one of his organs is ruptured."

David couldn't stop the desperate sound that came out of his mouth.

"What can I do?" Joe asked, his voice tight. "Did you call an ambulance?"

"Yes. Before I called Amy." David's hands were shaking now as he compulsively petted Christie's forearm while holding his hand.

"Dad, don't worry, he'll be all right," Amy insisted quietly, and it did make David feel better, even though he knew she couldn't possibly know that for sure. She checked Christie's skull with her fingers, looking for God knew what.

What if they kicked him it the head, or worse? Why is he not conscious? What if he has bleeding on the brain? Brain damage?

Fear overwhelmed David again and he forgot about Amy and Joe. He leaned down closer to stroke Christie's neck since his face looked too hurt to touch. He tried to reassure him. "I'm here, Christie. The ambulance is coming and Amy's helping too. I love you so much. So you fight for me, okay? You fight." Wet stuff splashed onto Christie's chest. Tears. "We can move back to the city if that's what you want. That's what I was coming over to tell you. I won't let you go. Won't give you up."

There was a distant wail of sirens.

"Dad." It was Joe's voice. He was squatting down next to David. His face looked guilty and pained. "I—I did text

Jessie. Jessie Robeson. I told him I'd found you with Christie. I'm.... Oh man. I'm so sorry, Dad. I had no idea he would do something like this. I was angry but... I would never.... I'd never wish anyone hurt like this."

David knew Joe was telling the truth. He wasn't a violent person. But Lord, was he going to make Jessie Robeson pay. "I believe you, Joe."

Amy was wrapping up a deep cut on Christie's arm. She looked up at David, her eyes soft. "I don't see any head injuries. He'll be all right. Please don't be so upset."

"But he's not conscious." David wiped tears and snot from his face with the crook of his arm. "Please, God."

"He has lost some blood, but not enough to be life-threatening. His pulse is slow but steady. He'll be okay, Dad. Joe, can you grab that afghan?"

Joe grabbed it and David helped Amy tuck it around Christie.

"I'm sorry, Dad," Joe said, still sounding guilty, though what he was sorry for, exactly, David didn't know. Maybe Joe didn't know either.

David nodded but his eyes stayed fixed on Christie.

"Me too, Dad," Amy said, her voice thick. "I didn't know you were so miserable. I love you so much. You know I'll support you no matter what."

"Okay," David said. "Okay."

See, my love, it's not so bad. You have to stay with me now. After all, we have a whole new life to lead, you and I. A new life together. A second chance for both of us.

As if he'd heard the silent plea, Christie shifted his hand in David's and squeezed.

ACT IV: FEAST

Epilogue

One Year Later

"His hands are so little!" a girl of about seven exclaimed.

"T. rex didn't need big hands 'cause of his teeth are *huge!*" Jeremy said. "He could *do* more with normal-sized hands, just like us." He made grabby gesture with his fingers.

"That's exactly right, Jeremy." David smiled at the little boy. The five-year-old was a firecracker, that was for sure.

He was giving a private museum tour to a large family group. It was clear this outing was chosen for the kids' sake, but everyone seemed to be enjoying it, even the texting teenagers.

"You can see similar features in some of today's reptiles—a large mouth and teeth, powerful back legs, and relatively small and dexterous forelimbs," David explained. "When we go over to the Reptiles and Amphibians wing, I'll point them out."

"I want to see more dinosaurs!" Jeremy insisted.

"Oh, we've got lots more to see here first. What are the scariest dinosaurs, do you think?"

Jeremy made a big show of thinking about it, putting his finger on his dimpled chin. "Raptors?"

"I think so too. Let's go check them out."

It was New Year's Eve day, and David, being low man on the museum totem pole, was working all day. He didn't mind. He adored just being *in* the New York Museum of Natural History, much less working there. Normally he worked in archives doing filing and processing and the tours went to docents better qualified than him. But they were all on vacation. Today felt a bit like being an understudy called in for the big show. He was relieved to find no one asked questions he couldn't handle or grilled him about his credentials. In fact, he felt like a million bucks by the time the museum closed at five thirty. It would be years before the natural history classes he was taking from the NYU extension resulted in a degree, but at least he'd had a taste of what it felt like to be an "expert."

A security guard named Frank waved to David as he left. "Have a good New Year's Eve! And say hi to Christie for me!"

"You too, Frank. Happy New Years to your family too."

He took the subway across the river to the duplex he and Christie were renting in Brooklyn. Inside the house smelled warmly of curry and naan, making his stomach growl.

He found Christie in the kitchen. "Hey, babe."

"Hey!" Christie turned from the stove with a big smile. They met in the middle of the room for a kiss. "How was your big debut?"

"It went well. Exceptionally well." David couldn't keep the pride from his voice.

"I told you! You know more about that museum than anyone."

"Well, that's not true, but apparently I know enough. It was fun."

"I'm so glad." Christie squeezed him tight before letting go. "Oh my God, Joe and Amy should be here any minute. I'm so nervous."

"It'll be fine."

David hadn't spared a worry for Amy and Joe's arrival all day, but he felt a spark of nerves now. They'd all come a long way since last New Year's. At this point he and Christie were so solid a Mack Truck couldn't run them down, but he felt less confident about his kids. This was the first time they were visiting his new place. He just wanted everyone to get along.

He remembered the horrible night that was last New Year's Eve. His eyes ran over Christie's face as he stirred something on the stove. He had a scar on one eyebrow and another on the middle of his lip where it had been split. His nose had been broken, and you could still see a bump. His arm was in a sling for weeks. But fortunately no permanent damage remained. They ran together most mornings, and Christie was as strong as he ever was. *Fierce Christie.* God, David loved him.

Evelyn Robeson had been cleared of any foreknowledge of the attack. But Jessie Robeson and his two friends were charged with a hate crime and each given ten years. And David couldn't find it in himself to feel sorry for them.

He cleared his throat. "I hope you didn't go to too much trouble." He walked over to the stove and scooped some tikka masala sauce off a spoon with a finger. Yum.

"Who, me?" Christie said, tongue-in-cheek.

"Uh-huh. This looks amazing."

"Do Amy and Joe even like Indian food? I totally forgot to ask."

"I have no idea, but they should like it. It's the best."

"Oh God. They'll hate it, won't they? I need a glass of wine."

"I'll get it."

David poured Christie a glass of merlot and had just handed it to him when the doorbell rang.

"They're here!" Christie ripped his apron off and shoved it in a drawer. He was getting way too worked up. David caught his hands and pulled him close.

"Breathe." David ran his nose along Christie's. "Repeat after me: I'm beautiful, I'm sexy, and, gosh darn it, people like me."

Christie laughed shakily. "Dork."

"Seriously." David gripped Christie's face with both hands. "I love you. Okay?"

Christie blinked his blue eyes and stared at David. He visibly relaxed. "Okay."

"So chill out, Stepdad."

Christie rolled his eyes. "Shut up! Technically I'm not."

"Yet."

Christie raised his eyebrows questioningly. David ignored him and went to answer the door. Yeah, he wanted to marry Christie. But he wasn't going to spoil that surprise just yet.

"Hey, Dad!"

Amy and Joe looked cold and a little nervous themselves standing on the stoop. David looked out at the taxi. "Can I pay the driver?"

"I already got it," Joe said.

"Oh. Well... come on in."

David took their coats and put them on a coatrack near the door. Their suitcases were set down and he gave them each a hug. It wasn't his family's way to hug, but he hadn't seen them in months. Besides, he'd already figured out sometimes the "way things had always been" wasn't good enough. He showed them into the living room just as Christie came out of the kitchen.

"Hey, guys! I'm so glad you made it safely," he said.

"Hi, Christie," Amy replied a little shyly. "Thanks for having us."

"Yeah, thanks," said Joe.

There was an awkward moment. David could tell Christie wanted to hug the kids too because it was his way to greet people with hugs. But he refrained, probably not sure his touch would be welcome.

"This place is really cute, Dad," Amy said, looking around.

"Thanks. We like it. Christie did a great job decorating. You know me. I'm a chair-and-one-mug kind of guy."

David gave them a little tour. When he put the farm on the market last spring, he was lucky it had sold quickly to a large Amish family. He got a good chunk of money for it, but some of that went to Joe and Amy and the rest into savings. He and Christie agreed they didn't want to buy a house right away. They wanted to be free to move around and travel if they decided to. But even though he didn't own the duplex, he was real proud of it.

The outside of their row house was unassuming old brick, but the iron railings, porch, and window frames were freshly painted. The inside was far better. The previous owner had remodeled and put in a new kitchen and faux hardwood floors. Christie picked out some modern-looking gray furniture at a discount place and accented it with bright rugs and paintings and pillows in purple, moss green, and gray. David loved how it felt modern and a bit sparse. It was low maintenance and classy.

"Really nice," Amy commented as he led them around. "You have good taste, Christie. I'm afraid I'm as hopeless as my dad about these things."

"I'm sure that's not true. How do you like *your* new place?"

Amy had graduated and gotten a nursing job at Lancaster General Hospital over the summer. She'd moved into an apartment with another nurse, but David hadn't seen it yet.

She beamed. "I love it! We can walk downtown to eat or go to the farmers' market. Or to do this...." Amy had kept on a paisley scarf when she took off her coat. She unwrapped it from her head now and took it off. They all stared.

"Oh, Amy!" Christie said, hand over his mouth. "I love it!"

"Do you?" Amy blushed and patted her short bob haircut. "I figured any man who wants to date me is going to have to be open-minded, so the hair is a first test. If he can't get past that, he's automatically disqualified." She laughed, but it was a nervous sound.

"You look... beautiful." David put his arm around her shoulders. "Your hair looks thick and healthy like this too."

"It's perfect," said Christie.

"It looks good, Am," Joe agreed.

David felt a twinge of guilt. Amy and Joe were still going to the Mennonite church, but Joe was no longer dating Amanda. He didn't tell David all the details, but David figured having a gay father had something to do with it. As for Amy... she seemed to be questioning a lot of things these days. And maybe that wasn't such a bad thing.

"Thanks again for coming," David told them both sincerely. *For giving us a chance.*

"Of course!" Amy said brightly. "We had to see the new place. And I want to hear all about your job and everything, Dad." She smiled at Christie. It was a bit tentative, but it was a smile.

"Anyone want a drink?" Christie asked. "We've got milk, Coke, apple cider, or wine. I hope you guys are hungry because I made way too much food."

"It smells good," Joe told Christie, looking right at him.

Christie swallowed. "Thanks, Joe."

"I'll help you get drinks." Amy took Christie's arm and they went into the kitchen.

When Joe and David were alone, Joe held out his hand. David was surprised, but he shook it.

"It's good to see you, Dad."

"You too. I appreciate this. I know it's not easy to accept the situation given your beliefs."

Joe nodded, looking away. "No. But you already know everything I'd say, anyhow, so I need to leave it up to you and Christie and God. We're still family."

David felt a dense ache in his chest, but he nodded. "Okay."

"Actually I wanted to talk to you about something. You know I did that mission trip to Sweden last summer. Well, there may be an opportunity to do a pastoral internship over there for a year. I'm seriously considering it."

"That's fantastic, Joe. Living abroad would be a great experience."

"Yeah. They have some different ideas over there, that's for sure. I've been praying about it a lot, and I think it would be good for me to spend some time there."

David knew which "different" ideas Joe was talking

about. The Swedish Mennonite church had embraced gay marriage, in part due to the law. Gay marriage was legal in Sweden, and it was *illegal* for churches to discriminate against it. But the Mennonite leaders there had accepted the change with grace and had a much more loving and tolerant view of homosexuality than did their brethren in the US.

"I'm very glad to hear it. I always believed nothing true can be threatened by expanding your horizons. God gave us a brain for a reason." *Even if it took me a long time to start using mine.*

Joe blinked at him for a moment, then changed the subject. "Dinner smells good. I guess you're still enjoying Christie's cooking?"

"Oh yeah. Do you like Indian food?"

"I'll try it."

David clapped him on the back. "Thanks, Joe. You're in for a treat."

After a delicious dinner, they all took the subway downtown. Christie led them to the least crazy areas of Times Square that still had a view of the ball. They had thermoses of hot cocoa, and the weather was a relatively balmy forty degrees. And when they counted down to the New Year, David took Christie into his arms and kissed him. He felt nothing but joy.

It wasn't just a new year for him; it was a whole new life. He was incredibly grateful.

THE END

BONUS: Cookie Recipe

Cherry Date Cookies

My mother used to make these cookies, so it's only right they are the first things Christie makes for David.

3 1/2 c white flour, sifted

2 c light-brown sugar

1 tsp baking soda

1/2 tsp salt

2 eggs

1 c butter, softened

1/2 c buttermilk

2 c dates, chopped

1 c maraschino cherries, chopped

1 c walnuts, chopped

Optionally you can add ¼ c of coconut flakes

Preheat the oven to 350F.

In a bowl stir together the flour, salt, and baking soda. In a separate bowl, combine the butter, brown sugar, and eggs, and mix until everything is incorporated and the mix turns light and fluffy.

Mix together the flour mixture and butter/sugar mixture until well combined, and then add the buttermilk. Stir in the dates, nuts, and cherry pieces.

Spoon drop the cookie dough onto a greased or Teflon cookie sheet, leaving at least 1.5" between drops. Bake 12-15 minutes. Cookies should be lightly browned. Don't forget they are in the oven.

BONUS: Tender Mercies Sample

The second book in the *Men of Lancaster County* series is called *Tender Mercies.* Enjoy this sample chapter.

Sample Chapter (Chapter 2)

"What the devil are you doing?" Father's voice boomed through the hayloft, frightening Samuel half to death. He was looking out the window with his back to the ladder, and he hurriedly did up the flap on his britches. He'd barely closed the buttons before his father was there, shouldering Samuel aside and peering out the window.

Humiliated, Samuel stepped back, his heart sinking. *Oh Lord, please don't let him see.*

But his father did see, and he understood. When he turned from the window, the stern, bearded face was set hard, and his eyes burned. "You have a sick, filthy soul!"

"No, Da! I was only lookin' at the sky."

"Liar! Don't make your sin worse by lyin' to my face!"

"Da...."

"Don't you move! Not one inch!"

Father moved swiftly to the hayloft ladder and climbed down to the main floor of the barn. Samuel knew he would return, and when he did, Samuel would be in for a world of hurt. He was nineteen years old, for land's sake, and he hadn't had a beating since he was fourteen. He avoided them by staying quiet and doing what he was told. But this.... He was in terrible bad trouble.

It was bad enough Samuel's father caught him touching himself. But that would likely warrant extra Bible study, not a whipping. What was worse was Samuel did it while looking out over a field. The only point of interest in the field below was their neighbor, young and handsome John Snyder, who was out there working a plow. His body was strong, and his muscles bunched under his white sweat-slicked shirt.... Even now the memory of the sight caused eddies of arousal to swirl amidst the fear in Samuel's belly.

It wasn't the first time he'd been caught at something like this either. He was found behind the schoolhouse with a boy when he was fourteen, their hands down each other's pants when the boy's father came around the corner. Samuel was driven home, and the man talked solemnly to his father. Samuel got the worst beating of his life that night. But he promised his father it was the only time he'd ever done anything like that, and it was mere curiosity, not his nature. He'd lied.

In the years since, that incident had eroded away his relationship with his father like rot in the foundations. Samuel sometimes looked up to find Da staring at him, suspicion and worry in his eyes. But Samuel ignored it, tried to prove he was a good worker, that he was an honorable man, that physical desire of any kind was not part of his makeup. Now one glance out the window had sparked those long-buried doubts in his father's mind, and all those years of hiding lay crumbled to dust at Samuel's feet.

His belly crawled with shame and self-loathing. Why did he do these things? Why did this desire torment him so? What was wrong with him? He was a grown man. He shouldn't still be getting beatings from his father, shouldn't be doing the kind of furtive, shameful acts that deserved them.

His father came back up the ladder. "Take your shirt off!" he ordered, his voice as dark and cold as a winter's night.

Hands shaking, Samuel stood, pushed off his suspenders, and began to unbutton his shirt. His fingers were graceless, fear robbing them of their usual dexterity. There was nothing he could say that would convince his father now. Any lie would only make things worse.

He laid his shirt neatly on a bale of hay and turned his back obediently to his father. Maybe if he showed humility in this, his father would be appeased. His shoulder dipped as his bad foot made the maneuver of turning awkward. As he moved, he glimpsed the large switch in his father's hand. His da kept a box of such switches in the barn, cut anew from green saplings from time to time. They were an excellent deterrent to his children but rarely saw use.

This was going to hurt. Bad. Samuel braced himself for pain. A few strokes, he told himself. Maybe three. Five at most. Then it would—

There was a faint whistling sound, and fire shot across his back. The pain was so sharp and fierce Samuel couldn't stop a cry and a half step forward.

Before he could begin to recover, another blow came, and another. He found himself half lying, propped up by the stacked hay bales and clinging to their rough surface. There was unfettered fury in the blows that rained down upon him. His da held nothing back, striking Samuel with all his might again and again.

Samuel lost count of the blows. His cries came in a

steady stream of agony and pleas. The fire in his back turned sharp and cutting as skin bruised, swelled, and broke open under the assault like a melon left to rot in the field. He felt blood trickle down his back. He twisted but couldn't escape the cruel lashes or the clouding effect of shock and pain.

Oh dear Lord in heaven, help me.

Through the fog of agony, he heard his father's ranting voice. "Shoulda known! That foot of yours is a sign from God about the sick, twisted nature of your soul! Your foot's not the abomination! You are! You lying, lustful, sick, devil-ridden...."

"Da, stop it!" It was Matthew's voice, urgent. "Da, please stop! You'll kill him!"

"Stay out of it!" His father shouted.

"I'm gettin' Ma. Ma! Ma!" Matthew was eighteen and the only one of Samuel's siblings he had any true closeness with. He heard Matthew's voice grow faint. Matthew would get mother. She would stop this, stay his father's hand. She had to. *Please, Lord.*

But the blows had already stopped, Samuel realized. The only sound was his father's harsh panting. The fear-fueled adrenaline that had kept Samuel mostly upright now vanished, leaving him exhausted, his senses overwhelmed with pain. He dropped his head into his arms, still propped on the hay bales, and sobbed. They were big, wracking noises he couldn't contain.

His father gripped his bicep firmly and tugged him upright. "Get to your feet. Now, boy!"

Samuel stood, shakily, and wiped at his eyes. He was ashamed of the tears, but he couldn't seem to stop them.

"You listen to me! You will go down that ladder and walk to the road, and you jus' keep on walkin'. I don't want you on this farm no more. Because if I catch you sinnin' again, I can't answer for what I'll do. And I don't need that on my conscience. Do you understand me?"

Samuel hitched in a breath and stared at his father in disbelief. He wiped a sleeve over his eyes again as if he couldn't trust his own senses. "But... but Da...."

"I mean it!" His father's face, his voice, were flat and merciless. "Take your coat and hat and be gone with ye. Here." His father dropped the switch, fished out his wallet, his mouth set in a white line, and took out a bunch of twenty-dollar bills. He shoved them into Samuel's hand. "Take this and don't never come back! I wash my hands of you."

Da turned and went down the ladder, not looking at Samuel again.

Samuel's ears were buzzing. His back throbbed and stung like it had been run through a thresher. His head swam. Nothing felt real, and yet surely this was too awful to be a dream. Surely the dream world was not so stark nor so cruel. He picked up his shirt and his black wool coat and black hat from where he'd lain it to the side earlier, before his world commenced to shatter. He stood for a moment, holding the clothes. He didn't want to put the shirt on. It was white, and it would quickly stain with the blood he felt on his skin. But he couldn't very well go walking down the road in March half-naked.

He put the shirt on, breathing through the pain as the movement stretched tortured skin. Then he put on his coat and placed the hat on his head, smoothing his long hair behind his ears with shaking fingers. He wiped the tears and snot from his face, swallowed the ache in his throat, and gingerly climbed down the ladder. The rough wood of the rungs felt too solid under his palms, the moment too important. *I've climbed this ladder a million times since I was a little 'un. I'll never climb it again.*

When he reached the driveway, he looked back at the farmhouse. He expected to see his mother or Matthew or Eliza, *anyone.* Surely someone would come out to say *Where are you going, Samuel? What's wrong? We'll talk Da 'round, you'll see.* But there was no sound from the house, and no movement except the flutter of a curtain as someone stepped back away from the window.

Da was keeping them inside. He wouldn't let them come.

Your foot's not the abomination! You are!

His heart shrank in his chest, withdrawing into the furthest reaches of his rib cage like an abused dog hiding in a doghouse. *Abomination.* He'd been cast out, sure to be shunned by the bishop. His family, Ma, Matthew, Jane, Sarah, Eliza, all his older brothers and sisters, cousins... they were all lost to him. He had nothing and no one. Dazed and in shock, Samuel turned and walked to the road. His normally mild limp, caused by his twisted foot, was exaggerated due to the agony of his back. He pathetically swung from side to side.

He turned right at the end of the driveway. And he kept walking.

Read more about Tender Mercies on the author's site. (https://www.elieaston.com/men-of-lancaster-county)

Dear Reader

Thank you for spending time with myself, River, and Brent. I planned a 4th installment of the Sex in Seattle series, one featuring a traveling tantric guy who worked for the clinic as a surrogate, but it spent years on the back burner. After taking some time off this past winter, I decided it was time to tackle River's story. I've always been interested in Eastern philosophy and took a few courses in college, though I am far (far) from an expert on the subject. That is to say, I'm more Brent's level than River's! I hope I intrigued you enough to do some searching on these topics on your own.

As always, I very much appreciate my readers posting recommendations for my books on social media and reviewing on Amazon and Goodreads. Thank you! Your reviews truly make a difference in drawing other readers and that helps me continue writing full time.

I appreciate my readers so much. It is awesome to hear from you and to know that I made someone smile or sigh. Feel free to email me: eli@elieaston.com.

You can also visit my website: www.elieaston.com. I have first chapters up for all my books and some free stories too. And you can sign up for my newsletter to get a monthly email about new releases and sales. (https://www.subscribepage.com/ElisNewsletterSignup)

My facebook group is a place to chat about Eli stories and get opportunity to read ARCs, excerpts from works-in-progress, and other goodies. (https://www.facebook.com/groups/164054884188096/)

Follow me on Amazon to be alerted of my new books. (https://www.amazon.com/Eli-Easton/e/B00CJUKM9I/)

I can promise you there will always be happy ending and that love is love.

Eli Easton

Men of Lancaster County Series

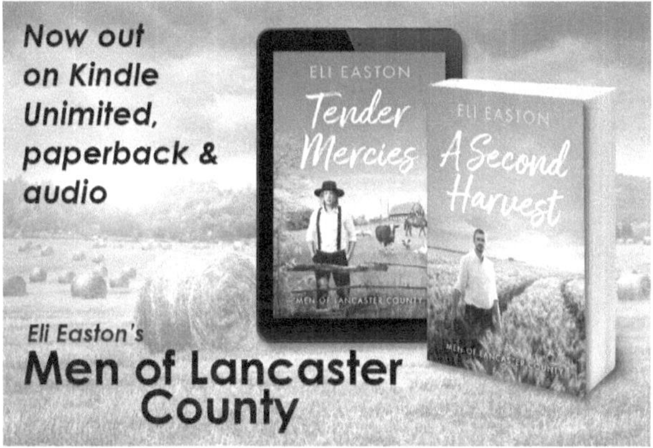

The *Men of Lancaster County* series features gay romances set in Lancaster County, Pennsylvania, a rural farming area with a large Amish and Mennonite community.

A Second Harvest – Mennonite farmer David Fisher, now widowed, believes his life is over before he's even hit 50. His kids grown, he runs his family farm by himself. But when a handsome young man from the city inherits the little house next door, and begins cooking for both of them, their friendship opens doors inside David he never knew existed.

Tender Mercies -Young Samuel Miller is shunned by his

Amish family when they discover his secret desire for men. Alone and without any resources, he answers an ad for a farm hand. Eddie Graber bought a Pennsylvania farm to start a farm sanctuary. But his boyfriend backs out, leaving him in dire financial straits. Samuel and Eddie come from different worlds, but they have a lot to teach each other about love, faith, and the healing power of mercy.

Read more about these books and check out the free first chapters at: https://www.elieaston.com/men-of-lancaster-county

Also by Eli Easton

Boy Shattered
Superhero
Puzzle Me This
The Trouble With Tony (Sex in Seattle #1)
The Enlightenment of Daniel (Sex in Seattle #2)
The Mating of Michael (Sex in Seattle #3)
The Redemption of River (Sex in Seattle #4)
A Second Harvest (Men of Lancaster County #1)
Tender Mercies (Men of Lancaster County #2)
A Prairie Dog's Love Song
Heaven Can't Wait
The Lion and the Crow
Five Dares
Robby Riverton: Mail Order Bride
How to Howl at the Moon (Howl at the Moon #1)
How to Walk like a Man (Howl at the Moon #2)
How to Wish Upon a Star (Howl at the Moon #3)
How to Save a Life (Howl at the Moon #4)
How to Run with the Wolves (Howl at the Moon #5)
Before I Wake
Blame it on the Mistletoe
Unwrapping Hank
Midwinter Night's Dream
Merry Christmas, Mr. Miggles

Desperately Seeking Santa
Christmas Angel
Family Camp (Daddy Dearest #1)
Angels Sing (Daddy Dearest #2)
The Stolen Suitor
Snowblind
www.elieaston.com

About the Author

ELI EASTON has been at various times and under different names a preacher's daughter, a computer programmer, a game designer, the author of paranormal mysteries, an organic farmer, and a profound sleeper. She has been writing m/m romance since 2013.

As an avid reader of romance, she is tickled pink when an author manages to combine literary merit, vast stores of humor, melting hotness, and eye-dabbing sweetness into one story. She promises to strive to achieve most of that most of the time. She currently lives on Puget Sound with her husband, dogs, and lots of very large trees.

Her website is http://www.elieaston.com.

You can e-mail her at eli@elieaston.com

Twitter is @EliEaston

Facebook: https://www.facebook.com/profile.php?id=100008994061782